"Cassie Edwards writes action-packed, sexy reads!
Romance fans will be more than satisfied!"
—*Romantic Times*

CASSIE EDWARDS
THE SAVAGE SERIES
Winner of the *Romantic Times* Lifetime Achievement Award for Best Indian Series!

CAPTIVE HEART

"We shall be home soon," he said. As he spoke the word "home," he pictured her there with him, not as a prisoner . . . but as the woman who would fill his lodge with sunshine . . . who would warm his bed and reach her arms out for him as she welcomed him.

Shawndee's heart skipped a beat, for she saw a tenderness in his eyes that made her feel she was much more than a captive to him.

If only things were different, she thought to herself.

If only they could have met under different circumstances. She imagined that she was in his canoe willingly and going to his home at Shadow Hawk's invitation, and not as his prisoner. It was hard not to see herself in his arms, to feel his lips pressed to hers, warm and passionate.

Other *Leisure* and *Love Spell* books by
Cassie Edwards:
TOUCH THE WILD WIND
ROSES AFTER RAIN
WHEN PASSION CALLS
EDEN'S PROMISE
ISLAND RAPTURE
SECRETS OF MY HEART

The *Savage* Series:
SAVAGE THUNDER
SAVAGE DEVOTION
SAVAGE GRACE
SAVAGE FIRES
SAVAGE JOY
SAVAGE WONDER
SAVAGE HEAT
SAVAGE DANCE
SAVAGE TEARS
SAVAGE LONGINGS
SAVAGE DREAM
SAVAGE BLISS
SAVAGE WHISPERS
SAVAGE SHADOWS
SAVAGE SPLENDOR
SAVAGE EDEN
SAVAGE SURRENDER
SAVAGE PASSIONS
SAVAGE SECRETS
SAVAGE PRIDE
SAVAGE SPIRIT
SAVAGE EMBERS
SAVAGE ILLUSION
SAVAGE SUNRISE
SAVAGE MISTS
SAVAGE PROMISE
SAVAGE PERSUASION

Savage
Honor

Cassie
Edwards

LEISURE BOOKS NEW YORK CITY

A LEISURE BOOK®

July 2001

Published by

Dorchester Publishing Co., Inc.
276 Fifth Avenue
New York, NY 10001

If you purchased this book without a cover you should be aware that this book is stolen property. It was reported as "unsold and destroyed" to the publisher and neither the author nor the publisher has received any payment for this "stripped book."

Copyright © 2001 by Cassie Edwards

Cover art by John Ennis
www.ennisart.com

All rights reserved. No part of this book may be reproduced or transmitted in any form or by any electronic or mechanical means, including photocopying, recording or by any information storage and retrieval system, without the written permission of the publisher, except where permitted by law.

ISBN 0-8439-4889-2

The name "Leisure Books" and the stylized "L" with design are trademarks of Dorchester Publishing Co., Inc.

Printed in the United States of America.

Visit us on the web at www.dorchesterpub.com.

In friendship and admiration, I dedicate Savage Honor *to my dear friend Steve Sandalis and his sweet wife, Katy! (And, thank you, Steve, for posing for the cover for* Savage Honor *and my next* Savage *series book,* Savage Moon!*)*

Savage Honor

WHO CARES?

As the clouds move in the skies,
I listen to the Indians' cries.
It hurts my heart and tears my soul,
How can the whites be so cold?
Do they not care what they have done?
Can't they hear the cries of the little ones?
One by one they're fading away,
Their land was taken in a passing day.
But I want you to know someone does care.
I wish I could have only been there.

—Diane Collett

Chapter One

It was 1784. The small room in the Silver Creek General Store was dark and dreary. It had the foul aroma of dried hides and tobacco. It also reeked of pickled cucumbers, which were packed in a tall, open crock that sat on the floor with a dead roach floating belly up on the top.

Eighteen-year-old Shawndee Sibley shuddered as she gazed at the roach. She was remembering the times she had bought one of the pickled cucumbers, enjoying its tangy, vinegary taste as she gathered supplies. She shifted her gaze to the wicker basket that she carried and hurried down one narrow aisle and then another, gathering household supplies for her mother, who sat outside in the buckboard wagon waiting for her.

Shawndee frowned as she thought of her stout, tight-lipped mother. She would be sitting with a long-barreled firearm hidden beneath a shawl right next to her on the seat, for of late her mother feared for her life. Shawndee's father, Caleb, had been knifed to death in a dark alley of Silver Creek a few nights ago.

Her father rested now in a pine box beneath a mound of earth behind Shawndee's home, for the people of Silver Creek would not allow her father to be buried in the cemetery. Too many thought him unworthy of lying amid the genteel dead of Silver Creek.

They despised Shawndee's mother just as much, and had tried all means possible to run the family out of town.

Now, even more determined than before her husband's death, Shawndee's mother would not budge. Her mother would not let anyone rule her life, especially not the narrow-minded people of Silver Creek. Her mother made her own rules and was determined to keep her Silverleaf Tavern open for business, even though it was against the law to have such an establishment in Silver Creek.

As far back as Shawndee could remember, her parents had moved from town to town, trading in whiskey. She was uncomfortable with this sort of life, not only because her family was looked upon as filth by all of the townsfolk of Silver Creek, but also because she was forced to hide her identity. This was a necessary precaution to keep the men who frequented her mother's drinking establishment from taking liberties with her while they were inebriated.

Shawndee walked down another aisle, reaching for a bar of lye soap, then placing it in her basket among the other things she was going to purchase. Today, as always, she was dressed as a boy, in breeches and shirt, with a wide-brimmed hat pulled down low over her thick golden hair.

Yes, when Shawndee began budding into a young lady, her parents forced her to dress and behave like a boy, and she hated every minute of it. She hated not being able to wear beautiful dresses and fancy shoes, and especially hated having to wear her hair in a ponytail when she was at home, and beneath a hat whenever she was anywhere else.

She had spent long hours in bed at night envisioning how it would be to wear a silk dress, with billows of frothy crinoline beneath it, and how she might look on a dance floor with a handsome man dressed in a fancy suit, twirling her frilly skirt around her ankles as she danced. Her hair would be worn loose and long and flowing down her back. Her cheeks would be flushed rosy with excitement. Her lips would be red, and her blue eyes would be sparkling.

But usually, just as she lost herself in such wonderful thoughts, drunken laughter erupting from downstairs in the tavern would remind her of reality. She must go on posing as the *son* of a woman who ran an illegal liquor establishment in Silver Creek, who had not yet been forced out of town because the sheriff of Silver Creek had refused to order the Sibleys to leave.

As Shawndee's mother had described Sheriff Tom Dawson, he was a man as corrupt as all hell, who enjoyed a drink of booze as well as the next fellow. He defended the Silverleaf Tavern as though it were a holy place of worship.

Shawndee sighed heavily as she moved down another dark aisle to avoid the women in fancy bonnets and beautiful dresses who were doing their shopping. She hurriedly slapped a long, twisted string of tobacco into her basket, hating the fact that her mother enjoyed a chew as much as a man. Her mother's teeth were stained and ugly; her breath smelled like a frightened skunk.

Yes, her mother was hard, through and through, as Shawndee herself would be if she fully accepted this life she was forced to lead.

But she clung to her dreams, where she could become the woman she prayed she'd be one day.

Shawndee had more than one dream. Another was her love of books.

She would love to be surrounded by them. She

went often and pressed her nose against the glass-paned window of Silver Creek's one-room library and watched the librarian at work, wishing *she* were there, the librarian herself.

Shawndee's time to watch through the window and dream was always short-lived, for as soon as the librarian caught her spying, she'd come outside and chase Shawndee away as though she were no better than a dog.

When that happened, Shawndee *felt* like a wounded puppy.

And then there was her dream of finding the perfect man. Yet she knew that as long as she was forced to behave and dress like a boy, that could never happen.

As she hid herself in a dark corner of her mother's tavern, she sometimes studied the men who sat at the bar, hoping to see one that might be different from the others.

She looked for one who seemed educated, who was dressed in fine clothes, who wore his hair clean and shaped just above his collar line, whose eyes were clear and not bloodshot from drinking himself crazy into the wee hours of the night.

Thus far, she had seen no man like that, not at her mother's tavern, or even walking or riding down the streets of Silver Creek. The townsfolk claimed that except for the Silverleaf Tavern, Silver Creek was a sin-free town, but Shawndee knew that many of the men of this town had skeletons in their closets. For it was those men, those *husbands*, who frequented the Silverleaf Tavern despite their wives' and church deacons' objections.

Eager to leave the dirty, smelly general store, Shawndee glanced down at her basket. She mentally checked the items there to be sure that she had gotten everything her mother needed.

She dreaded her next chore—paying for her selections while all the busybody ladies watched from a distance, as though she were poison, their faces pressed close together, gossiping about the son of the whorish woman who owned the only sinful place in their wonderful town.

Wanting to get it over, Shawndee went to the counter and hurriedly emptied her basket.

As the store clerk, a tall, lanky, bald man with thick-lensed glasses perched on his crooked nose, began adding up what Shawndee owed him, she heard the muffled footsteps of someone in moccasins. Surely an Indian had come into the store.

Intrigued by Indians, Shawndee turned and found a warrior only a few footsteps away from her. He stood at the counter with his arms heavily laden with pelts that he must have brought to the store for trade.

As the first store clerk continued to wait on Shawndee, another clerk stepped up to the counter and started taking the pelts from the Indian, stacking them neatly, one by one, on the counter.

Shawndee's breath was stolen away and she felt a strange flip-flopping sensation in the pit of her stomach when she saw *how* well muscled this man with the smooth copper skin was. He was wearing only a deerskin breechclout, revealing his broad, muscled, hairless chest, as well as muscled shoulders, arms, and legs.

Quite fascinating to her were the garters embroidered with fine appliqué that he wore just below his knees.

He also wore beautiful moccasins of the puckered-toe type, with a single seam up the center of the foot. The flaps of the moccasins were embroidered with quillwork in a running pattern of half circles, and above them were designs that looked like the zodiacal sign of Aries.

Shawndee was spellbound and could not take her eyes off the warrior. She loved his coarse, raven-black hair, which was worn long down his back, past his waist.

She was taken by the purity of his facial features as she saw them in profile. His chin, his jawline, his nose, were finely sculpted, as though made by a sculptor's skilled fingers.

And then he suddenly turned and caught her staring at him. She was mesmerized by his midnight-dark eyes, by the intensity and strength of his gaze.

Taken off guard, Shawndee gasped and stared

back at him, eye to eye. Then, remembering the danger of allowing a man, *any* man, to look upon her face for so long, she ducked her head.

She pulled her hat lower over her eyes and hurriedly finished her transaction with the clerk. She rushed from the store with her filled basket, placed it at the back of the wagon, then scrambled onto the seat beside her mother.

"You look like a frightened cat that's been told to scat," Jane Sibley growled as she reached over and placed a hand at Shawndee's chin so she could look into her eyes. "Daughter, did someone offend you in there? If so, I'll go in and horsewhip 'em."

Seeing the seriousness in her mother's dark eyes, Shawndee hurriedly explained what had happened.

"So you see, Mama, it's nothin'," Shawndee concluded, relieved when her mother snapped the reins over the team of horses and got them started away from the general store.

"I was just fascinated by a Seneca warrior, Mama," Shawndee added. "That's all."

"Such foolishness can get you in a heap of trouble," Jane grumbled. She reached up with her left hand and shoved a fallen lock of gray hair back into her tight bun. "Daughter, if that Injun was offended by you starin' at him, he might come lookin' for you and claim your scalp for his scalp pole."

"Mama, don't say such things," Shawndee gasped. She visibly shuddered at the thought, yet doubted that there was any real danger. The Seneca village was not far from the town of Silver Creek. It was located on the banks of the Genesee River upstream from Silver Creek. The Seneca were known for their peaceful ways, and for their ability to speak English, which they had learned from trappers and Jesuit priests. As long as they caused no problems, they were welcome in Silver Creek to trade.

Shawndee knew that some of the warriors came into town at night, and that her mother was guilty of selling them firewater, which was risky business.

Shawndee had watched her mother with the Indians and had studied their faces by the light of the moon, or by the faint glow of a lamp sending its light through a window, for the Indians were never allowed inside her mother's establishment.

Shawndee knew that she had never before seen the man she had seen today at the general store. There was something noble and proud about him that made her certain he would not stoop so low as to drink firewater. There was such dignity, such honor, such pride, in this warrior's stance.

No, surely such a man would never allow his senses to be clouded by whiskey.

Shadow Hawk went to the door of the general store and stared after the departing wagon. He could not forget the young lad whose eyes, the color of the sky and rivers, had seemed haunted by something. Frail and seemingly shy, the boy had fled the store almost as soon as their eyes had met.

Shadow Hawk was always hurt by the fear and mistrust of the townsfolk. He had lived a life of peace. Except for a few of his warriors whose judgment was clouded by whiskey, his band of Seneca never gave anyone cause to be afraid of them.

Shadow Hawk was curious about this white boy. When he had perused the boy's features, he had seen that they were not at all masculine, but instead resembled those of a delicate, beautiful young lady.

Yet how could that be? he puzzled to himself. No lady would go around dressed as a boy.

He decided it must be a quirk of nature that this boy had been born with the delicate features of a girl.

As Shadow Hawk stepped farther away from the door and got a better look at the woman who sat beside the boy, he grew cold inside. This woman and her husband were responsible for corrupting many of his warriors.

Surely this woman was the boy's mother. His parents must be the proprietors of the tavern where his warriors were supplied with *o-nish-uh-lo-nuh*, the firewater that stole their minds, logic, and energy, causing them to put their love of rotgut before their love of their people.

Doubling his hands into tight fists at his sides,

Shadow Hawk slid his eyes back to the young boy, who sat stiffly beside his mother. A plan came to Shadow Hawk's mind that made a slow smile steal across his sculpted lips.

Yes, through this boy he would make things right for his warriors.

If it wasn't for the firewater luring his warriors away from their usual clean, straightforward lives, all would be well at the Seneca village where Shadow Hawk was chief. Springtime in the valley of the Genesee River had never come with more promise. Myriads of passenger pigeons flocked in clouds that covered the sky for miles. The birds would soon be nesting in the open woods around the Seneca village, and thousands would be taken for food by the people. Newly prepared fields were springing to life with green acres of corn, beans, sunflowers, and squash.

Yes, things would soon change, he thought angrily, and he would be the one to bring about that change!

He went inside and finished choosing supplies in exchange for the pelts he had brought. As he left and walked toward the Genesee River where his canoe awaited him, a plan of abduction was building in Shadow Hawk's mind.

He must right the wrongs done his warriors. And if that meant taking the boy that he had seen today, so be it!

Chapter Two

A full moon rode the sky, casting dancing shadows everywhere. The air was warm. Fireflies flitted here and there, sending their sparks of flame across the land.

His midnight-dark eyes narrowed angrily, his jaw tight, Shadow Hawk stood in the shadows of a group of trees as he gazed intently at the rain-bleached, two-story house, whose long porch leaned precariously low at one end.

Tonight Shadow Hawk would station himself near to this place called the Silverleaf Tavern to see which of his Seneca warriors had come to trade for whiskey.

Shadow Hawk's warriors were never allowed inside the building as the white men were. They were treated as though they might be infested with lice, made to go to the back of the house where they stood outside on a smaller porch trading their pelts for rotgut.

Shadow Hawk, who had been appointed chief by his people after his chieftain father had grown ill two summers ago, was eager to reform his Hawk clan of Seneca, for theirs was the only one of the Seneca clans that had managed to survive the Revolutionary War.

It made Shadow Hawk's heart ache to recall just how badly the white people had shamed and tricked his brothers. The Treaty of Paris had ended the war. Britain had been forced to forfeit all of its holdings in the colonies that made up the United States.

But at the end of the war, the new American government had been in debt to the soldiers who had fought for it.

The government had decided to give the soldiers Indian land for back pay and sell what was left to reimburse government expenses.

Shadow Hawk grimaced at the tactics the new government had used to gain legal right to the land owned by the red man. They had claimed that because they had won the war with Britain, they had also conquered Englands' allies including the Seneca.

When the Seneca were not willing to give up their

land, the government then used other tactics to force them off.

Anger filled Shadow Hawk as he recalled how the white government had killed off as much of the Indian population as possible by giving certain clans blankets contaminated with the germs of smallpox.

Luckily, those blankets had not been given to Shadow Hawk's clan, but his people had not escaped the white man's depredations altogether.

The Hawk clan's crops had been heartlessly and methodically destroyed, causing many of the weakest and oldest of his people to die of hunger. The burial grounds of Shadow Hawk's Seneca clan now had graves that would not have been there had it not been for the fiery destruction of his people's fields.

But the problems facing Shadow Hawk's people now had nothing at all to do with the government's plans, and everything to do with the Silverleaf Tavern. He had even heard the townspeople call it a den of iniquity; there was talk that its owners must be forced out of this town where many white men's church steeples loomed high into the sky, proving the inhabitants' deep faith in their God, a faith that did not condone the consumption of whiskey.

The townfolk, like Shadow Hawk, believed alcohol was evil, as were the people who took money and pelts for it.

A deep rage filled Shadow Hawk as he thought of

warriors who were at one time proud and honest and who were now only shadows of themselves. Their decline had been caused by lack of hope for their future and by rotgut whiskey.

Shadow Hawk had done everything possible to make his people feel blessed for what they had; many other clans were now confined like penned-up dogs on reservation land.

But Shadow Hawk was afraid that if his warriors did not regain the bravery and courage they had had before the war, the Hawk people would also be forced from their land.

As he watched his warriors move stealthily, yet eagerly, toward the Silverleaf Tavern, Shadow Hawk's heart sank to see just how many men were being lured to the evil establishment. There were more than ten.

He studied their faces, the moon's glow identifying the warriors to Shadow Hawk. He recognized among them many whose future had held great promise prior to the war, among them his best friend, Blue Night. He felt the pain of regret deep inside his soul.

"Why, oh, why must they do this?" he whispered harshly to himself. "Do they not know the end result?"

He was afraid for his people's children, whose guidance came from adults who were setting the worst possible example.

It was hard for him to understand how this could be happening. His warriors had all been taught that it was the strict duty of every person to follow the paths of his ancestors and to resist any change that might destroy ancient customs. Those warriors who sneaked around in the dark, drinking rotgut, had turned their backs on such teachings.

Shadow Hawk could no longer see his men. They were now at the back of the house dealing with the evil white people.

Filled with loathing, Shadow Hawk glared at the house. The white people who lived there, who handed over the rotgut whiskey to his Seneca warriors, were even worse than the soldiers who'd come and tried to destroy the Hawk clan.

Oh, how often he had sat and watched this place, wondering how he could get back at those who wronged his people.

Now a smile curved his lips, for he believed he had come up with the perfect plan. The Silverleaf was the only drinking establishment in the area. If it was gone, his warriors could no longer spend their nights drinking, or waste their days in drunken sleep.

His warriors would learn once again how to be men!

He doubled his hands into tight fists at his sides as he moved his eyes from window to window. Inside the house, loud, raucous laughter could be heard. He could also hear a musical instrument called a piano blaring out its boisterous music.

His smile waned when he thought of what else, *who* else, was somewhere in the two-story house. The boy that he had seen at the general store . . . the boy that still puzzled him.

"How could a boy be beautiful?" he wondered to himself.

His jaw tightened when his thoughts returned to his plan. Yes, no matter how innocent the boy might be, Shadow Hawk would abduct him and use him as a bargaining tool to make his parents leave the area and take their rotgut with them.

Yes, even the white community would thank him for taking action. He had seen their rage against this establishment. It was not wanted. It was a place that brought shame to everyone, not only men with red skins.

What puzzled Shadow Hawk was why the top man in charge of this town, the sheriff, did not order the evil people away. Surely it was because he also was addicted to the firewater, and did not do his duty as sheriff.

In that lay the risk of what Chief Shadow Hawk planned to do. To stop Shadow Hawk from ridding the area of rotgut, the sheriff might retaliate against his clan of Seneca.

Shadow Hawk's only hope was that the townspeople would not allow their sheriff to stop him from chasing the evil ones away.

Yes, tomorrow night Shadow Hawk would seize the boy, then hope for the best. His people's survival as a clan depended on it.

Chapter Three

The soft glow of a lone candle flickered in the small room, where the smell of mold and mildew was always a reminder to Shawndee that she was in the attic of her home. She was sitting cross-legged in the middle of the floor in her hated boy's breeches and shirt. Her feet were bare. Her hair was still drawn back in the ponytail that was fashionable among men and boys these days.

She came to the attic as often as possible at night to get away from the unpleasantness of her mother's tavern. Besides, attics had always fascinated Shawndee.

Tonight she was surrounded by the memorabilia that had been carried from her parents' homes, from town to town.

The old, dusty books with their yellow, frail pages fascinated Shawndee the most. One by one she had read them by candlelight on those nights of escaping a world she detested.

Since her father's death, she had felt an urgent need to hide away from the tavern. At least while he was alive she had felt somewhat protected.

Now it was only herself and her mother, and their maid and friend Tootiba, an elderly Jamaican black woman.

Months ago, Shawndee's mother had told her that these books in the attic had been in her family for years. Since then, Shawndee had gone through the books, joyfully reading them by candlelight. Each time she chose a different one.

Tonight she had chosen a book that seemed the frailest of all those in her mother's collection. But she wasn't sure if she should try reading it, afraid that the pages might crumble beneath her fingers at the merest touch.

But after examining the title, which stood out boldly beneath the light of the candle, she was too curious not to choose it.

"Witches of Salem," Shawndee whispered to herself as she ran her fingers slowly over the title on the cover.

She arched an eyebrow, wondering why, of all things, her mother would have a book about witches.

The thought of witches conjured up all sorts of thoughts and visions in Shawndee's mind, none of which were pleasant.

She could not help recalling Tootiba's tales of witches flitting here and there on brooms beneath a bright full moon, and how their eyes flashed as though fire were in them, and how when they laughed it came out more like a cackle than laughter.

Shawndee had also been told about witches being burned at the stake, and how those witches came back from the dead in the form of ghostly apparitions in the night to haunt those who had set fire to the limbs and twigs at their feet.

She shuddered uncontrollably at such thoughts, then slowly opened the book.

Her eyes widened in wonder when she saw a list of names, above which was written: "In memoriam to the women below, who died in Salem."

This book had been written in memory of the women who had died in Salem, a place where witches had been burned at the stake.

Shawndee's heart pounded as she began reading the names, her throat constricting suddenly when she spotted the name of her great-grandmother . . . her mother's grandmother!

Gulping hard, she closed the book enough to give her a full view of the cover again.

The title *Witches of Salem* stood out now, as

though a soft glow illuminated it from behind.

Almost too frightened to open the book again, she started to lay the book aside. But now her curiosity was too aroused not to proceed.

She winced when a corner of one of the yellowed pages crumbled and fell away from the book when she opened it, again thinking that it would be better if she just put this book where she had found it and forgot that she had ever seen it.

But nothing could keep her from learning the truth. Again she studied the names.

Breathing hard, her eyes wide, she again closed the book. She couldn't stop seeing the name of her great-grandmother on the list of those who had died in Salem!

Were they really witches?

Could it be that her great-grandmother might have been a true witch? Then what of her grandmother? What . . . of . . . Shawndee's mother?

Shawndee had lived with her mother and had never seen her do anything that might suggest she was a witch.

The sudden sound of footsteps on the stairs that led up to the attic alarmed Shawndee.

"Mother!" she gasped out.

Her face suddenly drained of color. She did not want her mother to catch her reading this book. She realized now that it had been intentionally hidden from her, for it had lain beneath other books and a layer of old, crumbling, yellowed newspapers at the bottom of a trunk. She felt ashamed that she had even gone so far as to pry open the lock of the trunk.

Breathing hard, Shawndee glanced quickly at the open trunk, then at the book, and then at the door, which was still closed. She knew she had only a moment or two before being discovered snooping.

She hurriedly placed the book back in the trunk.

Her fingers trembled as she closed the lid.

Then she stared at the broken lock.

She glanced again toward the door.

Quickly, she swept up a shawl that she found nearby and spread it over the trunk. Just in time, for the door suddenly opened on its squeaky hinges. Shawndee was sitting on the floor trying to look innocent.

But when she saw who was there at the door, her eyes narrowed angrily. It was not her mother who had almost caught her in the act of spying. It was a man . . . a man she loathed with every fiber of her being.

And she could tell by the way he was leering at her, and by how unsteady he was as he stood there, his one hand tightly gripping the doorknob to help hold him up, that he was drunk.

"Chester Hawkins, what are you doing here?" Shawndee said in a gruff voice that sounded more like a boy's than a woman's.

Oh, she knew this man too well. He supplied her mother with whiskey for her establishment and he was always staring at Shawndee with a leering hunger in his eyes, as though he knew her secret . . . that she was a woman.

The very sight of him always sickened Shawndee. Tonight he wore drab breeches and a wrinkled, booze-spotted shirt. His brown hair hung in greasy wisps across his lean shoulders, and his yellow teeth were jagged.

His broad nose flared as he breathed.

His pale gray eyes were narrow and mean-looking.

Tonight he seemed to have sniffed Shawndee out in her hiding place. And despite the fact that she was dressed in her boy's attire, and that she even had her breasts bound beneath her shirt so that she looked flat-chested, Chester Hawkins seemed to know somehow that she was a young lady.

Or worse yet, perhaps he was attracted to her because he truly believed she *was* a boy.

"I've gotcha cornered now, don't I?" Chester said in a thick, drunken drawl. He chuckled as he started to take a step toward Shawndee, but stopped instead and got a wild, frightened look in his eyes when he heard footsteps on the stairs behind him.

Just as he spun around to try to make his escape, Shawndee's mother was there, blocking his way.

Shawndee winced when her mother began poking at Chester's chest with the bristles of the broom she held.

Gasping with fear, Chester had no choice but to edge away from Shawndee's mother with each fresh poke of the broom. Suddenly he let out a yelp of pain as she raised the broom and brought it down across his face, the bristles digging into his flesh.

Yowling, Chester tried to protect his face with his arms. But no matter what he did, the broom kept coming down in its attack.

"Stop, you witch!" Chester screamed. "I meant no harm. Please stop. Let me go!"

Shawndee slowly rose to her feet as she watched the anger in her mother's gray eyes darken.

And even though Shawndee detested Chester, she was glad when her mother finally stopped the attack and threw the broom halfway across the room, then stepped aside so Chester could escape.

Shawndee's eyes widened when her mother began cursing the man, yet this side of her mother's nature was not new to Shawndee. Her mother had been vituperative for as long as Shawndee could remember. She was a stout, big woman who cursed like a man, who could enter the fray against any man and emerge the victor.

But she never wore the clothes of a man. Tonight

she was dressed in a floor-length cotton dress with puffed sleeves and a white collar.

Her graying hair was in its usual tight bun atop her head. She wore no rouge, nor anything on her face that might make her look more feminine.

Jane Sibley seemed to enjoy looking bullish and strong, for she had to appear to be stronger than any man whom she might come up against on the rowdiest of nights in her tavern.

"Get out, damn you," Jane shouted. She waved a fist in Chester's face. "If you don't get out right now and leave my son Andrew alone, I'll be ridin' that broom I used on your face when I come after you some night in the dark. You don't want to even think about what I might do to you then."

That name "Andrew" always made Shawndee groan inwardly, for it was a name assigned to her to go with her male persona.

She hated the name as much as she hated playing this charade.

She wanted a man to draw her into his arms and speak her name—*Shawndee*, not Andrew.

She wanted to hear him speak it as he brushed soft kisses across her lips!

"Now git, Chester!" Jane said, pulling Shawndee's thoughts back to the moment at hand. "And remember what I said. I'll come after you. I'll even witch you if you so much as look at my boy again with eyes that say you want more than just a look."

38

Shawndee gazed at her mother with shocked wonder. Her mother had again used the term "witch" as she tried to convince this disgusting man to leave Shawndee alone. Why would she even think about such a thing, much less use the word as a ploy to frighten someone?

She looked quickly at Chester as he finally made it to the stairs. Eyes wide with fright, he hurried down the steps, stumbling and tumbling until he finally reached the bottom.

Alone now with her mother, Shawndee stared at her questioningly. In her mind's eye she kept seeing the word *Witch* on the book, and her great-grandmother's name associated with it.

And now Shawndee had heard her mother actually tell Chester that *she* was going to "witch" him!

"Mama, what did you mean by 'witching'?" Shawndee asked in a worried voice.

Jane laughed in a sort of cackle that until now Shawndee had never noticed.

It seemed like a laugh that you might associate with . . . that you might expect to hear from . . . a witch.

"Shawndee, you know I will use any ploy I can think of to keep the drunken sods away from my daughter," Jane said thickly.

"But, Mama," Shawndee murmured. "Must you resort to talking about 'witching' someone? Why would you even think of such a thing to say?"

"Keepin' you safe is my main concern," Jane said. "No matter what I have to say or do, or how I'm forced to do it, I'll keep those nasty men from pesterin' you." She visibly shuddered as she went and picked up the broom. "Especially that filthy-minded Chester."

Shawndee smiled weakly at her mother. She wanted to ask more questions about the subject of witches and what they might have to do with her family, but she didn't.

She was too afraid to know.

She *did* know that in the past, people who were accused of being witches were persecuted. Those that weren't burned at the stake were stoned to death.

Had her very own great-grandmother died in such a way?

The thought sent shivers up and down Shawndee's spine, for she didn't want to even consider that she might have witch's blood running through her own veins.

Chapter Four

Staying hidden, Shadow Hawk moved stealthily through the shadowed night from tree to tree, observing his warriors' behavior as they took turns drinking from their two jugs of whiskey.

Each time one of his warriors took a long, deep swallow, gulping the firewater as if it were a sweet elixir, Shadow Hawk's anger flared and grew fiercer.

They had not even been able to wait until they got into the forest, where their sins would be observed only by the night creatures and their disappointed chief. Instead, they had sat down on the steps of the back porch of the tavern and begun passing the jug from man to man.

Their behavior changed with the first long swig of the evil, fiery liquid.

Shadow Hawk had already decided before coming that he would not abase himself by going after his warriors within view of the white men who came and went from the establishment.

It was enough that the Seneca warriors were making fools of themselves without their chief being seen near the very place that was turning once valiant warriors into clumsy, bungling, shameful idiots.

He had planned not to go farther than the edge of the forest alongside the tavern owners' land. He had hoped to wait until his warriors entered the forest and stop them before they took one drink of firewater.

When, by the light of the moon, he had seen his warriors lingering on the tavern porch, passing a jug from man to man, each one more eager than the last to drink from it, Shadow Hawk had started toward his men, forgetting his earlier plan. But he stopped abruptly.

A man holding his face in his hands and yowling with pain ran out the back door of the tavern, with many other white men following to see what was causing the racket.

When the injured man stopped and began telling what had happened to him inside the tavern, and the Seneca warriors edged in among the whites to hear, Shadow Hawk had no choice but to stand his ground. A minute later, the injured man mounted his horse and rode away, leaving the other whites with the warriors, who then took turns drinking from something besides the jug. Shadow Hawk assumed it was whiskey in bottles.

Shadow Hawk knew his warriors were way beyond help when the white men went back inside the tavern and one of them brought out another jug for the Seneca. Shadow Hawk watched in dismay as his warriors staggered and laughed and giggled while they walked toward the forest.

It was then that Shadow Hawk decided to stay hidden and follow them for a while. If he were to show himself to them while he was filled with such rage at their shameful behavior, he would have little control over what he said.

He might even find himself banishing them from the Hawk clan, a move that would not only alter *their* lives forever, but also their families' lives. These men had women and children depending on them for their survival. Although they had already failed in many ways in their responsibilities toward their families, at least they kept food in their children's and wives' bellies.

No, banishment was not the answer. Being shamed by their chief should be enough. Until now, he had hoped they would come to their senses on their own.

He knew they were not proud of their behavior; nor did they enjoy the headaches and dark moods that came with putting firewater in their bellies.

But too much time had passed, and they had not shown any sign of giving up the evil habit. Shadow Hawk's patience had run thin.

After tonight, if those men drank even one more drop of firewater, he would have no choice but to make them stand before their whole clan and admit what they did, and why.

He doubted that any of these warriors would want that sort of punishment.

They had now traveled some distance from the tavern. Shadow Hawk decided that it was time to confront his men—men he had once trusted implicitly.

Especially one: Blue Night.

Blue Night had hunted with him on his first hunt as a child. Blue Night, who had always been Shadow Hawk's best friend, had learned to ride alongside him. They had sat and carved their first bows together, using them to practice their shooting. They had enjoyed their first smoke from a pipe together.

Shadow Hawk and Blue Night had even gone on their first vision quest at the same time. That quest had changed Shadow Hawk's childhood name of Small Bear to his adult name, Shadow Hawk.

Yes, Blue Night and the other warriors with him

were the last men Shadow Hawk would have guessed would become so faint of heart as to allow their lives to be guided by alcohol. Their confrontation with him tonight should be enough to shock them back into reality, for they all looked up to him.

Shadow Hawk hurried on ahead of his warriors, then made a quick turn to his left, which brought him directly in front of them, blocking their way.

The moon's glow was enough for the men to see the anger etched on their chief's face.

Blue Night was so startled he dropped his jug of whiskey, shattering it at his moccasined feet. The whiskey in the bottle splashed up onto his face, marking him with the shame he suddenly felt in the presence of his beloved chief . . . his beloved *friend*.

Shadow Hawk placed his fists on his hips. "I have watched tonight, I have seen the distortions of your faces and I have heard the false laughter brought on by the meaningless security of firewater," he hissed out.

His gaze moved slowly from man to man, purposely stopping when he came to Blue Night. "How can you allow yourselves to partake in this white man's filthy habit?" he said, his voice drawn. "Have you no pride? Have you no shame? Do you not know that by filling your bellies with firewater you are setting bad examples not only to each of your own children, but to all of the children of our Hawk clan?"

He paused, inhaled a quivering breath, and slowly lowered his hands to his sides. "My warriors, I have known you since we were all just old enough to take our first steps. How can our clan remain strong enough to keep our freedom from the white eyes when you care more for rotgut than for your very own people, who depend on you for their safe-keeping?" he said tightly. "If I asked you now, at this moment, to steady your hands enough to notch an arrow on your bowstring, you know that none of you could do it. Your hands are trembling. Your vision is impaired, as are all your senses changed because of the rotgut you have placed in your bod-ies."

He stared at the remaining jug that one warrior was clutching to his bare chest as though it were something as precious as a wampum belt.

The sight disgusted Shadow Hawk so much that he strode to Sky Eagle and angrily snatched the jug away from him.

While Sky Eagle watched, Shadow Hawk raised the jug high in the air, then threw it angrily to the ground.

As it broke into tiny pieces and the whiskey splashed all over the ground, spreading as blood would after a fight to the death between battling warriors, all was silent.

Even the hooting of an owl and the yipping of a

coyote were silenced by the crashing sound of the jug.

It was so quiet the warriors could hear each other's rapid breathing. They all understood their chief's anger . . . his shame . . . his determination to stop their wrongful behavior.

"I will not ask for apologies, for things have gone too far for mere apologies," Shadow Hawk said. He slowly shook his head. "But I do want you all to go home now. Pray for guidance. Pray for the strength to abstain from this vice that has you in its grip. My warriors, without you my power is lessened, and without me, your people's leader, all is lost for everyone of our Hawk clan. I have been chosen to lead, to keep our people from the grip of the white authorities. But how can I when there are no warriors worthy of leading? Yes, there are many more who have not discovered the lure of firewater. But *you* are the chosen few who are the backbone of our people, who were at one time the leaders, while the others were followers. Do you wish to lose your status among our people? If I should be forced to replace you with others more worthy, I shall."

The warriors turned and ran from Shadow Hawk toward home.

Shadow Hawk stood his ground and watched his men until they disappeared from view into the darkness of night.

Then he went and bent low over the broken jug.

The irritating smell of the spilled whiskey was harsh in his nostrils.

"What is there about this that lures men into its evil?" he whispered.

He straightened, knowing his speech was not enough. To make certain his warriors would not be tempted again, he had his other plan to carry out.

Yes, he still had a boy to abduct.

Chapter Five

Lamplight filled the town hall as did many women, who were attending a town meeting to discuss ways of ridding their fine city of Silver Creek of the one house of ill repute, where too many local townsmen were entertained after hours.

"We *must* find a way to rid the town of that filthy place," Carolyn Harper said, her blue eyes flashing as she rose to her feet. She was dressed in the same attire as the other women, in a suit with a crisp white blouse beneath the jacket, and white gloves. An assortment of fancy hats were perched on their heads.

"Let us not leave this meeting tonight without a plan to run the bitch and her son, and their black friend too, out of town," Carolyn added more forcefully.

"Yes. I thought when Caleb Sibley was knifed to death, that would be the end of the house of iniquity," another woman said in a shrill voice as Carolyn took her seat. "But it wasn't. Now his shameful hussy of a wife, his *widow*, is in charge."

"Worst of all, Sheriff Dawson looks the other way, condoning such devilish activity in this one-time beautiful, God-fearing town," another woman said, straining to see through her thick-lensed glasses. "As long as the sheriff reaps what that house sows, surely being paid well under the table by that shameful hussy, nothing will be done about the house."

Carolyn Harper stood up again. "It's up to us, the decent women of the community, to find a way to run off that evil woman, and the sheriff, too," she said forcefully. "Somehow we *must* find a way to wipe the slate clean so we can have a respectable town again."

Carolyn turned suddenly when she heard a rush of footsteps behind her as someone ran into the large room.

Everyone's gaze followed Carolyn's and saw that the intruder was Chester Hawkins.

They glared at him, knowing that he sold the liquor to Jane Sibley for her establishment.

He even now reeked of whiskey, and the blood

on his face indicated that he had surely been in some sort of brawl at the tavern.

Sarah James, the president of the women's group, who until now had been quietly listening to everyone else's viewpoints, rushed from her chair and went to Chester.

She placed her hands on her hips and glowered at him, her red hair and snapping green eyes proof of the fiery temper she was known to have. "Leave," she said, removing one hand from a hip to point at the open door. "Leave at once. This is a private meeting. You, especially, are not welcome."

Chester's chest was heaving. He was wild-eyed as he returned Sarah's determined stare. "I'll leave," he said between heaving breaths. "But first listen to what I have to tell you."

"You have nothing we ladies want to hear," Sarah hissed out. Again she determinedly pointed to the door. "You are worthless. So is anything you have to say."

"Just listen," Chester pleaded, his eyes begging Sarah. "You won't regret it."

He wiped a bead of sweat from his brow and flung it from his fingers to the floor beside him, drawing a gasp of disgust from Sarah as she stepped quickly away from this man dressed in cheap breeches and a wrinkled shirt that reeked of perspiration.

"Alright, just say what you have to say, then

leave," Sarah said, inching farther away from him.

"Let me tell you this much, I've had enough of that tavern and its owner, and whoever else resides in the damnable house," Chester snapped angrily.

He gingerly touched the welts on his face. He winced at the merest touch.

"Yep, I'm through with that nutty woman," he growled. "I don't need her business. I have many places along the river that pay well for my services."

Even though he knew it irritated Sarah, he took another slow step toward her.

He smiled crookedly when he saw how she winced at his proximity.

Then he looked around the circle of women, who had risen from their chairs and were silently watching him. "Listen well, women," he said, chuckling. "I have information that you need to know about Jane Sibley."

He smiled more broadly and stepped even closer to Sarah, yet his eyes were still on the other women. "Ladies, Jane Sibley is a *witch*," he said, enjoying the gasps his words produced.

The color even left some of their faces.

Some covered their mouths with their hands in horror. But it was their eyes that told him he had hit the right nerve. These women would take his bait and wreak his vengeance on Jane Sibley.

"Yep, ladies, Jane Sibley's a witch," he repeated.

He reached up and slowly ran his fingers over his aching face. "She did this to me with a broom, and then threatened to find me some night alone in the dark. She said she'd be riding on her broomstick, and that she'd *witch* me."

The women gasped in unison.

Again they grew quiet, then sat down on their chairs and scooted them closer together.

Chester watched as they began chattering like magpies, each telling something more shocking than the other.

"I *knew* there was a reason why some of my livestock died so mysteriously of late," one woman said. "Now I know why. They were bewitched!"

"More than once I've seen a witch flying through the winter mist," another lady said, causing quite a stir. "I just never told anyone because . . . because . . . I thought I might be looked at as daft."

"*I've* had strange things happen, as well, so I don't think you daft," one of the others said. "You see, more than once lately, my cheese and butter have gone suddenly, mysteriously bad." She thrust her chin proudly high. "You all know how clean my cooking utensils, especially my butter churn, are. It *must* be the witch putting a curse on my things."

"Our farm animals have been born with deformities," Sarah James said, drawing more hushed gasps from the women. "I now see why. All of our recent misfortunes were caused by that *witch*. She knows we want her gone. She is trying to scare us into keeping quiet about it."

Carolyn Harper cleared her throat nervously, drawing everyone's eyes to her. "Some of my household items have disappeared," she said, swallowing hard. "First there was my broom, then my—"

"Say no more," Sarah said, sighing heavily. "We know the witch is responsible for all of these things. She is an enemy of God. She will even bewitch our families if we don't get her out of our town." She paused, then said, "We must oust her as quickly as possible."

Smiling wickedly at the success of his scheme, Chester seated himself to watch. The women ignored his presence in their eagerness to make plans.

Chester reached his hand to his throbbing face and nodded. Yep, the foul-mouthed, obnoxious woman who had slammed the broom bristles into his face tonight *would* pay. He hoped the women would decide that the only way to truly be rid of the witch was to burn her on a stake.

He would proudly light the kindling at her feet.

He would laugh as she screamed for mercy!

And then he would have his way with her boy!

Chapter Six

Glad that the men down below were not too rowdy tonight, Shawndee snuggled into her thick feather mattress beneath a thin patchwork quilt.

Her hair lay like a golden halo around her head on her pillow and she loved the feel of her beautiful lacy nightgown against her flesh.

Always at night after she took her bath and washed off all smells of the tavern from her body, she was free to be the girl she had to hide from the world during the daytime.

Tonight the only thing that spoiled the serenity of her bedroom was the recollection of what had transpired in the attic only a short while ago.

The thought of Chester touching her made her insides tremble with disgust.

55

Worst of all was the realization that he lusted after her because he thought she was a boy!

How could a man have desires for . . . ?

Her thoughts were interrupted when the door creaked open and the soft candlelight revealed a figure standing there.

It was Tootiba, who was more of a friend and confidante to Shawndee than a maid and cook.

Tootiba was a West African native whom Shawndee's grandfather had acquired while he lived in Barbados, where he was a successful planter and merchant. Years later, he moved his family, including Tootiba, to Boston.

When Shawndee's grandparents drowned, her mother was left to fend for herself and Tootiba, which was hard, for her father had gone broke in bad business dealings.

At that time Shawndee's mother was only sixteen.

By the time she was seventeen she had fallen madly in love with Caleb Sibley, soon afterward marrying him and joining him in his business of selling whiskey.

Even before Shawndee entered the world, her parents were moving from town to town, selling their whiskey from taverns they always developed within their own home, leaving this or that town when they had exhausted their welcome there. Faithful and true to the family, Tootiba always accompanied Jane and her new husband wherever their whiskey business took them.

Tootiba had become close to Shawndee, as well, and protected her as though she were of her own flesh.

"Shawndee, honey, Tootiba is glad you are still awake," Tootiba said before entering the room.

Almost certain that Tootiba would have answers to the questions that were troubling her, Shawndee sat up. She brushed the quilt aside, hopped barefoot to the floor, and hurried to Tootiba.

Tootiba enveloped Shawndee in her warm, soft arms. Shawndee smiled. She could have placed her chin on Tootiba's head if she wanted to, for her elderly friend was quite short, which made her look even heavier and broader in the hips.

As Tootiba continued to hug her, Shawndee's smile faded, for she was aware of a smell that she had noticed often on Tootiba's clothes. It seemed to be some sort of herbal scent.

When Shawndee had first smelled it, she had thought the scent might be of kitchen herbs that Tootiba used while preparing the family's meals.

When Shawndee had grown old enough to recognize the scent of sage and other cooking spices, she knew that this smell on Tootiba's clothes had nothing to do with what she used in preparing food. It had more to do with whatever she did in the privacy of her room . . . concoctions she put together that she never shared with anyone.

But Tootiba *had* begun sharing tales with Shawndee about her native folklore, about voodoo, witchcraft, and omens.

Shawndee gathered from her tales that Tootiba might practice some of those things in her room, yet she had never questioned her about such practices. Shawndee's mother had always told her that Tootiba's life was her own when she was alone in her room.

"Shawndee, honey, you smell so sweet and good tonight," Tootiba said as she took Shawndee's hand and led her toward the bed.

"I sprinkled some of the perfume you gave me for my birthday in the water that I used to wash my hair," Shawndee said, recalling how Tootiba had taught her to do that when she was only a child of five. Even at that age she had learned to hate the smells in her house that came from the whiskey trade.

"On your next birthday I'll give you more perfume," Tootiba said, urging Shawndee back to her bed. "But for now, sweet chil', you mus' get your rest. I heard all about that Chester character and the fright he gave you. He oughta be horsewhipped. I'll do it myself if I ever get the chance."

Shawndee climbed into the softness of the feather bed, smiling contentedly as she rested her back against the headboard. Tootiba gently drew the blanket up to Shawndee's waist, then pulled a chair beside the bed and plopped down onto it.

"Shawndee, you ain't afraid no longer, are you?" Tootiba asked. She reached a hand out and brushed Shawndee's hair back from her face.

"No, not as long as you are here with me," Shawndee murmured, truly feeling safe in Tootiba's presence. No one could love her as much as this sweet, gray-haired woman. Not even Shawndee's mother, who seemed more interested in how she could make her next dollar than in her daughter's welfare.

"I've got my sharp-bladed machete if that man comes anywhere near our house again," Tootiba said, her chin firming with angry determination. "If you ever sees him comin', you just get Tootiba and show him the machete." She laughed throatily. "That Chester man'll take off runnin' so fast he'll look like a streak of lightnin'."

Shawndee laughed softly, then reached for one of Tootiba's hands and gently held it. Her smile waned and she hesitated, her brows drawing together.

"Somethin's still troubling you, honey. Tootiba can tell. Did you hear about that town meeting?"

"What town meeting?" Shawndee asked, startled.

"About your mama's tavern. Now don't you worry about that. Your mama can take care of herself."

Shawndee decided she had to ask the question that was tormenting her.

"Tootiba, tonight, before that man came, I . . . I . . . found something in that old trunk in the attic."

"Whatever you found is troublin' you greatly, sweet chil'," Tootiba said, gazing intently at Shawndee. "Does it truly have to do with a trunk? Or is it still that evil man? Chil', I tol' you he's not goin' to be able to get near you again, not as long as I have anyt'ing to say 'bout it. Or is it that trunk?"

"Chester did give me a scare, but he's not my concern right now," Shawndee said.

"Then don' you think it's best that you tell ol' Tootiba?" Tootiba said, her voice soothing and gentle.

Shawndee slowly took her hands from Tootiba's. "Tootiba," she said, "I . . . I . . . pried the lock open on the old trunk, and . . . and . . . looked inside. I have been so curious for so long, I just couldn't go another night without knowing what was inside it."

"You pried the lock . . . ?" Tootiba said, her eyes widening with surprise.

Shawndee lowered her eyes. "Yes. I know I was wrong to do that," she murmured. She looked up again at Tootiba. "I thought perhaps this trunk might hold some of my mama's earlier dresses from when she lived a more refined life. I had hoped to find things with lace, or perhaps dresses made of velvet. I even hoped to smell perfume on those dresses, so I could imagine the more feminine side of my mother."

"Yes, she was quite beautiful as a young lady," Tootiba murmured, her eyes taking on a distant look. "She was like a princess, your mama. Her locks of blonde hair looked like spun gold. Her eyes were warm, friendly, and filled with curiosity about life. And, Shawndee, you should've seen how thin and petite she was that day she met your papa. When she came home all excited about havin' met him in a store in Boston, it was like she was an angel with wings flying amid the white clouds of heaven."

"She was beautiful?" Shawndee said. She smiled at the thought of her mother being something other than the fearful woman she had become.

"Very," Tootiba said, sighing. "But let's get back to that trunk. What'd you find that makes you feel the need to confess 'bout openin' it?"

"You don't think I'm terrible for having snooped?" Shawndee asked anxiously.

"Chil', I'm surprised you waited this long to ease your curiosity about that trunk," Tootiba said. She laughed throatily. "So don't you fret none over havin' done it."

Tootiba took one of Shawndee's hands and held it. "Honey chil', tell me what's botherin' you about that trunk," she said, her eyes searching Shawndee's face. "You knows you can tell ol' Tootiba everythin'.'"

"Tootiba, I found a book in the trunk, at the far bottom. It had obviously been placed away from the other things so that it might not be found at all," Shawndee explained.

She swallowed hard when she saw a guarded look enter Tootiba's eyes. "Do you know the book?" Shawndee asked warily. "Have you seen it? Have you known all along what was in that trunk . . . that one of those things was a book that no one was meant to see, especially not me? A book . . . about . . . witches?"

"I was with your mama when she hid the book in the trunk," Tootiba softly confessed. She eased her hand from Shawndee's. "And you're right, she'd rather you hadn't found it."

"It's about witches," Shawndee repeated. "Tootiba, I saw my great-grandmother's name in the book, on a list of those who died in Salem. Tell me about it. Tell me about my great-grandmother."

When Tootiba's eyes wavered and she looked away, Shawndee knew that she should not have asked about her great-grandmother.

"You don't have to tell me," Shawndee said. "When I feel the time is right, I'll ask Mama. I don't want you to do something that might make Mama angry with you."

Tootiba turned her eyes slowly back to Shawndee. "It is best left for your mama to tell you," she said, her voice drawn. "But know this, sweet chil', none of the knowin' can affect the sort of person you've become. You are as pure as anyone can be."

"Because you have taught me the right and wrong of things," Shawndee said. She reached her free hand up to Tootiba and affectionately touched her fleshy cheek. "You, sweet Tootiba, are everything to me."

"As you are to me," Tootiba said, swallowing hard. "You are that daughter I never had. I'd protect you with my own life."

"I feel so ashamed for opening Mama's trunk and reading things that were not meant for my eyes," Shawndee said. She went to the window and gazed out at the darkness. Somehow tonight the dark seemed different. There was something sinister about it, something frightening.

"Just know this, Shawndee. You have nothing to fear from knowin' the contents of that trunk. But I do encourage you to forget the book about witches," Tootiba said, her words drawing Shawndee quickly around. "It is best not to let your mother know that you even saw it. Remember, *your* life will never be touched by witchcraft. Tootiba won't allow it."

"Witchcraft?" Shawndee said, her voice breaking. "Oh, Tootiba, since I do know that my family is somehow involved in such things, can't you tell me something more about witchcraft? About . . . witches?"

"I s'pose it can't hurt to tell you a little more," Tootiba said, sighing heavily. "But what Tootiba is goin' to say now is not fact or truth, just somethin' meant for entertainin' idle young ladies curious about Satan's work," Tootiba said.

"Satan's work?" Shawndee gasped out. She reached for the blanket and drew it up beneath her chin.

"Honey chil', witchcraft *is* Satan's work," Tootiba said, then smiled. "But remember, sweet thing, what I tell you tonight is for amusement only, not for serious concern."

"Alright, I'll only think of it that way," Shawndee said, forcing a laugh, for she did not see any humor in this discussion. She suspected that Tootiba was purposely trying to make light of a serious subject.

"Several nights in a row, long, long ago, when a child was wishing to be a grown-up so that she could go out on her own away from the poverty of her family, a tall man approached her," Tootiba said, reaching for a blanket at the foot of the bed and bringing it up to wrap it around her thick, slumped shoulders. "Sometimes this man appeared as a dog. Sometimes he appeared as a hog. Sometimes he appeared as a man. Nevertheless, however he came to this young girl, he asked her to sign his book and to do his work."

"Did she?" Shawndee gasped out.

"She refused him," Tootiba said, her eyes glistening. "She tried to run from him, but he turned into a dog and blocked her way."

"Then what?" Shawndee asked as she leaned up on an elbow. "Tootiba, what did he do to her then?"

"When he saw that nothing he said or did would make her do his bidding, he disappeared," Tootiba said, laughing softly. Then her smiled faded and she visibly shuddered. "But a very close friend of the child could not withstand him. He turned her into a witch. She could be seen flying through the air at night. Her laughter made even the forest animals run from her with fear."

"But the other child?" Shawndee asked. "How did she react to this friend who was now a witch?"

"She was such a devout friend," Tootiba said softly, "she continued to stand by her companion. This friendship caused the bewitched girl to change back to the sweet person that she was before the Devil came into her life. But . . ."

"But?" Shawndee said, leaning forward to look more intently into Tootiba's eyes. "What happened?"

"She was covered with terrible warts, and when she had her first child, the child suckled from one of those warts instead of her breasts," Tootiba said, her voice drawn. "You see, the Devil did not give her up entirely to the good world she so desperately wanted to be a part of."

"How terrible," Shawndee said, shuddering. "How sad."

"The child who suckled from warts to get her nourishment grew up healthy and had a child of her own, a *girl*," Tootiba said with a guardedness Shawndee did not understand, not until Tootiba finished what she was saying, then crept from the room, leaving Shawndee dazed by the truth that had come out of this latest tale.

The child, the daughter of that woman who had suckled from its mother's warts . . . was none other than Tootiba!

Chapter Seven

Even though Shawndee knew she was taking a chance of being seen by Chester, she had put all caution behind her, donning her boy's clothes again and fleeing her bedroom.

Thus far tonight, Shawndee had not seen hide nor hair of Chester Hawkins as she ran beneath the shadows of fully leafed trees or the taller shadows of the town's false-fronted buildings. Dressed in her boy's attire, with her hat pulled low over her brow, Shawndee blended well with the darkness.

She kept her eyes on the bright glow coming from lanterns in the windows of the town hall building. Lying in her bed after Tootiba had left, she had begun worrying about the town meeting Tootiba had mentioned.

And despite the danger of being alone on the dark streets, especially knowing that Chester would surely take the first opportunity to grab her, Shawndee had decided to find out why her mother was the subject of this meeting, and whether or not her mother's life was in danger because of it.

When she finally reached the two-story stone building where all of the town's civil affairs were held, Shawndee glanced in both directions down the street and along the board sidewalks. As soon as she saw that there was no one nearby to catch her, she bent low beneath one of the open windows and listened.

She cringed when she heard her mother's name spoken with a hatred that grated on Shawndee's nerves.

One lady poked fun at Shawndee's mother. Then another lady claimed that Shawndee's mother and her dead husband had brought decay to Silver Creek.

When Shawndee heard the word "witch" mentioned in the same breath as her mother's name, her spine stiffened and her heart skipped a beat.

Why, oh, why, was this happening? Shawndee was beginning to believe her great-grandmother might have been a witch.

But these women were talking about her *mother* being a witch!

What could have prompted such talk?

Did they know something she didn't know?

And what was worse, the women were now making plans about how to run her mother, the "witch," out of town.

It was terrifying for Shawndee to hear!

"No!" Shawndee whispered as one of the ladies spoke of not only running the witch out of town, but also her son and her black "voodoo" friend.

Panic grabbed Shawndee in the pit of her stomach as she realized just how serious the situation had become.

"I . . . must . . . warn Mother," she whispered to herself.

With a racing pulse, she turned to hurry home, but was stopped dead in her tracks when a hand swept around from behind her and covered her mouth to keep her from screaming. At the same time, an arm snaked quickly around her waist and lifted her from the ground, carrying her away from the window.

Shawndee's first thoughts were that Chester had followed her and was now carrying her off to have his way with her.

Knowing that she must do whatever she could to fight off her assailant, Shawndee grabbed hold of the arm that was around her and tried to push it away from her, but her captor was too strong for her to budge it.

She tried to wriggle free as she realized where she

was being taken . . . to the dark shadows of the forest that stretched for miles away from Silver Creek, where anything could happen and no one would be the wiser.

It was a dense, dark, dank place, where four-legged animals prowled and sought prey at night. She knew that wolves, coyotes, bears, and even an occasional puma were known to wander that forest.

If Chester got her far enough away from the town that no one would hear her screams, then he could have his way with her. Afterward, he would probably kill her and leave her for food for the wild animals.

But was it Chester who had abducted her? This man wore nothing on his arms, for it was bare flesh that she shoved against in her efforts to get free.

Also, the smell of this man was very different from Chester's. Chester always reeked of alcohol and tobacco. This man smelled fresh and clean, a mixture of river water and cedar.

Suddenly she saw the shine of the river through a break in the trees a few yards away. The moon was shining down on the river, giving the water a soft glow, as though a lantern were lit below the surface. The moon's glow revealed to Shawndee a canoe beached on the bank. She now realized it was this canoe that her abductor was moving toward.

When they reached it and he lifted her into the

canoe and placed her on her back on the floor, Shawndee was finally able to see who her abductor was.

She gasped when she saw that it was not Chester Hawkins.

It was an Indian.

It . . . was . . . *him*, the intriguingly handsome Indian whom she had briefly seen in the general store.

Shadow Hawk grabbed a knife from the sheath at his right side. He bent low over the canoe and placed the blade of the knife close to the throat of his captive. "If you value your life," he said flatly, "you will not shout for help or try to get away. You must cooperate with Shadow Hawk."

Shadow Hawk? Shawndee thought incredulously to herself. This man was Shadow Hawk, the young Seneca chief she had heard about.

Thank heavens, everything she had heard about him was good. She knew now that she had a chance of living through this latest ordeal.

Stunned, Shawndee forgot to speak like a boy. "Why have you abducted me?" she asked in a voice that was entirely feminine. "Are . . . you . . . going to rape me?"

She swallowed hard when she recalled what her mother had said about Indians and their scalp poles. "Are . . . are . . . you going . . . to scalp me?" she stammered out, frozen with fear on the floor of the birchbark canoe.

Realizing now that he had captured a young woman, not a *boy*, Shadow Hawk was stunned almost speechless.

He leaned closer to Shawndee and studied her upturned face. This close, the moon revealed a face of great beauty, with eyes and lips that mesmerized him.

He recalled now that in the store he had briefly thought there was something odd about the boy. But the store had been dark and his captive had been wearing a hat that hid most of her facial features. He had not been able to study her as he was doing now.

He gazed at her breasts beneath the blue denim shirt she wore.

His eyebrows rose, for he saw how flat-chested she was. He had never seen a woman whose chest was so flat.

His eyes went to her hair. When he had grabbed her, the hat had fallen away from her head.

He held his knife steady in one hand while with the other he reached up and untied the thong that held her hair in a ponytail.

He could hardly hold back a gasp of wonder when her hair tumbled down around her shoulders, golden, glistening, and thick.

He was taken by its richness, but most of all by its color.

Only a few other times had he seen hair the color of summer wheat.

Ah, he wanted so badly to run his fingers through it, to press it to his nose and smell it.

But seeing the alarmed look in the woman's eyes, and hearing her shallow breathing, he knew that he had a choice to make. Should he keep her now that he knew she was a woman, and not a boy?

"You are not a boy as I thought you were," Shadow Hawk said thickly, then grew quiet for a moment as he studied Shawndee even more closely.

"Who are you? What is your name?" he demanded as he moved the knife away from her.

"Shawndee," she said, trembling. "Shawndee . . . Sibley."

She could not stop staring at his face. No matter that he held her hostage, she was intrigued by just how handsome he was.

She knew now that he had mistaken her for someone else and that he would surely soon release her.

But did she really want that?

Might he not be the man she had always sought, the one who would take her away from the life she detested?

True, this man's skin was copper colored, and he wore clothes—a mere breechclout—that showed

73

his life was very different from the men she saw riding their steeds through Silver Creek.

This was an Indian whose customs were not her own. Nonetheless, frilly clothes seemed suddenly less important to her. Beaded buckskins or doeskin dresses would do! Even living in a tepee would be better than how she lived now!

Then she realized just how foolish she was to fantasize about such things at a time like this, when her life might be in danger. Now that Shadow Hawk had abducted the wrong person, what would he do to rectify the mistake? Would he decide to kill her to keep her silent?

She had no choice but to pray that he was a decent man who would not kill an innocent woman.

The way he was gazing at her made her feel less threatened. She wondered if he was as intrigued by her as she was by him. He seemed to be looking at her with wonder as he studied her facial features, then gazed at her beautiful hair.

"Shawndee," Shadow Hawk said, repeating her name.

"Since you know now that you have mistakenly abducted a woman, will you let me go?" Shawndee asked, her eyes watching his knife as he slowly lowered it to his side.

She sat up slowly.

She knew that she could try to escape now, for she believed that she could jump to her feet and kick the knife away from his hand. But she wanted to trust him.

"I promise not to tell anyone that you did this," Shawndee blurted out. "Just please let me go? Then . . . then . . . perhaps we can meet again at another time and place, as friends?"

If they had only met under different circumstances, she thought, it could have been magical. She sensed that he was attracted to her just as she was to him.

He had looked past her clothes to the woman within. Suddenly she felt oh, so feminine beneath the wonder in his eyes.

Confused and torn, Shadow Hawk searched his conscience. He had never planned to abduct an innocent woman.

But now that he had, would she not serve the same purpose as the boy he had thought he'd captured?

And was he not taken with her?

Would it not be wonderful to have time with her, to know her better?

His jaw tightened, and once again he raised his knife. "You are still my captive," he said throatily. "It matters not to me that you are a *wee-nighh*, woman. You will still serve my purpose."

He tried not to pay any heed to the way her eyes widened in fear, or how she gasped to learn that his intentions had not changed.

She stood up and moved away from him in the canoe, threatening to topple over backwards into the water.

"Why?" Shawndee gasped out, steadying herself. "Of what use could I possibly be to you?"

Seeing no need to supply her with answers, at least not yet, Shadow Hawk closed his lips in a tight, silent line.

When he saw her make a move toward him, he raised the knife between them again.

"Must I tie you to ensure that you will not try to escape Shadow Hawk?" he asked, his eyes flashing.

Afraid of being tied up, Shawndee anxiously shook her head. "No, please don't do that," she blurted out. "I won't try to escape. Honest. Just please don't bind my wrists, or my ankles."

"Just remember, woman named Shawndee, that my knife is a deadly weapon should you try to flee," Shadow Hawk said. He waded farther out into the river, dragging the canoe with him until he was knee-deep in the water.

"Yes, I can see its sharp edge," Shawndee said, shuddering involuntarily as she stared at it. "I . . . won't . . . try anything."

"Move to the front of the canoe and sit down on the seat," Shadow Hawk ordered flatly, his eyes never leaving her as she swallowed hard and did as he said.

He truly regretted having to treat this woman in

such a way, but he had not entered into this plan lightly. Once the people in the tavern cooperated and agreed to leave the area, he would relinquish his hold on their child.

But would it be so easy to let her go? This woman was beautiful, and she seemed so sweet.

Surely if she wore something besides boy's clothes, she would be as feminine as any woman in his village. Perhaps even more so, for none of them had made him look twice. None had made him realize the depths of his *ne-hagwenda-s*, his lonesomeness, his need of a woman he could call his own. Suddenly he ached to have a wife.

He desired *this* woman, even if she didn't have breasts enough to fill a man's hands. There was more to a woman's body than breasts.

He was eager to hear why she felt the need to dress in clothes that made people believe she was someone else, but for now, he had other duties to see to. He had his plan to carry out.

Later, he would find out as much about this woman as she would willingly share with him.

Now that Shawndee was sitting at the front of the canoe as he'd instructed, her hands gripping the sides, Shadow Hawk boarded the canoe himself.

He positioned himself behind Shawndee in the middle of the canoe, rested his knife on his lap, then picked up his paddle and sent the vessel up the moon-shadowed avenue of the Genesee River.

He could not take his eyes off the golden hair, the straight back of the woman, the lily-white hands that held to the canoe's sides.

His mind was filled with the entrancing loveliness of the woman's face, the litheness of her body beneath those terrible clothes, and even the name that her parents had given her.

It puzzled him why her parents would give their child a girl's name and then try everything in their power to turn that girl into a boy.

Shawndee was filled with many emotions, and strangely enough, fear of the Indian was not the most prominent. Her true fear lay back in Silver Creek, where her mother's life might at any moment be threatened by people who would do anything to rid their town of the woman they now called a "witch."

"Mama, oh, Mama, oh, *Tootiba*, what is going to happen now that I can't warn you about the threat?" Shawndee whispered to herself.

She felt totally helpless, and a sudden anger toward the Indian made her fingers leave the sides of the canoe to knot into fists on her lap.

Never mind the promise she'd made, Shawndee thought angrily. She *must* find a way to escape him!

And by hook or by crook . . . she would!

Chapter Eight

"Let's waste no time with this now that we know we have a witch living in our town," Carolyn Harper said, glancing over at Chester as he slipped out the front door.

She looked around the circle of women again, their eyes transfixed on her, some of their mouths gaping. "Let's treat Jane Sibley like a witch," she said. "Let's all go with torches to the witch's house and scare her away. We can threaten to burn her at the stake if she doesn't agree to leave."

A strange hush fell over the women as they looked from one to another questioningly.

Then one of the women who hadn't spoken before stood. "I can't imagine ever doing anything like that," Beth Sexton said in a squeaky, tiny voice.

She visibly shuddered. She reached a hand to her thin shoulder-length hair and nervously ran her trembling fingers through it. She was so thin and tall she made scarcely a shadow as the lamp flickered behind her on a table. Her pale eyes squinted through thick-lensed glasses.

"Aren't there any among you who share my apprehension about this?" Beth asked. "Don't you see that God may be frowning upon us at this very moment over . . . over . . . how we are speaking of another human being?"

"Haven't you heard a thing that's been said tonight?" a heavyset, round-faced woman said as she pushed herself out of her chair and stood with her hands on her hips, glaring at Beth. "We ain't dealin' with a human being here. She's a witch."

"There isn't any absolute proof that she is," Beth said, wincing when the other woman doubled her fleshy hands into tight fists at her sides.

Beth nervously looked away from her and gazed around at the other women. "Don't you all see that it's only speculation that Jane Sibley is a witch?" she said. "Are you going to let a man like Chester Hawkins get you so riled up about a woman that you . . . that you . . . would plan to go to her house with torches and run her out of town, even burn her alive if she doesn't agree to leave?"

"Not only *her* but also her son Andrew and that black woman named Tootiba," Carolyn said icily.

"What kind of woman would have a servant like her in the house? Don't you know she came from a place that practices voodoo?"

Beth softly argued, "I suggest we all go to our own homes tonight and think through everything we have discussed. Pray about it. Then when we meet again, let's take a vote. If the vote leans toward ridding the town of Jane Sibley, her son, and Too-tiba, then let us do it rationally. Let's not take torches like wild hoodlums. Let's invite them to a town meeting and talk like decent human beings about the problem."

"Haven't you heard a word anyone said about the strange things happening in this town?" Carolyn said, stepping away from her chair and standing in the center of the circle of seated women. She glared at Beth. "Beth, you have always been the timid one of our group. Well, this is not the right time for such behavior. Something has got to be done about that woman and her den of iniquity. What could be better than chasing her out of town? We have a good excuse now. Lord, she's a *witch*. Surely not even the sheriff will do anything to stop us."

"Yes, a witch is a witch," Sarah James said. "And voodoo is voodoo. We can't have anything like that as part of our community.

"Chester was right to come and tell us about Jane Sibley's threat to witch him," Sarah went on. "He understands the need to clean up our community.

Selling alcohol to our menfolk is one thing. But witching us in various ways is another. I say go and face her with what we know. I say show her the torches and she'll know we mean business. Chester is taking *his* business elsewhere. So don't you see? We've only got Jane Sibley and her brood to tend to."

"I agree that there should be no lenience as far as the witch's son is concerned," another lady said. "Is he not the son of a witch, with her blood rushing through his veins? Who is to say he will not use voodoo or whatever else witches use to protect his mother?"

"And I will gladly tell the black woman that she must leave, as well," Carolyn said, harrumphing. "She has surely brought her voodoo practices with her from Jamaica."

"I say let's waste no more time talking about this," Sarah shouted. She raised a fist in the air and shook it. "Let's get torches made and go and show that witch a thing or two tonight. The longer she's in our town, the more time she has to think of ways to witch us. I'm tired of worrying about it. Come on, ladies. Let's get the deed done and then after they are gone, let's burn the house and all traces of those who lived there."

Beth Sexton took a slow step away from everyone, then, sobbing, ran from the building.

A hushed silence followed inside the town hall.

Despite their brave words, they all had fears about what they were planning.

Then Carolyn stomped to the door. "Follow me," she shouted over her shoulder. "I know where we can find supplies to make our torches. My husband's general store!"

One by one the women left the town hall.

The moon cast dancing shadows all around them on the boardwalk as they made their way toward the general store.

No one said anything. Many of them were questioning the sanity of what they were about to do.

But still they proceeded onward. Their plans were made. Now all they had to do was carry them out.

When it was all done and behind them, they would pray for their own souls.

Chapter Nine

Shawndee said a quiet prayer that she would succeed in her effort to escape Shadow Hawk.

If she could reach land before him and hide long enough for him to give up his search for her, she would be able to get home to help her mother.

Her heart raced. She tried to fight off the fear that had caused her legs to suddenly feel as heavy as lead.

She needed every ounce of energy, and especially the full use of her legs, to get to shore before Shadow Hawk.

Realizing that now was the time to act, Shawndee sucked in her breath, held it, closed her eyes, then threw herself sideways over the edge of the canoe.

She plummeted into the cool, deep river, then forced herself upward again through the water, the moon's glow like a beacon as she gazed up at the surface. She exhaled a deep breath of air as her head broke free of the water.

She was acutely aware of a big splash behind her and knew that Shadow Hawk had dived into the river and was now in pursuit of her.

Skilled at holding her breath and swimming for a good distance beneath water, Shawndee inhaled a deep breath, then dove down and began making her way toward shore with long, deep strokes and kicking feet.

The moon was guiding her forward, its glow making her feel less alone in the deep.

But then it was gone.

She gazed up and realized that a sudden covering of cloud had swallowed the moon whole.

But wasn't that more in her favor than not? She needed to get to the surface for air to continue her swim. With the moon behind a cloud, she would be less visible to Shadow Hawk.

She began kicking her feet and legs to get herself to the surface, then felt something wrapping around one of her ankles.

At first she thought it was Shadow Hawk who had reached out and grabbed her. But she soon realized that it wasn't a man's hand that had her foot in its grip.

No!

She had managed to get tangled in some kind of debris. Panic filled her. She peered through the dark water to see what was holding her fast.

Then the moon came out again and sent its glow down toward her and she was able to see that her foot was caught in a twisted pocket of small limbs that were lodged in the fork of a fallen tree. The log rested on the bottom of the river, its branches reaching out like arms.

As she yanked and pulled and became more panicky when she still couldn't get herself free, she began swallowing great gulps of water.

She was afraid now that she was living her last moments of life!

Papa, she thought as blackness began overtaking her. *Oh, Papa, please . . . help . . . me!*

She knew that if she did not get free in a matter of seconds, she would be joining her father somewhere in the heavens.

Strange how she was no longer afraid.

Chapter Ten

Having lost sight of Shawndee after she dove underwater, Shadow Hawk swam more slowly, watching for her to come to the surface for air. He knew she could not stay below much longer. Having seen the direction she was swimming, he followed the same path through the water.

When she still didn't rise to the surface, it occurred to him suddenly that she might be in trouble. If she was too stubborn to come up for air when she should, she might have waited too long and lost consciousness. She could be drowning at this very moment.

Filled with panic over Shawndee's welfare, Shadow Hawk plunged headfirst into the darker depths of the river.

He was thankful that the moon had slid free of the clouds and lent him just enough light to be able to see around him.

When he finally saw Shawndee, his heart sank. He could see that not only was her foot tangled in brush, but she was also lethargic, which might mean that she was close to being unconscious.

She might even be dead!

When he saw her eyes flutter open as he reached her and began untangling the debris from her foot, he was relieved to know that surely he had reached her in time.

After finally freeing her foot, he wrapped an arm around her and held her close to his side, using his free arm to propel them toward the surface.

When Shawndee's eyes closed again and she lay limply in his arms, Shadow Hawk's heart sank, for he feared that he had been too late. If her lungs were filled with water, and she died, he doubted that he would be able to live with the knowledge that he was responsible.

He was relieved when he finally reached the surface and towed Shawndee to the riverbank.

How his heart would sing if she opened her eyes and he saw that she was going to be alright.

Panting hard, his heart racing, Shadow Hawk found the rocky bottom of the river with his feet. He gathered Shawndee into his arms, carried her from the river, and spread her out on the ground on her belly.

He gently arranged her face sideways so that he could see her eyes. But he grew cold with fear when he saw that she was still unconscious.

As he straddled her, he placed his hands on her and gently squeezed down on her back.

He wanted to shout a loud thank you to the heavens when Shawndee began coughing, gagging, and crying as water spurted from her mouth, until she finally subsided, lying still and breathing evenly.

Having succeeded at reviving her, Shadow Hawk crawled to his knees beside her.

Gently he rolled her over to lie on her back, then brushed wet tendrils of her golden hair back from her eyes.

"Thank you," Shawndee managed in a whisper. "I . . . truly . . . thought I would not make it."

"You are very much alive, and do not thank me for it. It is because of Shadow Hawk that you were in the water in the first place," he said, his voice drawn.

"No matter why I was in the water, you did save me and I . . . shall . . . forever be in your debt," Shawndee said, coughing softly.

She knew she should be angry with him, for she *wouldn't* have been put in such danger if he had not abducted her.

But the fact that he had rescued her, and that he

looked at her now with such guilt and gentleness, made her forgive him. At this moment in time what worried her most was how cold she was. She was shivering as her wet clothes clung to her. Her teeth were chattering and she saw that her fingers were blue.

"I see how cold you are," Shadow Hawk said thickly. "You must remove those wet clothes. I will go for my canoe and get a blanket from it."

He rose and started to walk away; then on second thought, realizing that while he swam out to his canoe she would have a chance to escape, he stopped and turned to her again.

With an arched eyebrow he gazed down at her.

Her eyes met and held his, and then her trembling lips moved gently into a soft smile.

"I'm too cold to go anywhere," she said. "I can tell you don't trust leaving me here alone. You can. I'm not only cold, I'm also weak. Please? Please go for the blanket. I'm so cold I ache."

Trusting that she would keep her word, and also knowing that she was too weak to escape, he gave her another long look, then turned and swam to his canoe. He soon had it beached and was standing over Shawndee with the blanket.

Shivering almost uncontrollably now, Shawndee was too cold to even care about undressing in front of a man for the first time in her life. She was too eager to get the wet clothes off and warm herself in the blanket to think about anything else.

Her fingers trembled as she slipped off her shirt, then saw Shadow Hawk staring at the cloths binding her breasts. She could see the puzzlement in his eyes, then was glad when he turned abruptly around and gave her privacy.

She hurriedly removed the tight, wet binding from her breasts and rushed out of her other things.

Then she reached for the blanket that Shadow Hawk was holding behind him with only one hand.

"It feels so wonderful," Shawndee said, sighing as she wrapped the blanket around her shoulders and snuggled it close to her body.

Seeing that Shadow Hawk still had his back to her, as though waiting for her to give the word that she was fully covered, she smiled. He was acting like a gentleman, treating her with gentleness and kindness. Perhaps she could convince him now to set her free.

"Shadow Hawk, am I still your prisoner?" she asked softly.

She gasped when he turned abruptly on a heel. The moon revealed to her that he was frowning as he gazed into her eyes.

"Can't you please let me go home?" she begged. She wished to confide in him and tell him how desperately she was needed at home, that she actually feared for her mother's and Tootiba's lives.

Yet how could she tell him of her fears without

also revealing things about her mother which she didn't want to explain to anyone, not until she was able to question her mother about the book and what she had found in it.

The mere chance that Shawndee was from a family of witches sent shivers up and down her spine.

She most certainly didn't want to confide such a thing to this man. She would keep her silence about it and wait and find a way to escape from him again. Only this time she would succeed.

"No, I cannot let you go," Shadow Hawk said, his voice drawn. "You are needed. There is a reason why I abducted you."

Shawndee's insides tightened. She gazed intently at him. "What sort of reason?" she dared to ask. "How could I be of any importance to you?"

"Are you warm now?" Shadow Hawk asked, trying to distract her. •

"Yes, warm enough," Shawndee murmured, still clutching the blanket around her shoulders to ward off the chill of night. She realized that he was purposely ignoring her question. It was obvious that she was still at his mercy and would remain so until she thought up a plan that would make it otherwise.

"Then we will proceed now to my village in the canoe," Shadow Hawk said.

Shawndee caught her breath and almost dropped the blanket when Shadow Hawk suddenly swept her up into his arms and carried her to his canoe.

After placing her there, along with her wet clothes, he boarded the canoe and pushed it out into the center of the river to begin his journey homeward again.

He watched Shawndee, worrying about how he was going to stay firm with her as his prisoner when what he really wanted was to have her as his woman.

He glowed with inner warmth at the thought of taking her to his blankets with him and teaching her all of the ways to love.

But he knew the foolishness of such thoughts. He realized she was only biding her time until she found a way of escaping him again. He smiled at her bravery . . . her courage . . . her determination.

She was the sort of woman a man would go to war over!

"I'm still so cold," Shawndee said as she looked pleadingly over her shoulder at Shadow Hawk.

"We shall be home soon," he said. As he spoke the word "home," he pictured her there with him, not as a prisoner but as the woman who would fill his lodge with sunshine . . . who would warm his bed and reach her arms out for him as she welcomed him.

Shawndee's heart skipped a beat, for she saw a tenderness in his eyes that made her feel she was much more than a captive to him.

If only things were different, she thought to herself. If only they could have met under different circumstances. She imagined that she was in his canoe willingly and going to his home at Shadow Hawk's invitation, and not as his prisoner. It was not hard to see herself in his arms, to feel his lips pressed to hers, warm and passionate.

Chapter Eleven

Haunted by images of that filthy-minded man in the attic eyeing Shawndee as though she were a juicy morsel he was going to consume, Jane Sibley left the crowd of drinkers to go to Shawndee's room.

As she went up the steep staircase, Jane eyed the flickering candles that were placed along the upstairs corridor in wall sconces; then her gaze settled on Shawndee's closed bedroom door. She hoped to find her daughter bathed and dressed in her sleeping attire, her hair loose and beautiful around her shoulders. She expected Shawndee would be resting on her bed, reading, with her door locked to intruders.

As Jane walked toward her daughter's door, she

did something that most would not think she was capable of doing. She prayed, but not aloud. Her prayers were always to herself, and most of the time they had to do only with Shawndee. Jane was doing everything within her power to provide for her daughter.

Of course, Jane knew that the way she did this was frowned upon by the genteel folk of all the towns in which she and her husband had established their taverns.

Widowed now, and knowing nothing but the liquor trade, Jane had no choice but to continue doing what she could to earn a living. Her main worry was how on earth her daughter was going to meet a decent man who would help her escape this sordid life.

Earlier on, when Shawndee was too small to remember, Jane had endured many embarrassments trying to attend church in each of the towns where she had lived. She had wanted her daughter to be raised in the house of the Lord, had hoped she might eventually meet the sort of man Jane wanted for her daughter, but when folks realized who Jane was, she was inevitably asked to leave.

Jane had given up trying the Lord's way long ago when Shawndee was too small to ask why. Jane had never wanted her daughter to suffer the embarrassment that she had endured at the hands of women who acted as though they were God's gift to earth.

Jane understood the trap that her daughter was in, living her life in the shadow of her "sinner" mother, and Jane knew that things had to change. She had enough money saved beneath the loose floorboard in her bedroom to finally offer her daughter another life.

But that required moving to another town where no one knew them. Soon Jane would tell Shawndee what she had planned.

Her eyes brightened and she smiled.

Tonight.

Why not tell her tonight?

Her steps became more eager, yet she was still upset about Chester Hawkins.

Oh, Lord, she hoped that Shawndee had learned her lesson about going to the attic where she could be found by any man who might sneak past Jane downstairs.

Jane stopped at Shawndee's door. "Shawndee?" she said. She spoke quietly so that the men downstairs would not hear, yet loud enough so Shawndee would know it was her mother outside the door.

"Shawndee, unlock the door," Jane said. "I've something exciting to tell you."

When there was no response, Jane looked toward the ladder that led to the attic.

Again images of what had happened there

flashed through her mind. What if it had not been enough to frighten Shawndee out of going there again?

The thought of Shawndee being so reckless made Jane determinedly place her hand on the doorknob and try it.

She said a soft prayer that she was worried over nothing . . . that Shawndee was just asleep.

Jane gasped when she found that the doorknob was turning. That meant Shawndee had neglected to lock it.

"How can she be so absentminded?" Jane whispered to herself as she hurriedly opened the door. She stopped when she found no candles lit.

But as her eyes adapted to the darkness, and she saw that her daughter's bed was empty, Jane's knees grew weak with fear.

"Oh, no, not Chester," Jane moaned as she hurried into the room and stood over the bed. She knew that the back staircase would allow someone to sneak upstairs without being seen, yet she did not believe that anyone would think to use it. No one went to the back part of her house where the kitchen and her office were located.

Jane did not believe Shawndee would be foolish enough to leave the house after dark.

"She must be in the attic again," Jane decided, nodding.

She did understand Shawndee's love of the old

books that had traveled with the household items from place to place through the years. Shawndee had even said she would love to be a librarian, a dream that might be possible if they could move elsewhere and assume new identities so no one would know of their past.

That was what Jane had in mind—to make her daughter's dreams come true. When Shawndee shed her ugly boy's clothes and wore feminine ones that would display her loveliness to everyone, the men would come clamoring to her doorstep to court her!

Jane silently prayed that Shawndee was in the attic getting a book to bring back to her room. She started to leave the bedroom to go to the attic, then stopped abruptly when something on the ceiling caught her attention. It was the reflection of flickering flames.

Stunned and puzzled, Jane swung around to go to the window to investigate, but stopped when a flurry of footsteps brought Tootiba into the room.

"Torches!" Tootiba said breathlessly, her dark eyes wide with fear. "Look out the window! Many women are there carrying torches! They've stopped at our house!"

Jane gasped in horror, then went cold when chants began outside, the sound of many women's voices being carried on the wind.

"Shawndee!" Jane gasped, paling. Where was Shawndee?

"Tootiba, Shawndee is missing," Jane blurted out. "Could she be in the attic?"

Tootiba lowered her eyes. "No, ma'am, she ain't," she murmured. "I was there lookin' for her myself when I heard the commotion outside. She's not there."

"Lord, Lord," Jane said, wringing her hands.

Tootiba turned wide eyes to Jane. "Where do you think she's gone?" she said, her voice now shrill.

Jane exhaled nervously. "Only the good Lord knows," she said, swallowing hard.

She doubled her hands into tight fists at her sides, and her eyes lit with fire.

"It's the people of this town who are the cause of whatever has happened to my baby," she said venomously. "Those damn hypocritical women. I'm going to tell them a thing or two. There ain't no way in hell they're going to frighten Jane Sibley with their shenanigans."

Huffing and puffing, Jane stamped past Tootiba and made a quick descent down the stairs.

When she reached the first floor, the drunken men crowded around her at the front door as she yanked it open to face the mob.

Determined not to allow the women of Silver Creek to see how hurt she was at being singled out again, Jane went out onto the porch and placed her fists on her hips as she stared down at those who held the torches.

As she looked from face to face, the fire's glow reflected in the women's eyes as though they were advocates of the Devil, she found a strange sort of peace inside. Suddenly she knew she would get through this embarrassment as she had always met the challenges of the past. She had the strength and courage to place herself above these prejudiced women, no matter what they said, or did, to her.

But tonight they were chanting something different from the taunts that had been hurled at her in other towns. A witch? Yes, they were calling her a witch!

As the shouting grew louder, Jane stood her ground, her tightened lips and jaw proof that these women did not frighten her one iota. Shawndee was her only concern. Jane had to get rid of this mob as quickly as possible in order to get Sheriff Dawson to help her find Shawndee.

Staring the women down instead of responding to them, she hoped she might unnerve them enough to chase them off.

She flinched and her heart lurched anew with each added shout. The women were now yelling that she had to leave town.

Tootiba inched her way out the door to stand behind Jane. She seemed as stunned as her mistress to hear the women accusing them of being witches.

They were now even ordering Jane and Tootiba out of town, saying they had only a few days to pack up their things and leave. They were saying that if Jane and Tootiba weren't gone soon, they would be burned at the stake.

Jane was stunned by the increasingly angry threats coming from the women. Then she saw Chester at the far edge of the crowd, smiling, his eyes filled with amusement.

Anger flashed through Jane, for she now understood that he had to be the one who was responsible for the women calling her a witch. She recalled what she had said about witching him.

Only now did she realize the foolishness of her words. She should have known that the local women would pounce on anything they could to use against her.

Jane had never thought that Chester would take her so seriously that he would tell someone else what she had said. But she now realized that she should have expected something like this from that twisted, disgusting man.

There was one thing positive about seeing him there with the women: He surely had nothing to do with Shawndee's disappearance. If he had Shawndee in his clutches, he would be taking advantage of every minute with her, not standing with these women . . . unless he had already used and discarded her!

Stunned by the savagery of the women, and afraid of what Chester might have done to Shawn-dee, Jane felt more threatened than she ever had in her entire life.

She had to think quickly of a way to handle this, of a way to make the women leave, so that she could look for Shawndee.

When Jane saw the sheriff riding up on his black horse, causing the women to scatter out of his way, Jane sighed with relief. She knew that if anyone could handle this situation, Sheriff Dawson could.

Because of his love of whiskey, and because he was lonely since his wife's untimely death and enjoyed talking with Jane, he would surely help Jane out of this newest scrape. And when that was done, he would find Shawndee!

Big and broad, sporting a wide-brimmed hat on his head and a reddish-brown beard that almost hid all of his facial features, Sheriff Dawson brought his steed to a rearing halt.

Still in the saddle, the sheriff yanked his long-barreled firearm from the gunboot at the side of his horse, then waved it in the air for all to see.

"Now I've about heard enough of this hogwash tonight," he shouted. "I've been back in those trees all the time, watchin' and listenin'. Now git home to your families, do you hear? Scat! Stop that gol'darn fussin'. Go mind your own business, do you hear?"

Then he lowered his gun, slid it into his gunboot, and gazed with troubled eyes at Jane. "And as for you, Miss Jane, I'd better not hear about any more witchcraft threats, or I'll be the one to set the fire that'll silence your words forever," he growled out as everyone stood and listened. "I don't want any witches in my town. If you don't want me thinkin' on you *bein'* a witch, you'd best talk and act like a normal human bein', or else."

"Tell her to leave!" Carolyn Harper shouted from behind him. "Tell her we don't want the likes of her here in our town."

Sheriff Dawson turned his eyes to the crowd and sorted through the women until he found the one who had spoken. "Now, Mrs. Harper, I don't think you hear so good," he shouted back at her.

Then he looked slowly around the crowd, glaring at each of the women in turn. "None of you seem to've heard," he shouted. "I told you to go home. Scat. Hightail it back to your homes. *Git*. Do it now or . . ."

He didn't have to say another word. The women scrambled away, their torches all tossed in one large heap in the road in front of Jane's house.

Jane still hadn't moved.

She stared at the sheriff as he turned and looked at her.

She was stunned by the sheriff's attitude toward her. He had spoken in such a cold, unfriendly, impersonal way, after having been her friend when no one else would be.

Lord, if she didn't have *him* solidly behind her in this latest crisis, how could she get through it?

And how could she ask him now to help her find Shawndee?

She had just lost all the respect she had ever had for this man. Someone who turned his back on you when you needed him the most was someone who never truly was a friend.

Holding back the strong urge to call the sheriff a sonofabitch, Jane stood her ground, her lips tightly pursed.

She was glad when he rode off. She hated this man now with a passion. But she was glad that at least he had gotten rid of the mob tonight.

She went cold when she thought of Shawndee. She was especially afraid for her daughter now. With no one to help find her, and feeling too threatened to go out into the darkness to search for Shawndee, she had no choice now but to wait . . . and . . . pray.

She had never been so afraid, or felt so helpless.

Chapter Twelve

When Shadow Hawk arrived at his village with Shawndee, it was the time of night when almost everyone was asleep. This gave him the privacy he needed to carry out his plan without interference.

He hoped to achieve his goal without having to involve his people in his unusual act of abduction. Although he was his people's *hasennowane*, their chief, he knew they would question his actions, which could bring trouble to them all.

He hoped for just the opposite result. He had one goal in mind—to help his people by removing a source of temptation.

Shawndee was aware of Shadow Hawk's silence; he seemed deep in thought. She walked quietly beside him in her squashy wet boots, the blanket still clutched closely around her shoulders. Although the Seneca did not live far upriver from Silver Creek, Shawndee had never wandered to their village.

Now that she was at the village, she was surprised to see that the Seneca did not reside in tepees. Instead they lived in long, gabled houses which appeared, beneath the light of the moon, to be covered with elm bark. The village overlooked the river from the hills of its western banks. She could see that the village was surrounded by gardens filled with many vegetables. The houses were scattered here and there in random fashion.

"Come into my longhouse with me," Shadow Hawk said, gesturing toward the door of his lodge. "There you can get warm by my fire and I shall give you something better than a blanket to keep around you until your clothes dry."

Shawndee hesitated and gave Shadow Hawk a guarded look.

Shadow Hawk saw the suspicion in her eyes. He understood.

Would he not also be suspicious if he had been abducted and taken to his captor's private lodge? Especially since she was a woman and he was a man, it was understandable that she was afraid of what lay ahead.

"You need not be afraid of Shadow Hawk," he said thickly. "You need not be afraid to enter

Shadow Hawk's longhouse. My home has many rooms, and I do not live alone. Purple Cloud, my *no-tha*, resides in my lodge with me."

"I did not understand the word you spoke," Shawndee said.

"In Seneca, I said 'father,' " Shadow Hawk said.

"Oh, I see. Your *father* lives with you," Shawndee replied. She had wondered if he might have a wife, perhaps even children.

A part of her was glad that it was only a father he shared his home with. Yet the more rational side of her wanted to shout that she didn't care who he lived with . . . that she wanted to go to her own home!

"Yes, my father," Shadow Hawk said. "He was our people's chief until he grew too ill to rule. He handed his chieftainship to me, his son, Shadow Hawk. My father has taken over the role of storyteller for our Hawk clan. He hopes to teach the children pride in their heritage again and take them on journeys backward into the forgotten yesterday."

He paused, then said, "The Revolutionary War changed many things for my people. I am trying to do what I can to set my people's lives back on the right track."

He started to reach a hand out to touch her lovely face, but when he saw her wince, he pulled his hand back and held it at his side. "Abducting you is one way I hope to achieve this," he said softly.

111

"Tell me why, please?" Shawndee said. "How could I be so important to you, or your people? I am only a woman who owns nothing but my horse, and who knows nothing that could be of value to your people. How could I have anything to do with your problems?"

"All I can say is that it is not so much you as your mother and father," Shadow Hawk said, then stepped ahead of her and opened the door. "Come inside. I will add wood to the fire. The heat will reach the room I assign you. You can rest in this room. Tomorrow we will continue our conversation."

"My father?" Shawndee questioned, her eyes wide. "My mother? It is because of them that you have done this thing to me?"

He gave her a harsh look. "Go inside," he said solemnly.

Believing he had said all that he would about his plan, Shawndee had no choice but to nod and do as she was told. But she would question him again and get the answers she needed from him.

She stepped slowly inside. The room was lit by flames in a firepit circled by stones in the center of the earthen floor. She watched the path of the smoke as it spiraled slowly upward; there was a hole in the gabled roof so that the smoke could escape into the sky.

"Come, *o-ne*," Shadow Hawk said, nodding to-

112

ward the fire. "Stand before the fire awhile. Let the warmth soak through the blanket."

Shawndee silently nodded, trying not to show her fear at being assigned a room, for surely he would lock her in and she would feel even more like a prisoner.

She was aware now that he didn't know about her father's death. Since she was certain that her mother was included in Shadow Hawk's plan, Shawndee decided not to disclose her father's death to him. Surely he would not hesitate to go to her house and take whatever it was he wanted if he knew that no man was there to protect the property. Yes, for now it was best left unsaid.

As she followed him into the longhouse, Shawndee looked slowly around to familiarize herself with everything.

The whole outer room was filled with stores of food. Long rows of corn hung along the roof poles that rested just above the upper platforms. Those braids of corn formed curtains that screened off the upper platforms except in places where there were small alcoves that probably held the personal possessions of Shadow Hawk and his father.

Besides the corn, she saw large quantities of smoked meat, dried fish, dried pumpkins and squash, and dried herbs of various kinds.

Along another platform on the wall she saw bowls made of bark and wood. Closer to the floor, other raised platforms were covered with reed mats or pelts, surely used as seats.

Clothing hung from the walls, or was folded in bark bins and baskets.

Around the fire were mats woven of corn husk over a warp of twisted elm bark fibers.

She could envision herself sitting there with Shadow Hawk, casually eating from wooden bowls with him, at his side because she wished to be and not as a prisoner.

If only it could be that way, she thought as she put her back to the fire, reveling in its warmth.

It was true that she was intrigued by Shadow Hawk. She tried to see down the dark corridor where he had disappeared. Somewhere down there, in one of the rooms that she could make out in the semidarkness, was his father.

She wondered how ill he was. Was he a kind, caring man, or had he ruled with an iron fist?

She doubted the latter, for he was Shadow Hawk's father and Shadow Hawk seemed not at all the sort who would be a ferocious leader. He must rule with kindness and understanding, for had he not been gentle with Shawndee from the very beginning?

Even when he had surprised her by coming up on her from behind in the dark, he had been gentle.

Even his voice had revealed his kindness. He had

not spoken harshly, or given cruel commands. Instead, his voice was beguiling.

Her thoughts were interrupted when Shadow Hawk came down the corridor carrying something fluffy and white.

When he came into the light of the fire and Shawndee could see what he held out for her, she caught her breath. She had never seen such a plush robe. Her eyes widened in wonder as she held it up against herself.

"This rabbit skin robe will be warmer and more comfortable than the blanket," Shadow Hawk said. Seeing her in his lodge, with the fire's glow giving her hair an even more golden sheen, and with her mystical blue eyes revealing that she did not fear him, Shadow Hawk wished more than ever that they had met under different circumstances. His feelings for her had already gone far beyond how he should feel toward a captive.

He cared for her.

He wanted to protect her.

He especially wanted to protect her from parents such as those she lived with. Surely they knew that they placed her in danger every night and day while she lived in a house where all sorts of men came and drank themselves senseless.

"Why are you looking at me like that?" Shawndee asked, blushing as she noticed him staring at her intently.

It was not a look that made her feel endangered. It was a look that made her believe he truly cared . . . and that he truly wished to protect her.

"You seem so vulnerable and innocent," Shadow Hawk said. He reached a hand to her pink cheek, a rush of pleasure spreading through him at the mere touch of her soft flesh. "I am sorry if I have frightened you. I will try to complete my plan quickly so that you can resume life as you wish to live it."

He drew his hand slowly away from her. "Perhaps you will decide not to join your parents again and live the dishonorable sort of life they offer you," he said. "When they leave this area, I hope you will not leave with them."

"Where would I go if I didn't?" Shawndee dared to ask, touched deeply by the gentle way he had touched her cheek, and by his openness in revealing his feelings for her.

"I have said too much," Shadow Hawk said tightly. "Come. I will take you to your room. You can change into the robe. Then you can rest on a bed of soft pelts and blankets. Tomorrow we will talk as we share the morning meal. I will then explain my plan to you."

"Why . . . not . . . now?" Shawndee asked.

"*O-ne*, now is not the right time," Shadow Hawk said, his voice guarded. He nodded toward the corridor. "Come with me now."

Knowing that he wasn't going to reveal anything

else to her, yet feeling safe nonetheless, Shawndee decided she would bide time until she could escape. She must go home to warn her mother about two different threats—the women of the community who saw her as a witch, and Shadow Hawk, who had some plan involving her family.

Shawndee followed Shadow Hawk to the first room off the corridor. A lone candle burned low on a table beside a platform that jutted out from the wall, covered with deliciously soft-looking furs.

"This room will be yours while you are my guest," Shadow Hawk said, smiling to himself when he saw how the word "guest" caused her to look questioningly at him.

He did not wish to call her his captive anymore. Soon he hoped, she would not be there in that capacity.

It all depended on her parents, whether or not they would listen to reason when he approached them.

"The rooms in my lodge have no locks," Shadow Hawk said as he stepped away from Shawndee and went to the door. "But do not get any notion of leaving my lodge. I will never be far from it, and if I find you gone, I will quickly track you down and return you to this room."

He frowned. "But then you would be securely tied—a *true* captive."

Ignoring the sudden burst of anger in her eyes at

his latest spoken threat, he turned on a heel and left.

When the door was closed, Shawndee slowly let the blanket fall away from her shoulders to the floor.

After slipping into the wondrously soft and warm robe, she stared at the door. But recalling his warning, she knew that for now she must stay put.

But tomorrow?

Surely she would find some way to elude him. She must find a way! Her mother's life depended on it.

And perhaps even her own, for could she truly trust the word of this Seneca chief?

Was he a smooth talker, who knew ways to make others trust him? Was she wrong to trust so easily?

Only time would give her that answer, but she didn't have much time. The women of Silver Creek might have already gone to her mother's home and ordered her from their city.

The worst scenario of all would be for Shawndee to return home and find her mother and Tootiba gone. She might never see them again.

Sobbing, her fear for her mother's and Tootiba's safety mounting, Shawndee crawled onto the soft bed of pelts. With the robe snuggled close to her body, she curled up and closed eyes.

Sleep was finally her reprieve from the worries that were eating away at her heart.

"Mama," she whispered in her sleep. "Tootiba."

And then she found herself whispering another name, a name that made her eyes spring open.

She had dreamed of Shadow Hawk!

In the dream he had been holding her and comforting her. In the dream his lips had come to hers in a sweet, wondrous kiss!

Trying to fight off the desires that had been awakened by her dream, Shawndee rolled over to lie on her other side.

But this time her eyes wouldn't close.

She found herself listening for Shadow Hawk's footsteps in the corridor, wondering which room was his.

Would he have trouble falling asleep, as well, because she was near?

She again tried to squeeze her eyes closed.

Sleep! If she could fall asleep and stay asleep, that would make time pass more quickly.

Suddenly she heard footsteps and the closing of the longhouse door. Shadow Hawk had not gone to his bedroom at all. He had left the lodge!

Her heart pounding, Shawndee got out of bed and went to the door of her room. Slowly, she began to open it.

Chapter Thirteen

She was alone in the longhouse except for an elderly, ailing man, who surely would not catch her snooping around. Shawndee stepped gingerly into the corridor, the earthen floor cool against her bare feet.

Seeing that the fire's glow was no longer so bright in the outer room, she went back to her room and took the candle.

Carrying the candle in its holder of clay, she crept from the room again.

When she heard snoring coming from a far-off room, she knew that Shadow Hawk's father must be sleeping.

This made her relax, for as long as he slept and Shadow Hawk was gone, she was free to do as she pleased. She would not try to escape, for Shadow Hawk was probably watching the longhouse from outside, but she could see more of his home.

She could not help being fascinated by him; he was so handsome and gentle-spoken, it was hard to remember that she was a captive, and he the captor she should loathe.

Strangely enough, when she thought of him, loathing was not the emotion she felt. She had heard that there was such a thing as love at first sight. Had she fallen in love with Shadow Hawk?

Afraid to answer that question, Shawndee tiptoed farther out into the corridor and stopped. From this vantage point she could see that at least four more rooms branched out on either side.

She was surprised at the size of this longhouse. When she had arrived at the village, she had seen that this lodge was much larger than most others in the village. The only other one as large was the one that seemed to be some sort of council house, where the business of the Seneca might be handled.

She could not help wondering if a meeting would soon be held there with *her* as the subject.

Thinking of herself being a pawn in whatever plan Shadow Hawk had thought up, she shuddered, then made herself think of other things.

Her eyes wide, her ears alert for the sound of Shadow Hawk at the door, Shawndee crept onward.

She started to go to the room opposite hers, then stopped when something above the front door in the outer room caught her eye.

When she was there earlier, she had not seen what was hanging in the gable of the longhouse above the door at the entry.

Studying it, she discovered it to be a wooden carving of a hawk's head.

She recalled now that Shadow Hawk had said his Seneca people were of the Hawk clan.

She concluded that the wooden hawk's head was some sort of symbol, perhaps denoting that the clansfolk of the Hawk dwelt within.

Turning, she held the candle out before her and looked more closely for what else she might have missed seeing in the outer room.

Her eyes widened in wonder when she saw that a buffalo pelt curtained one doorway instead of a wooden door.

The pelt hung from a pole across the doorway; the top of the pelt had been gathered, making it easy for one to slide it back and forth for entry or exit into the room.

Wondering if this was the only door with such a curtain, Shawndee tiptoed down the corridor. She found that the rest of the doors were made of wood.

"Why is this one different?" she whispered.

Too curious not to investigate, Shawndee tiptoed to the pelt, nudged it aside with her elbow, and, holding the candle away from the pelt, eased into the room.

She stopped and looked slowly around her. She was keenly aware of the smell of flowers in the room, yet she saw none.

The room seemed to be used for storage, for on one side there was a low platform scarcely more than knee high, upon which many folded pelts and blankets were neatly stacked.

Beneath the platform were a number of well-stuffed buckskin bags.

Again she was aware of the scent of flowers.

Could this be from some sort of perfume made by the Seneca? she wondered.

She couldn't help feeling a quick stab of jealousy to think that this perfume, surely made from crushed, dried roses and various herbs found in the forest, was meant for a woman . . . a woman loved by Shadow Hawk!

Yet where was the woman? Shadow Hawk had told Shawndee that only his father resided in this longhouse with him.

Had Shadow Hawk lied?

Or did Shadow Hawk plan to marry a woman soon? Perhaps these buckskin bags held some of the woman's personal things, which had already been moved into the lodge.

Or was Shadow Hawk widowed? Could these bags have belonged to his dead wife?

However she looked at it, she could not help feeling jealous of any woman who might have caught Shadow Hawk's eye. Shawndee knew that although she was being foolish, she did have feelings for Shadow Hawk that she had never felt for any other man.

The first time she had looked into his eyes, even moments after having been abducted by him, she had been drawn to him.

And now?

As she stood among the belongings of a woman who might soon be Shadow Hawk's wife, Shawndee regretted that she had not met him at an earlier time and under different circumstances. Did he not fit the description of the men in her dreams?

The only difference was that his skin was not white. He was an Indian. He was the sort of man who was normally forbidden to a white woman.

Although she was an Indian's captive, she knew that this man could never harm her in any way. She would never forget how he had saved her from drowning in the river . . . how his muscled arms had carried her to safety.

Just let a man like Chester Hawkins try to get near her while she was with Shadow Hawk. That weasel of a man would never be able to stand up against such a warrior as Shadow Hawk.

She smiled as she imagined Chester cowering in the presence of Shadow Hawk.

Knowing that she was allowing her fantasies to run wild, Shawndee returned her attention to the buckskin bags. Drawstrings held them closed, hiding whatever was in them from wondering eyes.

"No, I shouldn't," Shawndee whispered to herself when she got a strong urge to investigate further.

She did so wish to open at least one of those bags. Might not she discover where the smell of flowers was coming from?

If she discovered many beautiful feminine things in the bags, would that not confirm there was a woman in Shadow Hawk's life?

Did she truly want to know?

"I must see," Shawndee whispered. Her pulse raced and her cheeks grew warm with a flush as she knelt before the buckskin bags.

She set the candleholder on the earthen floor, her eyes never leaving the one bag where the ties seemed loose enough to give her easy access.

The candle gave a flickering light as Shawndee reached a trembling hand toward the bag. She was breathless with curiosity as she slowly opened the top of the bag, then reached inside to feel what might be there.

Her fingertips came in contact with something wonderfully soft, and she felt around it, studying the shape and size of it. She realized that what she was touching were clothes, and she pulled out one item.

When it was fully out of the bag, and she saw just how beautiful the snow-white doeskin, beaded dress was, she gasped in awe.

Never had she seen a dress as beautiful as this— not even those worn by the rich women of Silver Creek.

To Shawndee, this doeskin dress was far lovelier than any satin or silk dress she had ever seen.

It was so richly feminine, so wonderful to the touch.

She flinched as though she were shot when she realized that the perfumed scent she had smelled before was coming from this dress, and from the open bag, where other clothes were stored.

Again she could not fight the jealousy she felt at this discovery.

Who owned the dress, and where was she? Shawndee wondered, her fingers going over the softness of the doeskin again, and then fingering the lovely beads.

Suddenly her curiosity about the dress came second to her desire to put it on. It had been so long since she had been allowed to wear any dresses, she couldn't resist the temptation to slip into this one.

Her heart thudding with excitement, Shawndee stood up and changed quickly from the robe to the Indian dress.

She sighed as she looked down at herself. The

dress clung to her sensual curves, defining every inch of her as absolutely feminine.

And the doeskin felt so deliciously soft against her flesh, even better than the robe that she had discarded.

It felt as if her body was clothed in hundreds of rose petals.

She felt so deliciously feminine. So pretty!

But most of all, she felt cheated by having lived as a boy for so long. Although her parents had disguised her to protect her, Shawndee resented them now for having denied her the pleasures of her femininity.

If her parents had only found another way to make a living, things could have been so different for Shawndee.

But then, if things had been different, surely she would never have met Shadow Hawk and experienced these strangely wonderful feelings.

Shawndee knew now that she had fallen in love with this man who until tonight had been a stranger. She had found his arms and his voice comforting, so much so that she truly did not feel like a captive.

She hoped that whatever he needed to do before he could set her free would be done quickly, so that he might pursue her as a man pursues a woman.

"If he could only see me dressed like this," Shawndee whispered, gently pulling her long blond hair around so that it lay in waves across her breasts.

She ran her hands down her soft curves, pretending they were the handsome Indian's hands!

She closed her eyes and enjoyed this stolen moment, this fantasy of pretending that the handsome warrior's hands were there on her body.

She could almost hear his heavy breathing.

She could feel the desire that he felt as he touched her, heard the tremor in his voice as he asked for permission to kiss her. . . .

Shawndee gasped and tightened inside when she felt someone else's hands truly take the place of her own. Her knees grew weak at the thought of whose hands they had to be.

When she felt those hands turn her around and move to her face, his fingers gently tracing her features, Shawndee opened her eyes. She gasped when she found that Shadow Hawk *was* there, a look of wonder and mystery in his eyes.

Shawndee knew she should be mortified at having been caught where she should not be, and in a dress that was not hers.

Yet her love for Shadow Hawk took away all fear and shame. She was completely caught up by the moment, a moment when she was being fully awakened into the feelings of womanhood.

As Shadow Hawk ran his fingers through Shawndee's long hair, lifting it from her shoulders, then twining his fingers through it, Shawndee stood there, breathlessly allowing the intimacy.

She didn't even back away from Shadow Hawk when she saw his lips lowering toward hers.

She sighed and felt as though everything within her was melting when his lips claimed hers and his arms snaked around her and drew her next to him. Shawndee's head began to swim with a pleasure she had never known before.

A longing came with that pleasure. A strange, gnawing ache at the juncture of her thighs made her twine her arms around Shadow Hawk's neck.

Her pulse raced as she returned his kiss in a surrender that left her dizzy and weak. She could even feel the pounding of his heart against her own.

She was acutely aware of how his body was straining against hers, her breasts pressed hard into his bare chest.

Then a deep, throaty, ancient voice calling Shadow Hawk's name tore them apart.

But Shadow Hawk didn't respond immediately to his father's beckoning.

Instead he gazed at Shawndee with a look that made her heart sing, for she knew by the way he had kissed her and held her, and now by the way he was gazing at her, that he cared for her.

"Shawndee, I returned to my longhouse to place wood on my fire before retiring for the night. When I saw that the door to the room where I left you was open, I went there and saw you gone. I did not know where you might be, until I saw the flickering from the candle through the hide cover at the doorway of this room," Shadow Hawk said thickly. "When I came into the room and saw you, I was mesmerized, for I have never seen anyone as beautiful as you in this beaded dress."

He stepped slowly away from her, his eyes raking over her loveliness; then he gazed into her eyes. "But you are wrong to put on clothes that are not yours," he said. "You must remove the dress and place it back in its bag."

"I *was* wrong to do this," Shawndee agreed, slowly lowering her eyes.

Then she looked quickly up at him again. "I apologize." She swallowed hard. "I know it's none of my business, but . . . who . . . do the lovely clothes in the bag belong to?" She gazed down at the dress and again ran her hands down the front of it. "The dress is so beautiful."

"The clothes are my sister's," Shadow Hawk said softly. "She no longer lives in this longhouse. Nor does she wear such clothes. She is the Hawk clan's priestess. She wears the clothes of a priestess, and she resides in her own private dwelling, which is holy."

"Your sister?" Shawndee said, oh, so relieved that the clothes belonged only to a sister. "Your sister is a priestess?"

"Yes, and I am very proud of her," Shadow Hawk said.

"But I thought all priests were men," Shawndee said.

"Perhaps in *your* world," Shadow Hawk said. "But in the Seneca's, both men and women can attain priesthood, and they are called 'Keepers of the Faith.' They supervise religious rites and secret organizations such as the False Face Society, which performs the Seneca's most sacred event, the Mid-Winter Ceremony—"

Again the throaty voice called Shadow Hawk's name, causing him to go quiet and look toward the doorway.

He then gazed at Shawndee again. "Please remove the dress and leave the clothes where you found them," he said thickly. "Then return to your room."

Shawndee nodded anxiously, feeling a mixture of emotions. She was elated to know that the clothes belonged to a sister, not a past wife, or a future one. She was also thrilled that this man did have feelings for her, which he had proved by kissing her.

But another part of her felt despair over having been ordered to return to her assigned room.

Confused by her conflicting emotions, Shawndee undressed and replaced everything where she had found it after he was gone.

In the white robe again, she picked up the candle

and went back to her room, but her feet never seemed to touch the earthen floor.

It was as though she were floating on clouds.

She had never been in love before.

She had never had feelings such as she felt now.

Yes, surely the stories of people falling in love at first sight did happen, for it most certainly had happened to her, in one blink of an eye . . . tonight!

"And, ah, the kiss," she whispered as she ran a finger over her lips where his had been only a few short moments ago. She would never forget the thrill of his kiss.

Oh, how glad she was that he belonged to no other woman, that at least in her heart she could claim him as hers.

Sighing dreamily, she set the candle on the floor and crawled onto the platform bed. Smiling, Shawndee curled up on her right side amid the soft pelts and blankets.

Then her smile faded. She was again thinking about how foolish it was to allow herself to feel anything for someone who had taken her captive, who might even have plans that could harm either her or her mother.

Yet she truly could not see this man harming any woman.

Shadow Hawk came into the room and knelt down on one knee beside the bed. A dress was draped across his arm. "I have brought this dress for you to wear tomorrow, should you wish to," he said.

He was glad when she sat up, reached out, and took it, her eyes showing how touched she was by his generous gesture.

"What you did tonight was wrong, but forgiven," Shadow Hawk said. "But listen well, Shawndee, when I tell you never again to pry into private things while you are in the Seneca village. To the Seneca such a crime is as black as calumny and worse than murder, for it is a violation of our fundamental laws. This time you are forgiven because you did not know you were breaking the Seneca code of law."

Wide-eyed, and draping the dress across her legs, Shawndee anxiously nodded. "I will pry no more, anywhere," she said softly. She glanced down at the dress, then gazed at him again. "But I would like to know something."

"That is?" Shadow Hawk said, raising an eyebrow.

"I noticed the symbol of a hawk embroidered on the dress I took from your sister's bag, and now I see it on this one," she murmured. "Is that because you are of the Hawk clan?"

"Yes, it is our Clan's totem," Shadow Hawk said, nodding. He was pleased that she showed interest in his customs, for he hoped one day to teach her everything there was to know.

Again it all depended on her parents . . . on their cooperation!

"This symbol was used by our maternal ancestors, and will be used by our clan as long as we remain in existence," he said. "Members of a clan are related to each other by strong ties. The clan of the *Manamaguas*, which means 'hawk' in our Seneca tongue, is one of the leading political families of the Seneca tribe."

"I also saw the wooden carving of the hawk over the front entry door," Shawndee said. She sighed. "I am so curious about it."

"Curiosity is good sometimes, bad sometimes," Shadow Hawk said thickly. He stood, nodded to her, then left the room, forgetting to close the door behind him.

Not knowing how to take what Shadow Hawk had just said, Shawndee ran her fingers across the tiny hawk symbol on the dress.

When she heard the voices through her opened door, she tried to make herself live up to her promise never to snoop again, yet she was so curious to know what the voices were saying, for surely *she* was the subject being discussed between father and son.

She laid the dress aside, then went to the door and listened.

She recognized Shadow Hawk's voice, and the

throaty voice of his father. But it was impossible to hear what was being said.

And she would not let temptation draw her down the corridor to listen outside Shadow Hawk's father's door, for she knew that she had pried enough for one night.

Sighing, Shawndee went back and snuggled under the pelts and blankets; she soon found herself drifting asleep, but this time it was not pleasant.

In her dreams she saw hawks circling above her, their dark eyes following her. She tried not to see the sharp talons of their claws, especially when one by one the hawks began to sweep down toward her from the sky!

Suddenly she woke up, realizing that nervous perspiration had broken out in tiny beads across her brow.

"What could the dream mean?" she murmured.

She looked questioningly toward the door, which was now closed.

She knew that it had been open when she had gone to sleep.

That had to mean that Shadow Hawk had been there while she slept.

She tried not to connect the dream with him, for she did not want to be afraid of him. Her life depended on her staying strong. She had to look brave and strong in not only Shadow Hawk's eyes, but also his people's, for surely tomorrow she would come face to face with many of the Hawk clan of Seneca.

Chapter Fourteen

Shaken by his sudden sensual feelings for Shawndee, feelings that could get in the way of his plan, Shadow Hawk sat with his father. He realized that his mind had drifted again as his beloved father spoke to him, yet Shadow Hawk could not stop it, especially when it was Shawndee who now occupied almost all his thoughts.

Earlier, he had not been able to get her off his mind after sitting down with his father to talk; wondering if Shawndee could be trusted to remain in her room, Shadow Hawk had excused himself for long enough to go and check on her.

When he had gotten to her room and found that she was asleep, he had gone to her bedside and stood over her, to gaze at her while she was not aware of it. He had stood there, trying to unravel the mystery of how this woman had grabbed his heart when none other had done so before.

As he had watched Shawndee sleep, he had been overwhelmed by sensual feelings for her. Beneath the soft glow of the flickering candle beside her bed, he could see the thickness of Shawndee's eyelashes as they rested like golden veils upon her pink cheeks.

Her sculpted lips were partially open, revealing their true lushness, making him ache to kiss her again.

The soft curve of her face was framed by her wavy golden hair, which lay like a halo beneath her head . . . hair that had felt like spun silk to his fingers.

She lay on her side, and the blanket and robe had fallen away, revealing the fullness of her breasts to him. He had ached to reach inside the robe and fill his hands with her full, round breasts, to feel the silkiness of her flesh against his hands. He recalled how he had thought she was flat-chested at first, then later saw how wrong he was when she had unwrapped them.

As the ache of wanting a woman deepened, he felt guilty at being there while she trustingly slept.

He had hurried from the room and returned to his father, sitting down beside the bed, yet he was still unable to banish Shawndee from his mind.

"Shadow Hawk, my *i-ye-a-na*, my son, when you look at me as I talk, you are not seeing your *no-tha*," Purple Cloud said. He leaned on an elbow to get a better look at his son as the candle's glow played on his handsome features. "Shadow Hawk?"

After hearing his father speaking his name twice, Shadow Hawk was shaken from his thoughts. He blinked his eyes and shook his head as he met his father's questioning stare.

"*I-ye-a-na*, after you first came to me tonight, you excused yourself, then returned again and sat beside my bed, yet since your return you have not been yourself," Purple Cloud said in his old, quavering voice. "Shadow Hawk, I heard a woman's voice earlier in our longhouse. That is why I summoned you, to inquire whose voice it was, for I know it was not your sister's. Now that you are seated again beside your father's bed, and now that I have your undivided attention, do you wish to share with me who was in our lodge besides you and me?"

Shadow Hawk squirmed uneasily on the pallet of furs. He felt suddenly trapped, because he hadn't wanted to disturb his father with his plan.

Yet he had known he couldn't keep the woman's presence from him forever, nor her reason for being there.

If he had abducted a boy, not a woman, as he had

originally planned, it would have been a much easier thing to tell his father.

But Shawndee *was* a woman, and not just any woman. She was a vision of loveliness whom Shadow Hawk had become intrigued . . . enamored . . . with. And, ah, how beautiful she had been in his sister's beaded doeskin dress!

Yes, that was a sight . . . that was a moment he would never forget.

And the kiss?

It made him want a woman in his life, whereas until now, he had only allowed himself to think about bettering the lives of his people.

How could he even consider using this woman as a bargaining tool now, when he did not want to give her up to anyone, especially her immoral parents?

"*No-tha*, there is much I have to tell you," Shadow Hawk suddenly blurted out, realizing that he had momentarily become lost in thought again.

He hurried on and explained his full plan to his father and how it had changed since the person he had abducted was a woman, not a boy.

And since he and his father had always been open with one another, having always shared their deepest inner feelings and desires, he told him how intrigued he was with the woman.

Now finished with the most difficult part of his confession, Shadow Hawk waited quietly for his father to react.

"*I-ye-a-na*, everything about your plan is good . . . but I do not like to hear that you have become intrigued with a white woman," Purple Cloud said, his voice drawn. "No white woman is worthy of such a man as you. Do not allow her loveliness to bewitch you."

Purple Cloud paused, laid his head down on his pillow, then gazed at Shadow Hawk again and took one of his hands.

"*I-ye-a-na*, I have summoned you for another reason besides curiosity about this woman," Purple Cloud said. "As you know, *i-ye-a-na*, your *no-tha* has the disease that eats the lungs and makes people fade away to ghosts of their real selves . . . a disease that eventually claims its victim."

"Yes, I know. And, *no-tha*, the pain I feel over your illness is more than I can explain," Shadow Hawk said, his voice breaking. "*No-tha*, what can I do to ease your pain?"

"There is nothing more that anyone can do for my illness except pray for this old man's soul," Purple Cloud said softly. "But there *is* something that can momentarily place sunshine in my heart."

"What is that, my *no-tha?* Tell me, and I shall see to it," Shadow Hawk said quickly, for he was always eager to make his father's life more bearable.

"I know better than anyone that this old man's days are numbered," Purple Cloud said, swallowing hard. "I want one more time with our people as their storyteller. Prepare them for time beneath the stars and the moon with me, when they can sit around the outdoor fire and listen to my tales."

His father's grip on Shadow Hawk's hand tightened and he gazed intently into Shadow Hawk's eyes. "But, *i-ye-a-na*, get this business with your captive over with as soon as possible," he said tightly. "A captive can draw undue attention and trouble to the Seneca people."

"It will be done as quickly as I can," Shadow Hawk said, nodding. "But I need time to approach Shawndee's father, to convince him that he can have his daughter back in exchange for his promise to leave this area."

"Even if that means she will go, as well?" Purple Cloud asked guardedly.

"If that is what is necessary to restore the pride of our warriors, then, yes, I must look the other way as far as the woman is concerned and allow her to leave with her parents," Shadow Hawk said, his voice drawn with the pain of having said what he did not want to say.

He knew the chances were good that he would have to say good-bye to Shawndee soon.

He must be able to, for he was his people's chief, and they must come first, always, in his life. Women must come second, even a woman who was made in her mother's womb solely for *him*.

In life there was only one true love. Even without

knowing Shawndee more deeply than he did, he knew that she was on this earth to be his!

"I admire your courage more than ever before, *i-ye-a-na*," Purple Cloud said. "It is in your voice, it is in your eyes, that this woman who sleeps beneath our roof tonight is someone you feel deeply for. I, too, fell in love as quickly, as deeply, when I met your mother all those many moons ago. Each day of our lives, before she passed on to the other side three winters ago, due to the same disease that will soon claim your father, we realized that fate . . . that destiny . . . had drawn us together. We gave thanks often for our good fortune."

"I saw your love and I felt it," Shadow Hawk said thickly. "I regret that my own love must be unfulfilled. For I will return her to her parents if that is what is required to make things right for our people."

"Believe in the higher power above that another woman will pass before your eyes soon who will also attract you," Purple Cloud said. "Perhaps, *i-ye-a-na*, her skin will be the same color as yours. Would not that be better for you and our people as a whole? White men have taken so much from our people. No white woman deserves the devotion and love you would give her."

"When I see Shawndee I do not see the color of her skin," Shadow Hawk said. "I see—"

"You do not have to explain any more to me

145

about her," Purple Cloud said, interrupting his son. He patted Shadow Hawk's hand. "You do what you can to right things for our people, and however it comes out with the woman, you will have my blessing. I want your happiness, *i-ye-a-na*. If I know you are happy, then I shall walk the road of the hereafter with a smile on my old face."

"You are too good to me, *no-tha*, always so understanding," Shadow Hawk said, a sob catching in his throat as he leaned over his father and hugged him. "Life is not fair. First Mother was taken from me, and soon *you?*"

"My son, my son," Purple Cloud said as he stroked his son's back. "Now is the time for you to bring a woman into your life, and also sons. They will fill the emptiness in your heart once your father has taken his last breath. A wife, my *i-ye-a-na*. You do need a *neio*. If it is the white woman, so be it. So . . . be . . . it."

Shadow Hawk clung for a moment longer, then eased himself from his father's arms and sat straight-backed again beside the bed. He was not ashamed of the tears he had shed in the presence of his father, for they did not prove him to be weak, but strong. A man who cared deeply and loved deeply and was filled with compassion was the strongest of all. Tears sometimes were proof of such a man, or woman.

"Now tell me more, *i-ye-a-na*, about this plan,"

Purple Cloud said, slowly closing his eyes and sighing.

Knowing that he was tiring his father, Shadow Hawk hurried with what he had to say. "My plan is to first rid the area of this thing that has corrupted our warriors, then to clear our warriors' brains so they can become proud and productive again."

"*I-ye-a-na*, do not take long," Purple Cloud said in a voice barely audible to Shadow Hawk. "Since this white woman intrigues you, the longer she is around you, the more she will grow on you like the stars are married to the heavens."

Not at all surprised by his father's quickly changing attitude toward Shawndee, since quick changes in mood seemed to have come with this disease that was killing him, Shadow Hawk only grimaced slightly, then tried to put it from his mind.

"I *will* see this plan through as quickly as possible," Shadow Hawk said softly.

"Shadow Hawk, please go for Song of the Moon," Purple Cloud said, again sighing. "I know it is late and your sister is surely asleep, yet I need her. My soul hungers for the words she always has for this dying old man."

Shadow Hawk saw a smile quiver on his father's lips. "Our people's priestess," Purple Cloud murmured. "How proud I am that she was chosen for priestess, and that you were chosen for our people's *hasennowane*, chief. I can die knowing that I have done well in raising my children."

"As you have done well in everything you aspired to during your entire life," Shadow Hawk said. He reached a gentle hand to his father's wrinkled face. "There was never a chief as admired, as revered, as you. And our people still love you as much as ever."

"Our people's admiration for you, who are now their chief, grows each day," Purple Cloud said, slowly opening his eyes and smiling at Shadow Hawk. "You bring pride into all their eyes as your name is mentioned, or when you sit in council and they see your nobleness."

"Only because I am my father's son," Shadow Hawk said.

"I hope one day you will have a son who will say the same words to you as you are saying to me," Purple Cloud said. A low rumble of a chuckle breathed across his purple lips. He closed his eyes and gave a slight gesture with his hand toward the door. "Perhaps this old man needs words of praise from his daughter now, do you think?" He laughed softly again. "I do so enjoy hearing her voice. It is much like your mother's."

"Yes, sometimes when I hear Song of the Moon's voice I, too, believe my mother has entered our longhouse," Shadow Hawk said, in his mind's eye seeing his beloved mother and the smile that she always had for everyone. He missed her greatly.

Not wanting his emotion to show, Shadow Hawk hurried to his feet. "I shall go for Song of the Moon now," he said. He bent low and brushed a soft kiss across his father's furrowed brow, then hurried from the room.

Outside in the corridor, he held his face in his hands and wept for things he had no control over. He knew when it had all begun . . . when whites came to land that had belonged to his people from the beginning of time and made it theirs.

Yet he had fallen instantly in love with a woman whose skin was white!

He was pulled in many directions now and knew that in the end he would not be able to please everyone with the choices he made.

Wiping his eyes dry, he remembered the little boy of so long ago who first discovered that life did have its ugly turns, and how he had wept in his mother's loving arms over things that hurt him. He squared his shoulders and tightened his jaw and knew that it was the same now, except that he was a grown man and his mother was not there to comfort him.

He would continue taking the ups and downs of life, day by day, and do the best he could for himself, his family, and his people. When he took his last breath of life, as his father would soon take his, he would do so at peace with himself.

A man could do only so much and the rest was left to fate.

He went the limit with all of the challenges he was faced with and knew that in the end he always felt comfort, as though his mother's arms were there again, in knowing that he had done everything possible to right the wrongs that faced him and his people.

Just so would he face this challenge that now included the love of a woman! He would do what he felt was right, and hope that in the end not only he, but everyone else, would come out a winner.

But he did know one thing. He loved Shawndee and he would try everything within his power to make her his wife!

With that decided, he walked proudly down the corridor toward the front door to go for his sister. He was eager to tell Song of the Moon about Shawndee before their father told her. She would be less biased if she were to hear the news from Shadow Hawk himself.

It was always important for Shadow Hawk to get his older sister's approval, for she was everything good on this earth. And he knew he could trust her feelings.

As he stepped outside into the moonlight, he gazed up at the star-studded sky and said a soft prayer that Song of the Moon would approve of Shawndee, not as his captive, but as his woman.

Chapter Fifteen

Knowing his sister's door was always open to anyone who might need her at any hour of the night or day, Shadow Hawk opened the door and stepped gingerly into her longhouse.

The lodge fire cast a soft glow around the spacious outer room of the longhouse and into the long corridor that reached out from it.

Shadow Hawk went into the corridor, then knocked softly on his sister's closed bedroom door.

"Song of the Moon, it is I, Shadow Hawk," he said.

"Song of the Moon, I have just come from Father's bedside. He has asked for you."

"Give me a moment, Brother, to get into my robe and moccasins," Song of the Moon said through the

151

door. "I only went to bed moments ago. I am bothered too much to sleep. Each day brings us closer to our father's passing."

"Yes, that knowledge lies heavily on my heart, as well," Shadow Hawk said solemnly.

He felt guilty for having someone else on his mind besides his father.

Frowning and raking his fingers through his long, thick hair, he went down on his haunches before his sister's lodge fire and gazed into the dancing flames.

He could not help seeing Shawndee's lovely face everywhere he looked now.

Even in the fire.

He shook his head to clear his thoughts, for he could have sworn Shawndee's image *was* there, smiling at him, seducing him!

Then she was gone and all he saw were the glowing orange logs with flames lapping slowly around them like caressing fingers.

He was glad when he heard his sister's soft footsteps behind him and then felt her gentle, tiny hand on his bare shoulder.

"My brother, your shoulder is as tight as a skin that is drawn taut over a drum," Song of the Moon murmured as she moved her hand from him, then knelt down beside him.

Her midnight dark eyes gazed into Shadow Hawk's. "My brother, is there more troubling you tonight than concern over Father?" she murmured. "You and I have talked often about our father's fate and you came to grips with it. What has happened to change your feelings?"

She gasped low. "Oh, Brother, do not tell me that father has worsened so much that you believe he will not last another night," she said, swallowing hard. "Although I accept death because I know what comes after, an eternity filled with peace and happiness, I ache to know that Father's voice will be stilled soon, as will his laughter."

"No, I do not believe Father is worse than when you last saw him," Shadow Hawk said, momentarily struck by his sister's beauty. Since she was not married, she wore her hair parted in the middle and hanging long down her back, whereas married women wore their hair in a single braid.

Tonight his sister's hair lay lustrous across her shoulders.

Her eyes, which had a slight slant, were vibrant even though she had just awakened. Her high cheekbones made the loveliness of her face even more pronounced. She was petite, yet tall, and oh, so beautiful.

Knowing that what he had to say might shock her, Shadow Hawk looked away from her. He was a little ashamed to tell his sister that it was not so much his father that troubled him, but a woman.

And not only that, she was white, and she was his captive.

He felt he'd been wrong not to include Song of the Moon in his plan to abduct a white person.

He looked quickly at Song of the Moon again. "Big sister, I have something to tell you," he said, gaining courage from the steady, sweet smile she gave.

Song of the Moon settled down beside her brother and drew her soft fur robe more closely around her shoulders. "I am certain Father knows that you have had to awaken me to bring me to him at this hour of night, and will not expect me to move as quickly as I would if it were not so late, so I am sure he will not expect me to suddenly appear at his bedside. Tell me, little brother, what else is on your mind besides our father?" she asked.

She reached over and took one of his hands and fondly squeezed it. She laughed softly. "Did you not know that big sisters are always ready to help little brothers?" she murmured. "When I am with you, my title of priestess comes second, you first."

"I am touched by your devotion to me," Shadow Hawk said. He lifted her hand to his lips and gently kissed it, then released it. "I thank you, big sister. *Taubut.*"

"Tell me, *o-ne*, what is troubling you?" Song of the Moon said softly. She rested her hands on her lap as she waited for his explanation.

"There is this woman . . ." he began, purposely avoiding his sister's eyes. He stared into the flames of the fire as he got farther into the story of how it happened that a woman instead of a boy was captive in his lodge.

"A captive woman?" Song of the Moon said, trying hard not to reveal her shock at what her brother had done. She trusted his judgment in all things and believed that even though he had made a mistake in taking a woman instead of a boy, his plan would work in his people's favor in the end.

Shadow Hawk looked slowly at his sister. "As I said, she was supposed to be a he," he explained, his voice tight. "I hope that even though I have made a mistake, the end result will be the same."

"I am sorry if I showed surprise at what you have revealed to me, for I do trust you, little brother, and know that whatever you do, it is well thought out beforehand," Song of the Moon said reassuringly. She put a gentle hand on his arm. "It *will* work out, even though the plan has changed somewhat."

She lowered her hand. "But it is not a usual thing for our people to take captives," she said guardedly. "This is something that must have eaten away at your heart before you did it."

"Yes, it was hard, but I saw it as the only way," Shadow Hawk said. He nervously raked his fingers through his hair and gazed into the fire again. "But I have not told you the full extent of my worries."

155

"There is more?" Song of the Moon asked, her eyebrows arching.

"Yes, there is more," he said, his voice guarded.

"Tell me," Song of the Moon said in a soothing voice that was filled with love and caring. "Tell me the rest, little brother, and then I must go to *no-tha*."

Shadow Hawk moved quickly to his feet. "*No-tha*," he said, gasping softly. "How could I take time away from Father by asking you to stay this long to listen to my troubles?" He gestured with a hand toward the door. "Go to him. He needs you more than I."

"I know Father well," Song of the Moon said. "Although he was awake moments ago, asking for me, by now I am almost certain he is asleep again."

She rose to her feet and took Shadow Hawk's hands. "So, little brother, continue what you have to say," she softly encouraged. "Unburden your heart. You will then be better prepared for what lies ahead."

"Yes, it will be better if I tell you everything. The more I think about what I have done, the more I believe our people should all know," Shadow Hawk said, nodding.

"If you feel that everyone should know, then tomorrow call a council and tell our people," Song of the Moon encouraged. "But tonight it is only you and your sister. Tell me what you feel comfortable in telling."

"Song of the Moon, as you now know, it was my plan to abduct a boy, not a woman, use the boy for the purpose I revealed to you, and then discard him. But now all is changed," Shadow Hawk said, his gaze wavering. "The boy is a woman . . . an alluring, beautiful *wee-nighh*. I am so attracted to her, I am not certain that I can use her in the way I planned to use the boy."

He saw shock registering in his sister's eyes, but knew that if he did not confess his feelings now, he might not be able to later. It was very hard to talk about. It was terribly hard to dwell on the mistake he had made, and what had happened to his heart because of it.

"Go on, little brother," Song of the Moon urged. "Get it all said. Then you will be more at peace inside your heart."

"Song of the Moon, I am enchanted by this woman," Shadow Hawk blurted out. "Every moment that she is in my care, my feelings for her deepen more and more. I could so easily give my heart to her . . . even now, I fear that I love her."

Song of the Moon's eyes widened. Her lips parted in a slight gasp.

Then she went to Shadow Hawk and embraced him. "My little brother, this is something that only you can work out inside your heart," she said softly.

"You are a wise man. Whatever you decide about the woman will be right, not only for you, but also for our people."

"But she is white, and . . . she . . . is my captive," Shadow Hawk said, easing from her arms.

"She will always be white, and that is something you must accept, but she will not always be a captive," Song of the Moon said. "When she is truly free to return your love, will she? Does she also care? Or does she hate you?"

"There is no hate in either of our hearts," Shadow Hawk said thickly. "It was clear in her kiss that she cares for me as I care for her."

Taken aback by this latest confession concerning the kiss, Song of the Moon was momentarily at a loss for words.

Then she patted him on the arm. "You will do what is best for both yourself and the woman . . . and your people," she said, trying not to allow him to see her alarm over his relationship with the white woman. "Only you can decide how you will treat this woman from here on out—as a captive still or as a woman who has stolen your heart."

She paused, then said, "Brother, is this woman relaxed, or fearful, when you are around her?"

"Sometimes relaxed, sometimes wary," Shadow Hawk said solemnly. "When we kissed, she was not a captive. I was not Indian, or her captor. We were two people whose hearts had become as one."

Song of the Moon was quiet for a moment; then she laid a comforting hand on her brother's arm. "My brother, it is not best for you to be so torn," she said solemnly. "Never forget who you are. You are *sennhawane*, chief."

She took his hand. "Take me to her," she said. "Let me see this woman who has you feeling foreign to yourself."

"Yes, that is best," Shadow Hawk replied.

They went to his longhouse.

Shadow Hawk took her to Shawndee's room and stepped aside as Song of the Moon stood over Shawndee. While Shawndee slept, Song of the Moon studied her.

Shadow Hawk and Song of the Moon exchanged quick glances, then left the room and stood in the corridor.

"My brother, I can see why you are captivated by this woman," she murmured. "By the candle's glow I saw how beautiful she is. And there is such an innocent quality about her. She has the face of someone whose life is guided by goodness."

"But, Song of the Moon, her parents are those who have brought sorrow into our people's lives. They have lured our warriors down the wrong path with their firewater," Shadow Hawk said thickly. "Could Shawndee's outward appearance camouflage her true inner self? Can someone who has been raised in an environment of evil truly turn out to be good?"

"Brother, you have allowed yourself to feel deeply for this woman; surely you do not see traces of evil in her," Song of the Moon said. "Not every man's personality is molded in the exact image of those who bring him into the world. Each person has his own identity . . . his own ideas of right and wrong. I did not see any trace of evil on this woman's face, nor did I feel an aura of evil as I stood near her."

Feeling relieved to receive the confirmation he had so badly wished to hear, Shadow Hawk grabbed her into his arms and hugged her. "You always know what to say to your brother to make him feel right," he said.

"You will know in time if your sister's feelings about this woman are true," she murmured. "For now, you must continue to follow your own instincts . . . your own heart."

She eased herself from his arms. "I will go now to our father," she said. She stood on tiptoe and gave Shadow Hawk a quick kiss on his cheek, then walked away from him toward their father's room.

Shadow Hawk watched her go, then gazed into the room at Shawndee. He realized he had one more place to go before retiring for the night.

He needed to pray.

He had received his sister's guidance. Now he needed direction from high above.

He grabbed a blanket and left the longhouse for a bluff where he would be closer to his Great Spirit, where the sky would become an extension of himself and his prayers.

Chapter Sixteen

A sneer on his face, Chester Hawkins waited at the back door of the tavern for Jane Sibley to answer his knock. What he had to say was private, and he wanted no one to see him going into Jane's house at day break.

He shifted his feet nervously and gazed at the forest behind the tavern.

He had set a plan in motion to get what he wanted from the tavern lady: time with her son, Andrew. He had ambushed and killed the sheriff and had placed his body in the forest, close enough to Jane's house to cast blame on her if she refused to go along with his plan.

After Chester had heard the sheriff warn Jane about her witchcraft threats he had realized that

163

she would be the obvious suspect if anything should happen to the sheriff.

"Yes, it'll work," Chester whispered to himself. It had to.

He reached a hand up to his face and was once again filled with hatred for Jane Sibley when he felt the scabs where her assault with the broom had injured him.

The door suddenly swung open and Jane Sibley was standing there, her eyes narrowing with hate when she saw Chester.

"What in tarnation do you think you're doin' comin' to my home after what you tried with my . . ." Jane said, stopping just short of saying daughter.

"I've come to make a bargain with you about your son, Andrew," Chester said, a small stream of drool rolling from one corner of his mouth. His pale eyes were anxious.

"You don't need to waste any more words with me," Jane said, placing her fists on her hips. She stepped closer to Chester, and he cowered away from her. "Git, Chester. I warned you about comin' back here. What you did, or *tried* to do in my attic, turns my stomach." She moved her face closer to his. "*You* turn my stomach."

"You'd best listen to what I have to say or you'll be in a peck of trouble," Chester said, stepping away from her. His jaw tightened. "Hear me out. If you don't, I'll have the law knocking at your door within the hour."

"Hell's bells what are you talkin' about?" Jane fumed. "Sheriff Dawson is on my side. Not yours."

"It didn't sound like he was your ally last night." Chester said, his eyes dancing as he saw her flinch. "Now listen well, Jane. You truly don't have a choice."

Yes, Jane knew very well that the sheriff had turned on her, yet she still hoped she could change his attitude the next time they were alone and could talk things through.

There was a part of her that hated the man because of what he had said, yet the part of her that was so lonely since Caleb's death needed the companionship of Tom Dawson. They had spent many long hours over coffee, not booze. She respected him because he had treated her justly in the past.

She truly believed his harsh words tonight were part of an act to make it look as though he was upholding the law in this town.

"Knowin' your sort, and what you are capable of doin', yes, I guess I'd better listen," Jane said. She was still afraid that Chester might have something to do with Shawndee's disappearance.

"Sheriff Tom Dawson lies dead just beyond your property line in the forest," Chester said, closely watching Jane's reaction. She gasped, went pale, and grabbed hold of the door frame to steady herself.

"No," Jane said, her pulse racing as she gazed past Chester toward the forest.

She then looked Chester square in the eye. "You're just telling me that," she said. "But why? What could be your motive for saying such a thing?"

"Because it is true," Chester said, chuckling. "Do you know how I know? I placed his dead body there after killin' him myself."

Jane teetered, then started to grab for the long, thick-bladed machete that stood just inside the door to use on polecats such as Chester Hawkins.

But Chester was quicker.

He slid a knife from a sheath at his right side and placed the sharp blade at Jane's throat.

"Like I said before, listen well, Jane, or I'll add your body to the one that's already in the forest," Chester said, his voice tight.

"How could you?" Jane said, inching her hand away from the machete. "Why?"

"When I'm sober and my mind is alert, everything I do is well calculated and planned," Chester said icily. "I've contrived all of this to give me an opportunity to bargain with you."

"Lord, I hate to ask what kind of bargain you have on your twisted mind," Jane gulped out, seeing Shawndee in her mind's eye.

"I'm sure you know," Chester said, chuckling. "I'll make sure no one finds the sheriff's body. In exchange, you'll allow me some time with your boy." He motioned with the knife. "Of course, I know that I could kill you and then have all the time I want with Andrew. I could even take him far away so you'd never see him again. But my needs are too varied. I don't want a lasting relationship. I only want a short time with Andrew and then I'll skip town and you and Andy'll never hear from me again."

"You wouldn't get one mile up the road before I told the whole town what you'd done," Jane threatened. "I'd tell them you killed the sheriff and raped my child. You'd have a noose around your neck so quick you'd wet your pants."

"I've thought of all that and I know you wouldn't do it, not after I've planned this out so well," Chester said. "Must I remind you that it'd be your word against mine? Everyone would believe that you'd killed the sheriff. I would convince those who doubted it. I've never done anything in this town to arouse suspicion, except supplying you with booze."

"You are truly despicable," Jane said, swallowing hard. "And I do believe that no one sees it but me."

"Then you'll cooperate?" Chester said, anxiously looking past her into the house. "All I want is to be with Andy one time. Then you have my promise you'd never see my face around here again."

"You repulse me," Jane hissed. "What you have on your mind sickens me." She shuddered. "And quit callin' my child Andy. It makes it sound as though you two are buddies. You . . . are . . . anything *but*."

Then she sighed heavily. "But the last laugh is on you, Chester. You see, chances are that you won't get the chance to call him by any name. It seems you've come too late for my Andrew," she said, her voice breaking. "He's gone. He's disappeared. I even thought you might be responsible."

Chester's eyes widened. He shakily lowered his knife to his side. "He's gone?" he gulped out. "He's missin'?"

"His bed wasn't slept in last night," Jane said, a sob almost choking her. She wiped tears from her eyes. "So get on with you, Chester. I've got more worries on my mind than fightin' off the likes of you."

She gazed toward the forest and slowly shook her head back and forth. "And now even Tom Dawson is dead," she said. Her eyes narrowed angrily as she turned them back to Chester. "You are the lowest of—"

"Let me go and find Andrew for you," Chester said, interrupting her. "I know the area well enough to search for him. I might even have a clue as to where he might be."

"I suspected no less," Jane said, her jaw tightening. "Now I suppose you'll tell me that my child's disappearance was a part of your plan. Where do you have him? You've only come today to taunt me. Isn't that right?"

"I had no idea he was missing," Chester said tightly. "If I had abducted your son, do you think I'd be foolish enough to come to your doorstep and play games with you? No, Jane. I don't have your son, but I have an idea who might."

Jane's heart skipped a beat. "Who?" she asked guardedly.

"I saw Chief Shadow Hawk sneaking about not far from your house last night," Chester said. "Maybe he saw the lad and wanted him, as well. Indians are known to take captives. A young, healthy boy could come in handy with chores, or whatever else the Indians might have a mind to do to a young, dainty thing like Andrew."

"An Indian?" Jane gasped, picturing those who came almost nightly to her back door for whiskey.

In a drunken stupor, could one of them have abducted Shawndee? She had heard too many good things about the young Seneca chief to suspect him of abduction. But those who had forgotten their culture to lose themselves in whiskey just might.

"Jane, I promise to find Andrew and bring him home to you, but only if you promise that I can have my way with him for one full night," Chester said smoothly.

"I'll never give you permission to be with my child in such a sinful, ungodly way," Jane said, visibly shuddering.

"Do you prefer for the Indians to use him?" Chester said. "Let me go and find the boy for you."

Feeling an urge to retch, Jane grew quiet and stared down at him for a moment.

He might be the only one who could find Shawndee.

She tried not to think of Sheriff Dawson lying dead so close to her house, or how he had died, and at whose hands.

All she could think about was her daughter.

She would do anything to protect Shawndee, even if it meant she had to put her trust in this filthy-minded man until Shawndee was safe beneath her roof again.

And then heaven help this man who was leering at her and imagined her at his mercy. The minute Shawndee was safely inside her house, Jane would make this man pay for his sins, even if she had to hang for the crime she would commit to rid the world of such a man as he.

"Chester, I have no choice but to ask you to go and find my son," Jane said, her voice tight. "Although the men of Silver Creek depend on me to serve them whiskey, none of them have befriended me. They see me and my child as white trash. No one could care less about Andrew's safety. Yes, go and find Andrew for me."

"You'll keep your side of the bargain and let me have time with him when I get him home safe and sound?" Chester said anxiously, wanting her to say it. Part of his vengeance would be knowing that she was beneath the same roof where her son was at the mercy of a man she loathed. That would double the pleasure for Chester!

"When I make a bargain with someone, it is kept," Jane said somberly. "I expect you to keep your part of the bargain, too. If you so much as touch my son before bringing him home, you will regret it."

She leaned into his face. "If you don't bring Andrew home untouched, you will see the worst of what a witch can do to a man," she hissed out, seeing no choice but to use the threat of witchcraft again to scare this man into doing what he promised to do. Since he had already spread the word around town that she was a witch, this new threat could not do her any more harm.

"What . . . do . . . you mean?" Chester gasped out, nervously running a finger around his shirt collar.

"I think you know what I mean," Jane said, chuckling. "Witches have many ways to make their point. If I am forced, I will show you exactly what witches do to men who deceive them."

He slowly backed away. "What's to keep you from witching me after I get Andrew home safe?" he gulped out. "How am I to trust that you won't use your powers against me before I get Andrew to his room?"

"Getting my child home safe is all that matters to me," Jane said. "My powers will only be used if you don't keep your word. Bring him home untouched. That is all you have to worry about."

"I promise to do what I've said I'd do, but I still expect you to hold up your end of the bargain when I arrive here with Andrew," Chester said as he slowly backed down the steps.

Although she knew that she was lying, that she could never allow this man to assault her daughter, Jane again told him that she always kept her promises.

He gave her a final nod, then ran across the yard.

When she saw him enter the outer fringe of the forest, she cringed, for she knew now that someone she had once admired lay there, dead.

"All because of a man's twisted mind," Jane said, swallowing hard.

Tears streaming from her eyes, she went back inside the house. Not even wanting to talk to Tootiba about what had just occurred, she hurried into her private office and closed the door behind her.

She sat down behind her desk and put her head in her hands. She prayed to herself that her plan would work, that she had scared the weasel enough to keep him from harming Shawndee.

When he returned with Shawndee, she would have to get the courage to do what she must to stop him from harming her daughter.

For her child, Jane would do anything.

Even murder a man.

If only her father had not lost his wealth. If only her mother had not died shortly thereafter. If only she had not had to marry Caleb to survive. . . .

Shawndee was the only good thing that had come from that marriage to Caleb.

That she might lose Shawndee now, after all that she had done to keep her well and safe, tore at the core of her being.

"Lord, I'm not one to pray all that often, but please bring my daughter home to me," she softly entreated.

Chapter Seventeen

Shawndee awakened to the sound of children playing and laughing. The happy sounds wafted through the thin walls of the longhouse from somewhere outside.

She sat up and listened more carefully. She was surprised to hear children playing because she did not think it could be very late in the morning. She scarcely ever slept past sunrise.

Yet everything in her life was different now. She was among strangers, being held prisoner.

And then she thought of the chief who led those strangers—Shadow Hawk, the man who had not only abducted her, but who had also stolen her heart.

She had tried to fight those feelings, yet had lost the battle already.

Sighing, and trying to keep Shadow Hawk out of her thoughts, Shawndee stroked her long, slim fingers through her thick, golden hair to comb out the night's tangles.

While doing this she scooted over to the edge of the bed and was quickly reminded again of Shadow Hawk.

The dress that she had left folded neatly on a blanket beside the bed brought a thrill to her heart as she thought of where she had gotten the dress, and the look in Shadow Hawk's eyes as he had handed it to her.

She sensed that he would prefer her to wear a dress; the breeches and shirt she usually wore seemed wrong now.

"And I *shall* wear a dress today," Shawndee murmured.

She gazed down at the lovely robe that she had slept in. She grabbed its edges and drew it closer to her skin, sighing at the softness of it. She knew that many hours must have been spent making this robe and wondered who had done it for Shadow Hawk. Would its creator resent the fact that a white woman was wearing it?

With the exception of Shadow Hawk's ailing father, she doubted that anyone else in his village

176

would ever know that she had been there, once she was allowed to return to her home.

"He must let me go today," Shawndee whispered as she slid the robe off and stepped down onto the damp, cold earthen floor with her bare feet.

She had second thoughts about wearing the dress. If she was going to leave the village and return to the life where everyone thought she was a boy, it might not be a good idea to put it on.

"No, I mustn't," she said aloud, her jaw tight.

She looked around for her other clothes.

When she didn't see them, she concluded they must be out by the fire, drying.

She glanced at the robe. Should she put it on to go and get her clothes?

She looked slowly back at the beautiful dress, aching to wear it.

She nodded determinedly.

Yes, she would wear it, but only for as long as it took to get her other clothes. Then she would politely hand this dress back to Shadow Hawk and demand to be set free!

Today she would not mix words with him. She would tell him that she was tired of playing this game, a game that might cost her mother's life.

Even if she had to reveal the truth about her mother to Shadow Hawk, to get his understanding, she would.

Something else caught her attention, something

lying with the carefully folded blankets just inside the door of the room. Someone had come in the night and had placed the blankets there, along with a pair of beautifully beaded moccasins. It seemed they had been put there for her to use. She supposed that Shadow Hawk had brought them.

Smiling, wanting to prolong this fantasy, which included beautiful clothes, robes, and now moccasins, as well as the most handsome man in the world, she went to the shoes and got them.

Carrying them gingerly in the palms of her hands, as though they were as delicate as tiny birds, she went to the bed, sat down, then slid her feet into the moccasins.

She sighed, for she had never felt anything so deliciously soft on her feet.

Oh, how wonderful it would be to wear them forever and toss her hard-soled leather boots out the door.

Standing, putting her full weight on the moccasins, and again running her fingers down the soft dress, she was not aware of someone slowly opening the door, then standing there, watching.

Shadow Hawk's heart thumped wildly as he stood just inside the room. Shawndee's back was to him, yet as he gazed at her, delicate and lovely in the dress and moccasins, he knew he could not help loving her.

With her long, golden hair flowing down her

back, and the dress revealing her tininess as it clung to her perfectly shaped figure, she was a vision.

When she suddenly realized that she was no longer alone, she swung around and saw him there. Her sweet smile touched him deep inside his soul.

More and more he realized that there was no way he could use her as a bargaining tool. He could not even think of saying good-bye to her. He was convinced that she was nothing like her mother, who was so brash, so hard, so unlikable.

Somehow the Great Spirit, or her God, had looked out for her and protected her and taught her to be someone good and loving.

"You are so beautiful," Shadow Hawk suddenly blurted out. "I have never seen anyone as beautiful."

A blush rushed to Shawndee's cheeks. She lowered her eyes bashfully. "Thank you," she murmured.

Then she looked slowly at him again and saw that today he was dressed in fringed buckskin and moccasins that had the same design as on those she wore. And he wore a beaded headband, even though his raven-black hair was drawn back today and worn in one long braid.

The clothes fit snugly, revealing to her the muscles that she already knew he had.

And his face!

Ah, his handsome face, so sculpted and perfect.

His midnight dark eyes mesmerized her until she found it hard to remember the forceful words that she had planned to use today to convince him that he must set her free. At this moment, all time stood still, all wrongs were forgotten, and there was only Shadow Hawk.

"Come with me and take food beside my lodge fire," Shadow Hawk said, stepping aside. He gestured toward the door with a hand. "There is a large pot of stew brought by one of the village women, as well as freshly baked cornbread. Come. We eat, and then we talk."

That word "talk" seemed to shake Shawndee from her reverie, for she did have something vastly important to say to him this morning.

Yes!

Her mother!

She must convince him that she had to go and see to her mother's welfare.

"Yes, I must admit that I am very hungry," Shawndee said, her eyes meeting and holding his. "Thank you for inviting me to eat with you."

She almost melted inside when he reached for her hand and held it as he led her into the outer room, where the delicious aromas of food greeted her.

She saw that he had placed mats woven of corn husks and twisted elm bark fibers beside the fire. When he dropped his hand from hers and gestured toward the mats, she nodded quietly and sat down on one of them.

She watched his every move as he set two wooden bowls near the fire and bent on one knee close to the huge blackened clay pot that hung over the flames. She had heard these pots called *gadje pots*. They had serrated rims which flared out with designs of parallel lines arranged in triangles.

She watched Shadow Hawk use a ladle to dip out the stew into the bowls, and noticed that the ladle appeared to be made of curly maple. It had a dove carved on the long, wide handle.

After both bowls were filled, Shadow Hawk handed one to Shawndee and took one for himself.

They began eating with wooden spoons, silenced by their eagerness to consume the delicious stew. Shawndee thought it was made from venison and wild vegetables from the prairies and forests.

After two bowls of stew and much cornbread were consumed, and their empty bowls were set behind them on the earthen floor, Shawndee started to plead her case, but was stopped when Shadow Hawk began talking.

"My plan to talk with your parents must be delayed, at least until tomorrow," he said thickly. He noticed that Shawndee winced and narrowed her eyes angrily.

"There is no other way," he explained. "My people are preparing themselves for something special tonight. It is for my father that this is being done, as well as my people. I will do nothing to disturb these plans. Of late, there has been too little to bring light and excitement into my people's eyes."

"But you said—" Shawndee began, but he interrupted her.

"It is my father's request that brings my people together tonight, for this will be his last time with them in such a way," Shadow Hawk said, his voice drawn. "My *no-tha*, who is our people's storyteller, will do something that makes his heart sing. He will lift his people to the fairylands of pure imagination as he tells his stories to them."

"But—" Shawndee again tried to say.

"My *no-tha* will transport my people to the land of magic," Shadow Hawk continued in an effort to make Shawndee understand the importance of the storytelling event tonight. "Father will give the hungry minds and yearning souls wings upon which they may fly away from reality. You see, Shawndee, the Seneca storyteller is the storehouse of our knowledge."

"Shadow Hawk, I see that this means a lot to you, but my mother is . . . is . . . in danger," Shawndee pleaded. "She is as important to me as your people, as your father, is to you."

"My father's days are numbered on this earth, and he knows this," Shadow Hawk said thickly. "Tonight is his, Shawndee."

"Please listen to my plea for my mother's safety," Shawndee said, a sob lodging in the depths of her throat. She moved to her knees and faced Shadow Hawk. "Please set me free? Like you, I have concerns about my own family. Just before you captured me, I heard something that could be very dangerous for my mother. I have to go and warn her. You must allow it!"

Shadow Hawk lifted an eyebrow. "Does not your mother have a husband to protect her?" he asked, his voice drawn.

Seeing that she had no choice now but to reveal the truth about her father's death, Shawndee sighed deeply, then sat down before Shadow Hawk and gazed into his eyes pleadingly.

"My father is no longer alive," she began. "He was recently murdered. Now it is only myself, my mother . . . and Tootiba."

"Your father was murdered?" he gasped out.

Shawndee hung her head as tears burned in the corners of her eyes. "Viciously," she said, visibly shuddering. She looked again into his eyes. "I don't want to talk about that. It pains me too much. But don't you see now? With my father gone, my mother is so alone. She . . . her life . . . is being threatened. She doesn't know it. I must go and warn her."

Silence reigned between them as Shadow Hawk digested this latest news.

"It was your father with whom I would have talked. I planned to exchange you for his promise never to sell alcohol to my warriors again," Shadow Hawk said. "Of course, when I discovered you were a beautiful woman, and then when I grew so quickly to care for you, well, my plan changed. I did not want to use you as a bargaining tool."

He rose to his feet and began pacing the floor, his fingers kneading his brow. "So much is confusing now," he said, his voice drawn.

Realizing now exactly what he had planned to do, and understanding his confusion, Shawndee felt more hopeful than before.

She jumped to her feet and stood before him. "Shadow Hawk, let me go to my mother," she said, her voice determined. "After my mother knows about the plot against her, she will have no choice but to leave the area. With the women of Silver Creek and the Seneca against her, surely she will see that it's too dangerous to stay in the area."

"Are the women of Silver Creek angry because of firewater?" Shadow Hawk asked warily. "Is that the reason they plot against your mother?"

Shawndee's eyes wavered. The women were angry about Jane's tavern, but they were also accusing her of witch craft.

"The women do not like their men going to my mother's establishment," Shawndee said, looking slowly up at him. "They . . . hate . . . her."

Shadow Hawk placed a gentle hand on Shawndee's shoulder. "Tomorrow is another day," he said, truly hating to disappoint her by not doing as she wanted. But at this moment, the welfare of his father came before anyone else's, especially a woman like Jane Sibley!

"What . . . do . . . you mean, tomorrow?" Shawndee asked warily as she stepped slowly from him so that his hand dropped away from her. "Are you saying I must wait . . . until . . . tomorrow?"

"Yes. Tomorrow we will decide how to approach your mother, but today I must focus on the request of my father," he said thickly.

"How can you make me wait?" Shawndee said, her anger now turning to hurt. "I thought you understood me, even cared—"

"I do care, but my father has to come first at this time," Shadow Hawk said. "He wishes to have one more time with his people for storytelling. I wish to be there to hear him, to join with the others to laugh, and to praise this old man who has given his all to his people from the day he took his first breath of life."

"But one more day of waiting to help my mother might be too late," Shawndee said, her voice breaking. "Please let me go and talk to Mother. By the time you are free to come tomorrow, you will see that your battles have been won by *me*. Mother will be made to see reason. She truly has no choice this time. Too many are against her."

"I must not chance that she will not listen to reason as *you* tell it," Shadow Hawk said solemnly. "You and I must go and face your mother together for council."

He placed a gentle hand on her cheek. "Shawndee, I wish for you to join me tonight to sit with me as Father brings sunshine into my people's hearts," he said softly. "I wish to share this sunshine with you before we are forced to enter together into things that might not be pleasant. I do not expect your mother to immediately cooperate with what I have to say to her. If she does not . . ."

He stopped short of telling Shawndee how he would react if her mother disappointed him. He was not even sure himself what he would do.

"You want me to sit with you, to let your people stare at your captive?" Shawndee said, her voice breaking. She slapped his hand away. "I think not!"

"It is not in that way that I will take you amid them," Shadow Hawk said, understanding her anger and hurt. "When you sit beside me, they will not see you as my captive, but as something more."

"Something more?" Shawndee gulped out. "What do you mean?"

His response was only to smile at her. Then he said, "I have duties to my people today that will take me away from you. But my lodge is comfortable.

186

Stay beside my fire on soft cushions. The day will pass quickly into night, and then I will be with you again."

Shawndee knew she had no choice but to do as he told her. And she was stunned that he was going to introduce her to his people as someone other than his captive.

It made a sweet thrill sweep through her to think that he did care for her in a special way.

She cared, oh, so deeply for him.

Yet she couldn't understand how he could ignore her concern about her mother. Why didn't he allow her to do something about it?

Shawndee watched Shadow Hawk leave. Restless, she began pacing. Then she sat by the fire for a while. She peered out the door and watched the beautiful copper-faced children at play.

Her gaze followed the women, whose duties seemed varied. Some cooked on outdoor fires just outside their lodges, while others went to bring fresh water from the river, and others sat and sewed in the shade of their lodges.

She watched elderly men who sat, cross-legged, beside the large outdoor fire, sharing talk and smokes from their long-stemmed pipes.

She was fascinated by the girls of her own age, who looked so beautiful as they moved about, their long hair bouncing on their shoulders, with young braves following, teasing them.

Shawndee wondered how it would feel to be among those girls, dressed as beautifully as they, with young fellows obviously interested in them.

Her childhood had passed by quickly without the pleasure of having girls her age as friends. It hurt even now as she thought of the loneliness she had felt.

Weary of thinking about past hurts, and tired of watching others who were free to do as they pleased while she was made to stay put, Shawndee sat beside the lodge fire again, lost in thought.

As more time passed and Shawndee was still alone except for the old man who stayed in his room at the far end of the corridor, she grew even more restless.

She found herself wandering from room to room, touching things, looking at the varied objects of the Seneca way of life.

When she came to what she assumed was Shadow Hawk's bedroom, her eyes were drawn to a storage chest beneath his bed.

His warning about such things being forbidden to everyone but the person who owned them plagued Shawndee, but she could not take her eyes off the chest.

Finally, that side of her that was led too often by curiosity made her forget his warning.

Her pulse racing, she knelt down beside his bed and slowly pulled the chest out from beneath it.

There was no lock on the buckskin-wrapped chest, but still she knew that it was too private for her to consider opening it.

Yet so badly did she wish to see this private side of Shadow Hawk's life, so badly did she wish to know everything about him, she lifted a trembling hand to the chest.

Breathing hard, she slowly lifted the lid, then grew pale as the lid fell back, revealing something too awful to contemplate.

"Scalps," she gasped aloud, staring at the many scalps that lay among Shadow Hawk's personal belongings.

She couldn't believe that Shadow Hawk could have such an evil side to his nature that he would actually take scalps from human beings!

But there they were, proof of a side of him that she never would have imagined.

There was a red scalp, a black one, and even . . . a palish sort of golden one.

Shawndee's hand trembled as she reached up to her own hair. She recalled how Shadow Hawk had run his fingers through it.

Did he want it as a trophy to add to those he already had in his chest? Did he plan to do away with her after he settled things with her mother? When he had admired her hair, even touched it, was he even then dreaming of a time when he could take it from her head?

Truly, deeply afraid for the first time since she had been brought to the Seneca village, Shawndee made sure she put the chest back exactly the way she had found it, then rushed to her assigned room and huddled in a corner, her heart pounding.

Again she lifted a hand to her hair. She closed her eyes and tried to fight off thoughts of her hair hanging from a scalp pole and blowing in a gentle breeze.

She visibly shuddered.

Chapter Eighteen

Night had drawn its dark shroud over the village outside. Shawndee knew that soon Shadow Hawk would come for her, to take her to the storytelling event that he had told her about.

Haunted by the scalps she had seen in his private trunk, Shawndee had decided not to cooperate as much as Shadow Hawk probably expected. He would expect her to wear the lovely buckskin dress tonight as he took her among his people.

She was sorely tired of being forced to please him, and tonight she had a surprise waiting for him when he entered this prison of a room.

She was breathless as she waited for the door to open. Her feelings for him were so contradictory, it made her heartsick. The scalps had given her a sense of revulsion. If he was responsible for taking them, how could she ever feel the same about him?

She lifted her hand to her hair, which was tied back again in a ponytail, a thong securing it in place.

She shuddered every time she recalled Shadow Hawk admiring her hair. She tried to block out her fear over how this abduction might end after Shadow Hawk succeeded with his plan.

Instead she forced herself to remember how she had felt before seeing the scalps, how every thought of Shadow Hawk had sent her senses reeling with an ecstasy that was new to her.

She had known it was wrong to allow herself to fall in love with her captor, but nothing could stop the way one's heart reacted to someone so mesmerizing.

"Mesmerizing," Shawndee whispered.

Yes, that was the only way to describe Shadow Hawk.

Now, since she had decided to fight her feelings for him and concentrate on escaping his clutches, she must think the worst of him. She must forget those moments when he had held her, kissed her, touched her. . . .

Her knees grew weak when the door opened and Shadow Hawk stepped into the room.

The sight of him drew her breath away. She would have to fight even harder to remember that she must no longer trust him, that she should perhaps even hate him.

A beautifully fringed and beaded doeskin outfit sheathed his muscled body. A beaded headband that matched the beads on his outfit held his hair back from his face. His beautiful midnight dark eyes shone in the candle's glow as he gazed at her with disbelief.

He had reacted as she had expected. Drawing on the inner strength that she had always had since childhood, the strength that had helped her through troubled times, degradation, and unhappiness, she thrust her chin out stubbornly, her lips tight, her eyes flashing. She took a step toward Shadow Hawk so that he could not doubt her defiance.

"You are wearing the clothes of a boy instead of the dress?" Shadow Hawk said, his voice filled with puzzlement. "Why?"

Not wanting to blurt out that she did this to purposely antagonize him, she held her tongue.

"And now you refuse even to talk to Shadow Hawk?" he asked. He took a slow step toward her.

When he saw that this gesture made Shawndee flinch and take a shaky step away from him, he stopped and studied her eyes in an effort to find answers there.

He reached a hand out to her and gestured toward her hair. "You even tie your hair back as you did before coming to my lodge."

He sighed, looked over his shoulder toward the front door, where the sound of music and laughter could be heard. His people were gathered outside beside the great fire to hear his father's stories.

He had just helped his father to the platform where he now sat upon plush pelts, smiling as his people took their seats around him, their eyes wide, their ears ready for stories.

And now Shadow Hawk wished to introduce to them his woman, whom he hoped would soon please his heart by accepting his offer of marriage.

Of course, he knew that much must be achieved before this could happen, but he hoped that the arrangements could be made before his father died.

His father had urged him to marry and have sons. Shadow Hawk did not expect his father to live long enough for him to bring his first child into the world, for that would take many sunrises and sunsets.

But he had hoped his father could take his last breath smiling, knowing that his son was happy, and that his son would soon father many children.

But now?

Tonight everything had changed along with Shawndee's attitude.

Then suddenly it came to him what might have caused the change.

Had he not refused to let her see to her mother's welfare when she felt that she must? Had he not given her a full day to think about this, so that her anger toward him could build?

He saw the defiant anger in her eyes and stance. Yet there was something else in her attitude, too.

Had she not flinched and taken a step away from him? Would not fear cause such behavior?

It puzzled him as to why she should be afraid of him now, when she had not seemed afraid earlier. Not even moments after he had abducted her.

He was too proud to ask her about any of this, for such questions would make him look weak. He had come to her now for a purpose. His father would soon begin his storytelling. Shadow Hawk would not miss it for the world.

And he had wanted Shawndee to enjoy it, as well, so that by listening to the tales of his people, she might understand and love them.

"Come," Shadow Hawk said, stepping aside so that she could leave the room. "Father will not begin his stories without his son listening. You will listen with me. My people know of your presence in their village. I went into council with my warriors. They have spread the word to their families."

He looked past her at the doeskin dress that lay in a heap at the foot of the bed.

He stiffened, for the dress seemed to have been thrown down in anger. He looked at her and realized that she knew he had seen the dress.

He decided that if she wanted to play out a battle of wits with him, he would join her.

He hoped that once she sat among his people, regaled with his father's stories, her mood would soften and she would again be the Shawndee that he had grown to know.

"No one makes my father wait," Shadow Hawk said. He went to Shawndee and placed a firm hand on her elbow. "Especially not a woman who chooses to look like a boy."

Although she was fighting her feelings for Shadow Hawk, Shawndee knew that her heart was losing the battle. She forced herself to remain strong and defiant.

But as she stepped outside into the light of the huge outdoor fire in the center of the village, and she saw the crowd of Seneca seated on blankets facing an old man on a platform, everything that had been strong inside her fell apart.

She gave Shadow Hawk a quick, pleading look.

He caught the look in her eyes and for a moment regretted exposing her to this newest ordeal. Still, he knew the importance of her hearing the tales, and of understanding the bond he had with his people, especially his father.

He could only hope that after she sat awhile, listening, she would get caught up in the magic of the stories and once again become the woman he had grown to love.

"Must I sit in the midst of your people?" Shawndee said in a whisper that reached only Shadow Hawk's ears. "I feel like such an intruder."

"You are with their chief, so no one will look at you as an intruder," Shadow Hawk said, his voice not so authoritative now. His feelings for her were evident in his gentle tone.

"But still I would rather not . . ." Shawndee said, more loudly than she had intended.

She heard a rustling behind her and looked slowly around. Her words had traveled to his people.

It seemed that all heads and eyes were now on her. She saw how shocked people were by her clothes.

Gasps of horror reached her ears, and she knew that Shadow Hawk had not prepared them well enough. Yet how could he?

He had thought she would be wearing the lovely clothes and moccasins which had made her feel, oh, so feminine . . . even beautiful.

She now regretted having chosen to wear the damnable boy's clothes again, but the damage had been done. She could not turn back time and pull the delicious dress over her head, or sigh with heavenly pleasure as she slid her feet into the moccasins.

She must get through these next moments as she was, and then she would finally put this behind her.

Blushing and feeling awkward, Shawndee turned her eyes away from Shadow Hawk's people. She stepped closer to him. "I wish to return to your lodge," she entreated softly.

He ignored her, taking her hand and leading her toward the waiting crowd.

He bent near and murmured, "I do not understand why you chose to displease Shadow Hawk tonight by wearing those clothes."

"Perhaps you should think more about how *you* can please *me*," Shawndee whispered back heatedly.

He gave her an annoyed glance, then sighed and looked away from her, knowing he must make the best of things now. He would allow nothing to interrupt his father's voice lifting high into the sky as he told the revered tales of his people.

When they had made their way through the gawking crowd to the blanket that he had prepared for himself and Shawndee, Shadow Hawk gestured toward it.

"This is where we will sit and listen," he said, glad when Shawndee hurried onto the blanket.

Shadow Hawk gave his father a nod, then sat down beside Shawndee.

His father had refused Shadow Hawk's offer to meet Shawndee earlier. Purple Cloud had said that this was not the time for him to exchange words with the white woman. Later, when the storytelling was done, he would meet with Shawndee.

Shadow Hawk saw through his father's words. Purple Cloud wished to learn the woman's reaction to the stories; in that way he would discover her true feelings for the Seneca, as well as for Shadow Hawk.

Then Purple Cloud would meet and talk with her, for he would know how to behave toward her. If he saw that she had not been moved by the stories, he would know that she was wrong for his son.

If she was touched by the stories, then just perhaps he would accept that Shadow Hawk had chosen wisely.

What disturbed Shadow Hawk was that Shawndee had begun this test on the wrong foot. By wearing the boy's clothes, she had begun to earn his father's disapproval.

Shadow Hawk and Shawndee were unaware of being watched by someone other than the Seneca. Chester Hawkins was standing in the shadows of the forest, snickering.

His eyes gleaming, Chester chuckled to himself as he thought of the irony of things. He would be rescuing Andrew from one fate, only to subject the boy to something that he might feel was worse than death. It had been in Andrew's eyes how he despised the very ground that Chester walked on.

But to be saved from scalping and death at the Seneca village might make Andrew so grateful he would do anything to please old Chester Hawkins!

In time, Chester would know all of Andrew's reactions.

But for now Chester was too afraid of being caught to stay so close to the Seneca village. He would go into hiding again near enough to keep watch on who came and went from the village.

With luck, an opportunity would soon come for him to grab Andrew. He must wait, though, until the lad was alone.

He shuddered as he recalled Jane Sibley's threats. He believed that she had enough knowledge of witchcraft to make him pay dearly if he didn't return Andrew to his mother, as promised. He didn't want to even think of the ways a witch might torture a man!

With nervous sweat pearling on his brow, he crept away through the thick brush, stopping only when he thought he was far enough away not to be detected.

Hunkering down behind the bushes, he kept his eyes on the village, wondering why the crowd was assembled facing the old man.

The wind brought a voice to him. He tried to hear what was being said, but he was too far away to make it out.

The voice had a soothing quality. It made Chester realize just how tired and sleepy he was. He settled down beneath a tree and rested his back against its trunk, his head nodding as sleep claimed him.

•

Chapter Nineteen

After Shawndee was able to relax, she became quickly entranced by Shadow Hawk's father. She could tell that his illness had aged him before his time, yet his lined, copper face radiated tranquillity, proving that he was facing his eventual death with peace in his heart.

She also noticed that if he were not sitting on the bench which had been placed before the central fire, he would be a tall, lean fellow.

And, ah, how he was dressed. His attire was almost as colorful as the tales she expected to hear him weave. Just now he was greeting people one by one as they passed by him, hugging him in greeting.

As Shawndee admired Purple Cloud, so did the storyteller's son. Shadow Hawk noted his father's long, white flannel overshirt, which was bound with blue ribbon. It was embroidered richly with colored moose hair.

He also wore a *gustoweh*, a cap of soft doeskin quilled in a herringbone pattern. White down feathers of a heron, drooped from the crest, and the lone feather at the tip was from the tail of a young eagle. Also from the tip rose a little tassel of red moose hair held on by fish glue.

Two bags hung from a loop on Purple Cloud's belt. One bag contained his pipe and tobacco, and the other was filled with lumps that had filled Shadow Hawk with curiosity as a child.

But now he knew what those lumps were. They were the trophies that reminded his father of his stories—bear teeth, shells, bark dolls, strings of wampum, bunches of feathers, bits of bark with hieroglyphics.

His father had been proud to be his people's *hoskwisaonh*, their storyteller, proud to be the one who took his people on journeys backward into the forgotten adventures of yesterday.

His father was called by the children an "Old Warrior in the woods," a person who entertained with tales of past glories . . . wonder stories of the ancient days.

Shawndee absently grabbed Shadow Hawk's hand when his father's tired old voice began. *"Hauh, oneh, djagaondys."*

The people responded in unison, *"Hauh-oneh."*

Shawndee gave Shadow Hawk a quick questioning look, but glanced back at Purple Cloud when he spoke again, much more forcefully and louder.

"Kakaa!" Purple Cloud said, raising a hand in the air as a gesture to silence everyone around him. *"Gakaa!"*

Hushed silence fell over the crowd, and everyone who had been standing sat down on their blankets or mats.

Shadow Hawk explained that this was the beginning of the storytelling time, that the marvels of old were about to be unfolded. Everyone would stay silent, to listen.

Shawndee strained her neck to get a better look at what Purple Cloud was doing.

Her eyes widened when he plunged a thin, shaky hand into a mysterious-looking bag that hung at his waist, and drew from it a bear's tusk.

"Hoh!" he exclaimed as he held the tusk up into the air for all to see. "The bear! As you all know, it is a part of a child's initial training to learn why the bear lost its tail, why the chipmunk has a striped back, and why meteors flash in the sky! Seneca children, listen well tonight as I relay to you a tale of *Nyagwai*, the bear. Do you all wish to hear it?"

Shawndee looked quickly around her as everyone spoke one quick word in unison, *"He,"* which she knew must mean "yes" for Purple Cloud went immediately into his story, sometimes speaking in English, other times in his Seneca tongue.

She became entranced by the tale, and wondered why at intervals during the story many of the Seneca people exclaimed *"He."*

Shadow Hawk watched Shawndee's expression during the storytelling and was happy to see how eagerly she attended each and every word, even trying to understand the Seneca words.

He saw that she was puzzled by the way his people interrupted the storytelling, saying *"He,"* which some might think was an impolite thing to do.

He decided to make sure that Shawndee did not think his people rude when in truth they were proving to Shadow Hawk's father that they were intently listening.

"Shawndee?"

She turned and leaned closer to him.

"My people say *"He"* at times while my father is telling his story to prove they are listening to him," Shadow Hawk whispered to Shawndee. "If there is no frequent response, storytellers stop and inquire what fault was found with the story."

"Truly?" Shawndee whispered back. She smiled. "I doubt anyone would go to sleep while your father is telling his stories. I have never heard anything as interesting."

"It is a breach of courtesy for a listener to fall

asleep, and it is also an omen of evil," Shadow Hawk whispered.

"I feel discourteous by talking while he is talking," Shawndee said.

"My father did look our way a moment ago, but he smiled instead of frowning, for he knows that his son would only speak at such a time as this to explain things to you," Shadow Hawk said. He was suddenly aware that Shawndee had not released his hand.

He glanced down at their twined fingers, then gazed into her eyes. He no longer saw the defiance that had been there earlier. It seemed that the tales were weaving their way into her heart, making her feel the mystique and lore of his people as he'd hoped she would.

Had she not, he would have known that however she might soften in her mood toward him, he could no longer think of her as someone he would want to share his life with.

Feeling herself falling in love with Shadow Hawk again, and still uncertain about how wise it was to give her heart to him after seeing those dreadful scalps in his trunk, Shawndee looked quickly away from him.

She listened to his father again, but allowed her hand to remain twined with Shadow Hawk's. For the moment it was wonderful to pretend that she was a part of his world; that the future could link them as man and wife.

"Children!" Purple Cloud exclaimed, capturing Shawndee's complete attention again, especially when all of the children replied in unison, "*He*," to the old storyteller whom they obviously revered.

She looked from child to child, taking in the radiance on their faces and in their beautiful dark eyes; for a moment she saw another child, one that had formed in her mind's eye, one that was being held by Shadow Hawk, a child that she had just given birth to. A son!

She shook her head to clear her thoughts, and again listened to the storyteller, glad that she had something to focus on besides her intense feelings for a man she doubted she could ever have.

"Children, you have all been taught that to listen to stories in the summer makes trees and plants lazy, as well as animals and men. In the summer, storytelling makes scanty crops, lean game, and shiftless people," Purple Cloud exclaimed, then smiled. "But as you know, this is summer and your storyteller *still* speaks to you. You are all wise and know why. This old man is telling his last stories. He could not wait for winter, when the year's work is over and all nature slumbers. Tonight I have come to you for the last time to sit among you to make you laugh; to make you love life. I have lived long and well. I have loved life. I have loved my people with every beat of my heart."

He raised both of his hands heavenward. "I encourage all of you not to be sad at my passing," he said thickly. "I encourage all of you not to linger long on mourning your past chief who is your present storyteller. Just remember how I sat among you, happy, fulfilled, and eager to walk the road of the hereafter with the loved ones who have gone before me. Rejoice, my people, on the day my spirit drifts over to the other side of the mountain! Rejoice when you know that I have gone far beyond it into the heavens! I will look down upon you smiling, for I will be at peace, as should you be, knowing that I am where I wish to be."

Everyone grew stone quiet, their eyes focused on Purple Cloud.

Tears fell from some.

But many of the Seneca smiled peacefully at their beloved senior warrior, for they knew that he had spoken from the heart and was accepting death with a joyousness only those who had lived a good life could know.

Purple Cloud lowered his hands and gazed at Shadow Hawk. He gestured with a hand toward his son and smiled. "I am leaving you in good hands," he said, nodding. "My son, your chief, will continue leading and protecting you."

Purple Cloud lowered his shaky hand and grew

solemn. "Since the arrival of white eyes on our land, life has become more challenging," he said tightly.

He gave Shawndee a quick somber glance that made her flinch and tighten her fingers around Shadow Hawk's.

He looked slowly away from her and faced his people again. "But as you know, sometimes there are whites who are good through and through," he said. "It is for each of you to know who is and who is not to be trusted."

Shawndee became aware of several Seneca slowly turning their eyes to her.

But the glances were brief and soon all attention was on Purple Cloud again as he prepared to tell one last story.

Shawndee tried to put her brief moment of uneasiness behind her as she again listened to Purple Cloud's words.

"*I-newaengegeode, Haunio-djadao, dii-us!*" Purple Cloud loudly exclaimed.

Curious, Shawndee leaned closer to Shadow Hawk.

"What did your father say?" she whispered.

"He has just announced his intention to recite a *ga-gaa*, a folk tale, to our people," Shadow Hawk whispered back as his people answered "*He.*"

Shawndee smiled at Shadow Hawk, then listened to the tale. When it was done, the people rose to their feet and began filing past Purple Cloud, each of them giving him a small gift of thanks. She saw that sometimes it was a lone bead, a small round brooch, pinches of native tobacco, a carved nut, a strand of sinew for thread, or a small bag of tobacco.

"The gifts are called by the Seneca word *dagwaniatcis*," Shadow Hawk said to Shawndee, this time not in a whisper, for everyone was talking aloud now, discussing the excitement of the evening, the wonders of this man who could spin tales that touched their hearts. The crowd had been thrilled by his dramatic recitation, sometimes moved to uproarious laughter, sometimes made to shudder with awe.

Shawndee herself felt a strange glow, as though the stories had reached far inside her, touching her deeply.

It had made her want to know more, to experience again the thrill that the stories had given her tonight.

But she was afraid that after tonight her life would change back to the way it had always been. She doubted she would even see Shadow Hawk again, for if her mother was too stubborn to do as Shadow Hawk requested, who knew what would happen?

The scalps she had seen suddenly flashed before her mind's eye again, but disappeared just as quickly when he placed a gentle hand on her elbow and helped her to her feet beside him.

"We go now to the council house where food has been prepared for tonight's celebration," Shadow Hawk said, already walking her through the crowd toward the large longhouse. She could see smoke rising from four smoke holes, instead of the usual one that was found in the smaller, residential lodges.

Most of the day, Shawndee had smelled the tempting aromas of food cooking in the other longhouses. The women seemed to put their hearts into the meals they prepared for their families. Shawndee who had not been taught to cook, wondered if she could ever learn how to please a man with food she prepared for him. Or would he wish he had taken a different woman for a bride?

"Shawndee?"

Shadow Hawk's voice brought Shawndee from her thoughts. She gave him an awkward smile as she hesitated. "Taking me to the council house for food might be too much for your people, especially your father," she said.

She glanced over at Purple Cloud, who was being helped to the council house by two muscled warriors.

"No one will question my taking you there," Shadow Hawk said, continuing to walk her toward the lodge. "If it is my decision, then so be it."

Shawndee smiled weakly, then grew silent as he took her inside with him. She was glad when he did not force her to sit in the middle of the crowd. They sat back from the others while Purple Cloud remained the center of attention. He sat now by the largest lodge fire of the four, receiving hugs and laughing and patting the children lovingly as they came for their own hugs.

After everyone was seated and Shawndee could get a clear look at everything around her, her eyes widened when she saw the varied assortment of food that was placed on a bench not far from where Purple Cloud sat.

The food was served with much grace and dignity as one matron ladled steaming hull-corn hominy from a large black kettle over the main fire into neatly carved bowls.

Several other women then passed the filled bowls around until everyone had one, as well as a wooden spoon.

As everyone began eating the delicious-smelling hominy, Shawndee realized just how hungry she was. She ate until her bowl was empty.

Shadow Hawk reached over and took her empty bowl and placed it into his. "Did you enjoy?" he asked, turning his face up to smile at the matron who took the bowls from him.

"It was delicious," Shawndee murmured.

They had no time for further conversation, for

the next portion of the meal was being offered on a small wooden platter for each person. It was a mixture of meats, the most plentiful being roasted venison. Like the others, Shawndee ate the meat with her fingers.

When she saw what came next, her eyes widened. A bowl of fat was passed to each person, and then boiled corn bread. As Shawndee watched the people dip the bread into the bowl of fat, she shivered. The fat looked thick and unappetizing. She hated to think how it would make the corn bread slide down her throat and then lie heavily in her stomach.

"Eat," Shadow Hawk said between bites. "You will soon discover just how good it is."

Shawndee smiled wanly at him, but when he waited for her to eat, she knew she had no choice.

She dipped the corn bread in the fat, closed her eyes, then brought the greasy mass to her mouth and quickly shoved it inside.

She gulped hard as she swallowed.

Then her eyes opened in surprise. Never had she tasted anything as delicious as this.

She gave Shadow Hawk a wide-eyed look of wonder.

"Don't you know by now that you can always trust Shadow Hawk?" he said teasingly.

The scalps rushed before her mind's eye.

She quickly blinked the image away.

When a matron came and stooped next to Shawndee, holding a box of corn husks, she gazed at them questioningly.

"They are for your greasy fingers," Shadow Hawk said.

He reached for one and gave it to Shawndee, then took one for himself.

"Wipe your fingers with the napkin; then the napkin will be thrown into the fire by the waiting matron," Shadow Hawk said.

The "napkin" was rough against Shawndee's fingers, but she knew this was a part of the eating ritual tonight, so she took one and wiped her fingers.

She smiled and gave the soiled "napkin" back to the matron, as did Shadow Hawk.

More food was then consumed until Shawndee felt as though her belly might pop.

She sighed with relief when the main portion of the meal came to a close and a bowl of *onegadaiyeh*, "hot fluid," a fragrant tea made from the tips of hemlock boughs mixed with a dash of sassafras, was given to each individual.

"Dessert is now served, and then we will return to my longhouse," Shadow Hawk said, smiling a thank you to a matron as she handed him and Shawndee each a dish with generous slices of sugar-nut bread to eat with the tea.

With her first bite, Shawndee felt as though she might be entering heaven. It was sweet, yet tangy, one of the best things she had ever eaten. Neither Tootiba nor her mother had ever troubled themselves with such delicacies in the kitchen.

"I hope I can learn how to make this delicious dish," Shawndee said without forethought.

"You can cook well?" Shadow Hawk asked, raising an eyebrow.

Shawndee blushed and lowered her eyes. "No, not even boiled water," she murmured, then giggled as she looked slowly up at him.

"I know how this is prepared," Shadow Hawk said, smiling. "As a small child I watched my mother prepare this for our family's evening meal."

She listened intently, smiling as he told her how the sugar-nut bread had been prepared . . . made by mixing white corn flour with pulverized maple sugar, into which hickory and hazelnut meats were added, the whole being molded into a cake held in shape by husks and then boiled until done.

Just as Shadow Hawk finished what he was saying, the entire group of Seneca loudly said, *"Oguhoh."*

She looked quickly around her when the revelers began rising to their feet, smiling, talking, laughing.

"When a feast is finished, it is polite for everyone to say *'Oguhoh,'* which means delicious," Shadow Hawk said, placing a hand beneath Shawndee's elbow and helping her to her feet.

She watched as everyone began filing past Purple Cloud again, giving him more hugs. Then she moved along with Shadow Hawk out of the council house beneath the moon and the stars.

"I will escort you to my lodge and then return and help my father," Shadow Hawk said as he walked with Shawndee toward his longhouse. "After I get Father comfortably in his bed, then you and I will sit by my lodge fire and talk."

They left the smells of venison and steaming maize pudding and hull-corn hominy behind, and entered Shadow Hawk's lodge.

Shawndee watched him walk away from her. He smiled over his shoulder at her. "I will not be long," he said, then stopped and went back to her. He gently touched her cheek, then turned and left.

Even a small gesture like his touching her cheek made Shawndee's insides feel as though they were melting.

"What am I to do?" she whispered, sighing as she sat down on a mat before the fire.

She couldn't stop thinking about the hidden scalps, but at the same time she was deeply touched by the stories she had heard tonight, and by the way Shadow Hawk was so attentive to her.

Tomorrow everything could change back to the way it had been before Shadow Hawk entered her life. Tomorrow she might have no choice but to return to her own world, which was dark, dreary, and unhappy.

It would be hard to forget Shadow Hawk and the way he made her feel.

Sighing, she pulled her knees up before her and hugged them, thinking about that moment when Shadow Hawk had kissed and held her. How could a man so gentle ever remove someone's scalp?

Soon Shadow Hawk and his father would return to the lodge. Not wanting to come face to face with either of them just now, Shawndee scrambled to her feet.

Sobbing, she hurried to her assigned room and closed the door between herself and Shadow Hawk and his father. How she regretted her snooping, which had changed everything from a world of wonder to a world of doubt!

Chapter Twenty

After returning to the longhouse with his father and seeing that Shawndee wasn't waiting beside his lodge fire as he had expected, Shadow Hawk had at first become alarmed. He'd feared she might have tried to escape. He had helped his father into his room. Then, with a pounding heart, he'd gone into Shawndee's room, sighing with relief when he found her there, asleep.

As he knelt down beside her, he marveled at how beautiful she was. Surely she was dreaming, the dream god guiding her soul on its dream journey.

Her position struck him as very odd. She was lying on the floor far from the bed, with her legs drawn up close to her chest.

He could not understand why she had come back

to this room even though he'd asked her to wait for him beside the fire. And why had she chosen to fall asleep on the floor?

Bending low beside her, he looked more closely at her face as she lay with one cheek on the cold, earthen floor. Shadow Hawk saw something that truly puzzled him. There was a lone tear slowly drifting down Shawndee's cheek.

That proved she had only been asleep for a short time, and also that she was sad. But why? She knew he would not be holding her captive for much longer. Was she still resentful of the fact that she had been taken captive?

He did know that she had begged to be set free so that she could warn her mother about some plot. She had even said that her mother was in danger. . . .

Gently he brushed his thumb over her cheek, the coolness of the tear absorbed by the warmth of his skin. Disturbed by so many questions, especially concerning how she truly felt about him, Shadow Hawk moved his hand away from her and went to his own room.

He paced for a while, then sighed deeply and changed from his full buckskin attire into his breechclout. He would look in on Shawndee one last time tonight, and then he would go to the bluff and seek solace and prayer beneath the stars. Perhaps he would learn answers that would help him understand this woman he loved, who seemed to love him one moment and then fear him the next.

He went back to where Shawndee still slept so soundly on the floor. Again he was uneasy about her being on the cold earth. He reached his arms gently beneath her and lifted her up, stopping when her eyes began slowly opening.

Shawndee melted inside and awoke fully when she felt herself in familiar arms. The warmth and loving of those arms was like an elixir to her aching heart. Although she wished to fight off her feelings for the man who held her, she could not help leaning her head against his powerful, bare chest as he carried her from the dark room to the light and warmth of his lodge fire.

"Why did you not wait for my return?" Shadow Hawk asked thickly as he looked down at her.

Where her cheek rested against his bare chest, her flesh was soft and warm, her long, thick lashes brushing his skin as she closed her eyes, then opened them again and gazed up at him with a soft sort of apology in their depths.

"You ask me, but I cannot tell you why," Shawndee murmured. She truly wanted to forget why she had gone to the other room, tormented by feelings that had made her suddenly afraid of not only Shadow Hawk, but also his people.

The scalps in his trunk came back to her mind's eye in a flash.

But with one blink of an eye and sheer willpower, they were gone again, for she did not, she *could* not, see how such a gentle man as Shadow Hawk could have taken the scalps.

She most certainly could not believe that he had ever looked at her hair as a prize he wished to place with the others.

His arms, his voice—they both proved that he cared too much for her ever to treat her with cruelty.

"You cannot tell me because you choose not to?" Shadow Hawk asked, stopping beside the fire.

He stood there for a moment longer before placing her on a mat. "Or do you not tell me because you cannot remember?" he asked thickly. "Did sleep rob you of the memory of why you left the warmth of my lodge fire?"

"You do not truly wish to know," Shawndee murmured, looking almost apologetically at him.

"If you think it is best not to tell me, then do not say it," Shadow Hawk said, though he wished she would confide in him.

"It is best not said," Shawndee said, looking quickly away from him.

"Then I will not question you again about it," Shadow Hawk replied, wishing he could carry her to bed and make love to her all night.

All that lay between them was his brief breech-

222

clout and her pants and shirt. In a matter of moments their bodies could come together as one.

For now, he must brush thoughts such as those from his mind. All good and wonderful things came in time—even getting her to trust him enough so he could prove just how deeply he felt for her.

Making love to her would demonstrate all of the feelings she had awakened inside his heart.

If she returned that love, then he would know he and Shawndee had been brought together because it had been destined from the beginning of time. He believed that if he looked heavenward now, he would see their names written in the stars.

Knowing that he had allowed his thoughts to go far beyond what was possible at this moment, when he was just regaining Shawndee's trust, he smiled at her and placed her gently on a mat. Beside it was another mat where he would sit.

Yes, he saw the love in her eyes that he had seen before. No amount of tears could wash that emotion from her eyes.

And now, as she smiled at him while he sat down beside her, he knew that whatever had drawn her away from the fire was no longer inside her heart, troubling her.

As their eyes met and held, and he reached to brush a soft curl from her cheek, the touch of his hand caused her to shiver sensually. He knew without a doubt that all was right between them again.

223

He wanted to hold her.

He wanted to tell her how much he loved her and show her in the way only a man in love can show a woman. He *was* in love with her, so much he felt foreign to himself, for he had never loved like this before.

He had never met anyone like her.

He had never been touched deep inside his soul as she touched him.

"Is your father alright?" Shawndee asked, shaken by her feelings, which seemed to grow more sensual the longer she sat with Shadow Hawk.

"Yes, Father is happy now that he has had the chance to share his stories with his people one last time," Shadow Hawk said, glad to have something to say that momentarily broke the sensual tension between them. He needed things to be right before he took her in his arms and kissed her tonight. He expected more than kisses. Heart and soul, he wanted her.

But he must take it slow . . . and . . . easy . . .

"When I left my father in his bed, he had a smile on his face as he drifted into a sweet sort of sleep," Shadow Hawk said softly.

"Your father told so many interesting tales tonight," Shawndee said. "I was quite taken by the myths of your people. But I am surprised to learn that your people are superstitious."

While listening to the tales tonight, she had

found herself comparing some of the superstitions of his people with witchcraft.

Could his own background help make Shadow Hawk understand and accept her ancestry? Then she reminded herself that it was foolish to think of their having a future together.

He would have no reason to care even if she were a witch. His whole reason for being with her was because of a plan to get her mother's whiskey out of his people's lives.

Yes, tonight might be their last night together.

She would cherish each and every moment.

"Yes, you might say that some superstitions enter into our Seneca beliefs," Shadow Hawk said. He was glad to see that she was truly interested in his people. If things worked out, he would bring her home with him after he met her mother, and he would teach her all the Seneca customs as his wife!

"Tell me," Shawndee said. She crawled over to him and rested on her knees before him. She thrilled inside when he reached a gentle hand to her hair and brushed golden tendrils back from her face.

"I truly wish to know more about you . . . your myths . . . your people," she murmured. "Especially your belief in superstitions."

"There is in the heaven world a Master of Life and Souls," Shadow Hawk began. "He allows his subordinate spirits to rule the earth-world and concerns himself generally with his own realm. Souls that return to him are taken apart and readjusted so that they may function properly in the immortal realm."

"Please tell me more," Shawndee said.

"My Seneca people believe in beings such as wizards, witches, and sorcerers," Shadow Hawk said, his eyes holding Shawndee's when he saw a guarded look enter hers. "These beings possess an evil *orenda* and seek to destroy innocent people, while virtuous persons may be given a good *orenda*, which is always more powerful in the end than the evil *orenda* of witches and sorcerers."

What he said about the evil *orenda* of witches made Shawndee shiver. Would he not see her as an evil *orenda* if he knew about the book in her mother's attic that suggested she came from a family of witches?

"What might the evil *orenda*, or witches, do to those who are innocent and good?" Shawndee asked guardedly, remembering how her mother had told Chester she would "witch" him.

"You might better ask what is done to those who are found to have the evil *orenda*," Shadow Hawk said thickly.

"Tell me," Shawndee said, swallowing hard. "What is done to the evil ones?" She refrained from saying "witch" again, afraid that if she did, Shadow

Hawk might look deep inside her and see that she herself was a witch.

"My people do nothing to them, but the evil ones are punished nonetheless," Shadow Hawk said, his voice drawn as he looked past Shawndee and gazed into the flames of the fire. "Bees might sting the lips of the evil one, or his tongue might swell and fill his mouth, or snakes might crawl into the evil one's bed and choke him while he sleeps."

When he heard Shawndee gasp and saw how pale she was, Shadow Hawk reached over and took one of her hands. "I am sorry," he said. "I should not have described such horrible things to you. Only those who prove to be bad are punished. They are then made to believe in an earth holder, a great creator who gives all things useful to man, and who is the source and ruler of health and life."

Believing that he could never love her because of what she might be, and knowing that he might discover the truth about her heritage, a heritage that even frightened herself, Shawndee leapt to her feet and stumbled away from him, sobbing.

Stunned by her strange behavior, Shadow Hawk turned and stared disbelievingly at her as she rushed from the warmth of this outer room back to her cold bedchamber.

Angry at himself for bringing up things that might frighten Shawndee, Shadow Hawk leapt to his feet and hurried after her.

When he got to her, she was stretched out on her stomach on her bed, her deep sobs tearing his heart to shreds.

Hoping to make things right for her again, Shadow Hawk sat down beside Shawndee and placed gentle hands on her waist. He urged her up into his arms where he held her close.

Her arms twined around his neck, and her sobs subsided. When their eyes met and held as she gazed up at him, he could not help kissing her.

She returned the kiss, and he kissed the salty tears from her lips, his hand reaching inside her shirt and claiming a breast. He heard her quick intake of breath and knew that at first it was from the shock of what he was doing, and then from sheer pleasure as he kneaded the breast, her nipple growing hard against his palm.

Shadow Hawk brought his lips close to hers. "I love you," he whispered. "I am sorry if I frightened you. Let me kiss it away?"

"Yes, yes," Shawndee whispered against his lips, her head spinning from the pleasure his hand on her breast was giving her. His lips had made her forget everything but their love for one another.

Oh, Lord, she *did* love him.

Heart and soul.

She had loved him from the moment she had first seen him.

His lips met hers in a frenzy of kisses.

He leaned slightly away from her, enabling him to reach his other hand inside her shirt to claim her other breast.

As he felt the wondrous softness and heat against his palms, his head began to spin in a way that was new to him.

But he had never loved a woman before.

But he did now . . . every fiber of his being cried out for her.

All of their differences meant nothing to him. All he wanted was to make love with her.

And he knew by the way she was breathing, by the way she was clinging and kissing him, that she felt the same as he and wanted to be with him just as badly. She was straining her body against his, pushing her breasts into his hands.

"I want to make love with you," Shadow Hawk whispered against her lips. "My body, my mind, my soul cry out for you. Do you feel it, as well?"

He slid a hand down and felt the pounding of her heart against the flesh of his palm. That told him the answer she seemed to find hard to admit.

"Tell me no and I shall leave your bed," Shadow Hawk said, yet even without her permission he could not help sliding a hand lower, where the flesh of her flat stomach quaked with pleasure as his fingers eased down inside the front of her breeches.

He heard her quick intake of breath and saw her eyes close languorously when his fingers sought and found the soft fronds of silken hair that lay over her womanhood.

Shawndee gasped with pleasure as Shadow Hawk dared to slide his fingers down through the hair and touch the sensitive place that he found wet and ready for such pleasuring.

Slowly he slid his finger over her, back and forth, and then his full hand went across her and he pressed his palm where she opened herself to him.

"I have never felt anything so heavenly," Shawndee whispered, her voice sounding drunken and strange to her. This change, too, she realized, came with the passion that his hands were creating inside her.

No man's hand had ever been where she had allowed his to go. And she wanted more.

All her worries were swept from her mind by the pleasure that dominated her whole being.

"Touch *me*," Shadow Hawk said, his voice husky as he reached for one of her hands. He held it steady as her eyes met his with a questioning look.

"I don't know if . . ." Shawndee choked out, her pulse racing so hard she felt she might faint.

"Touch me, and then if you wish to stop, I shall leave you until tomorrow when I plan to take you to your mother," Shadow Hawk said, his heart thudding like hammer blows inside his chest as she allowed his hand to slowly take hers where she would discover the true strength of his need for her.

His manhood was tight and hot and throbbing.

He had made love to many women, but none had caused him to feel like this. None had made his heat almost too much to bear!

"I'm not sure," Shawndee murmured as he took her hand closer to where she saw his thickness pushing against his breechclout.

She knew what that was, even though she had never seen a man nude before. She had guessed how a man should look, and had already imagined how well endowed this handsome man must be.

She was soon to know.

Shadow Hawk disregarded Shawndee's hesitance, for he felt that once she got past her initial fear of making love, she would relax and allow herself to enjoy the most precious gift of life that the "Master of Life and Souls" blessed man and woman with.

Shadow Hawk and Shawndee were one in heart and soul. Making love would seal their love for eternity.

Shawndee was guarded about what she was about to do, yet her heart told her that everything they did together was right. They were in love.

And she now knew that no matter what she said or did, he would love her no less.

Her thoughts were swept away again, and all she was aware of was how her hand was sliding down the inside of his breechclout. She was only moments away from touching his manhood.

A part of her was afraid. Yet the part of her that was ruling her heart tonight ignored her fears.

As her fingers finally found him—hard, long, throbbing, hot, and eager for her touch—she sighed and let his hand guide her fingers around him until his manhood was snuggled tightly within her grip.

She had felt him flinch and gasp when she first touched him. She was very aware now of his rapid breathing as his hand showed hers how to move on him.

When he groaned, she gazed up at his face and found his eyes closed, his jaw tight, and his teeth clenched.

She yanked her hand away. "I did not mean to hurt you," she said, pulling her hand from inside his breechclout.

Chuckling, his eyes opening, Shadow Hawk slowly slid his breechclout completely down and allowed it to fall to the earthen floor.

Shawndee saw his nudity for the first time in the slight light from the outer-room fire. She scarcely breathed as he leaned low over her on the bed and slowly undressed her.

Her own body was now bare in the fire's glow.

Shadow Hawk's eyes and hands moved slowly over her as she stretched out on the bed.

"Your body is more beautiful than a man could ever imagine it to be," Shadow Hawk said huskily, moving so that he knelt over her, his knees resting on the bed on each side of her.

He brushed his lips against her flat belly, causing her to moan with pleasure.

Then he moved his lips up and was soon sucking on one of her nipples while both hands kneaded her breasts.

"Be not afraid," he whispered as his lips moved to her ear. His tongue flicked inside it. "What we are about to do is done with love."

"I have never . . ." Shawndee whispered back as one of his knees slowly parted her legs.

"Would you rather wait?" Shadow Hawk asked, for he had never forced himself on any woman. All women he had taken to his bed had come willingly because they wished to become a wife to their chief.

None had ever pleased him enough.

Not until now!

Making love was not even required for him to know that Shawndee was his one and only love.

Her body was crying out for something she had never been aware of before; his hands, his lips, his tongue awakened every nerve in her body. Shawndee knew that waiting now to make love would be the hardest thing she would have to endure in her lifetime.

No, she would not force this denial upon herself. She had waited too long to find someone like Shadow Hawk, and to feel totally like a woman, to make herself wait until another time.

"Please?" she found herself whispering as she arched herself up toward him. "I need you so badly. I do not wish to wait. I don't believe I could and . . . and . . . keep my sanity."

"You need not wait any longer," Shadow Hawk said huskily.

He guided his throbbing member to where she had opened herself willingly to him.

As he placed himself at her entrance and stopped, he brushed soft kisses across her lips.

"I do love you," she whispered against his lips, her pulse racing as she felt the heat of his manhood where she was throbbing, warm, and wet.

She pressed herself up against his heat, then shuddered as he began probing, slowly, easily. He kissed her with passion and swept his arms around her to hold her as he gave one last shove that sent him past the thin barrier of her virginity.

The pain surprised Shawndee, but his kiss, his arms molding her close to his body, swept the pain away and she was quickly aware of a wondrous sort of spinning inside her head. Slowly the pleasure built into something magical with each of his strokes within her.

As though practiced, she swept her legs around his hips, drawing him more deeply inside her.

His thrusts were swift now.

His lips were demanding as he continued to kiss her.

His one hand went between them and he kneaded her breast.

She reached down and splayed her fingers out across his tight, muscled buttocks, then gasped when wondrously pleasurable feelings flooded through her until she seemed to see great bursts of sunshine as she reached the peak of her passion. Shadow Hawk groaned as he reached his own climax, thrust, held, and then rolled away from her, spent and breathless.

"I had no idea it would be like this," Shawndee murmured, still aware of a sensual throbbing deep inside her where he had filled her with his seed.

"Nor I," Shadow Hawk said, his voice filled with awe. He sighed and turned on his side to face Shawndee. "I have never experienced such bliss until tonight, with you."

"Bliss—yes, that is the word I would use to describe my own feelings," Shawndee said, smiling dreamily as she rolled over and stretched out on her back.

When she felt his lips moving slowly over her body, his tongue finding places that until tonight she had never known could feel such pleasure, she closed her eyes, moaned, and again felt herself being transported to paradise, but this time only by his tongue, lips, and fingers.

When she was back down on earth again, she gazed in wonder at him over what he had just done. He smiled and brushed her lips with kisses.

"However we choose to make love is right between us because we are of one heartbeat, you and I," he said huskily. "Nothing you could say could make me love you less than I do at this moment. And soon, when things are settled in both our lives, I want to speak vows with you that will make us man and wife."

A sudden alarm went off inside Shawndee.

She scooted away from Shadow Hawk, grabbed a blanket, then left the bed and hurried from the room. She sat down before the fire, which had burned down to ashes.

Stunned by her behavior, especially after what they had just shared, Shadow Hawk drew a blanket around his shoulders and went out to sit beside her.

"What did I say that was wrong?" he asked, trying to meet her gaze. She ignored him, staring quietly into the firepit. "What did I do that was wrong? Did I hurt you? Do you regret having made love?"

Shawndee looked quickly over at him. Never had she wanted to put doubt inside his heart again, yet she knew now that she had. She felt trapped by truths that she knew she should reveal.

Yet she wasn't even sure, herself, what was truth. Was she, or wasn't she, from a family of witches?

Either way, she knew she owed it to him to tell him what was truly troubling her.

She suddenly blurted out what she had discovered in her attic.

"My mother might even be a witch," she said, her voice catching. "If *she* is a witch . . ."

A warning shot through Shadow Hawk's brain. If Shawndee's mother was a witch, might Shawndee also become one someday?

Then he remembered what his sister had said when he had worried aloud about Shawndee. He knew that goodness could overcome bad, and that a man's love could help any woman overcome her weaknesses.

"Shawndee, we must all accept what life brings us," he said gently. "If it is bad, we overcome it and become a better person because of it."

He drew her into his arms and embraced her. "I love you," he said thickly. "Let me be the one to help you fight off any evil that might try to enter your heart. Let me help you forget all that troubles you. Let us rejoice in what we have found together. Rarely does one find such a love as you and I have found."

"I know," Shawndee murmured. "But can it truly be enough? I . . . I . . . remember what you said about how witches are treated, the *orenda*—"

"You are not a witch, nor shall you ever be," Shadow Hawk said firmly.

With him encouraging her so, she wished she could ask him about the scalps. But seeing this wonderfully good side of him made her realize that it would be best never to question him about such things. How could she let him know she had doubted him so?

"I will settle things with your mother soon, and then I want to bring you home so that we can be man and wife," Shadow Hawk said huskily. He lifted her chin and brought her eyes level with his. "Do you wish to be my wife?"

"I wish for nothing else," Shawndee murmured. "But are you certain? We have known each other for such a short time."

"Are you certain about your feelings for *me*?" he asked in return.

"I love you with all my heart and soul and know I could never love anyone else," Shawndee said. "And, yes, I do want to return with you and stay with you forever."

"Then so be it," Shadow Hawk said huskily. He swept her up into his arms and carried her to his room. The pelts on his bed were thick and plush, and a candle glowed warm beside it.

As they began making love again, Shadow Hawk

knew that he must get what he needed from her mother, regardless of how her mother behaved when she heard that she had lost her daughter to a Seneca chief!

Chapter Twenty-one

Realizing that she was smiling as she woke up, Shawndee reached out beside her for Shadow Hawk, then turned, frowning with disappointment when she found he was not there.

She saw the impression of his body in the blankets where he had slept and ran her hand caressingly over them. She was filled with delicious memories of the time spent with Shadow Hawk in his bed.

She never would have guessed that making love could be so wonderful.

She never would have guessed that one man could change her into someone she hardly recognized this morning.

The world didn't seem so forlorn and drab today.

And even though she was still worried about her mother, she felt warm and special this morning. It seemed that nothing could lower her spirits.

She smiled again when she felt the warmth where Shadow Hawk had lain. He had not been gone from the bed for very long.

As she sat up, the blanket fell away, and she looked down and gasped when she saw that she had slept unclothed a full night with a man.

A blush rose to her cheeks when she thought of how her mother would react to what she would call shameful behavior. Shawndee did feel a little ashamed to know that she had given herself fully to a man before any vows were spoken.

"But not just any man," she whispered.

A soft smile quivered across lips that felt somewhat swollen from the many kisses she had shared with Shadow Hawk.

No, she thought as she stretched her arms above her head and yawned dreamily. It was not just any man that she had given herself to. It was the man she loved and would marry after she saw to her mother's safekeeping.

"Oh, Mother," she sighed aloud as she realized that another full night had passed and she still had not gone to warn her mother about the women of Silver Creek.

Her lips pursed stubbornly, Shawndee hurried from the bed and grabbed a blanket to cover herself. After wrapping it around her, she rushed from the room.

When she stepped out into the dark corridor, she stopped and listened to the silence of the long-house. She gazed down to the far end of the corridor and wondered about Shadow Hawk's father, and whether Shadow Hawk might be there looking after him.

She was tempted to go and see. She wished to hurry him along with whatever he had to do this morning so that they could leave as soon as possible for her mother's house. He *had* promised to take her there today. Just before going to sleep last night, he had promised to be gentle with her mother as he explained how his warriors' lives were being ruined by her alcohol, and warned her that it had to stop.

Shawndee, in turn, had told him that she believed her mother would heed his warning, especially after she told her mother about the danger she was in from the townsfolk.

Yes, perhaps today would be the last time she would see her mother and Tootiba. When her mother fled to another town with faithful Tootiba at her side, she would surely travel far before settling down again.

Shawndee hoped her mother would find a place where she could live out the rest of her days in respect and peace.

Knowing that Shadow Hawk might return at any moment from wherever he was, Shawndee decided to get dressed. She went back to her room and tossed the blanket on the bed.

Then she stood where the fire's glow from the outer room fell on two different outfits.

Shadow Hawk had brought her boy's clothes into the room and folded them neatly on the end of the bed. Even the cloths that she had used to bind her breasts were there, reminding her of just how far she had gone to look like a boy. She hated the disguise now more than ever.

But Shadow Hawk had also spread the doeskin dress out across the bed, displaying its loveliness so that she would see it upon entering her room.

She smiled, for she knew that he had arranged the dress in such an alluring way as a hint for her to wear it today instead of the garb he detested.

"I do love the dress so much," Shawndee whispered aloud as she ran a hand across its softness.

She traced a finger over the hawk design. One day soon it would have a true meaning for her. When she married Shadow Hawk, would she not become a part of the Seneca? Would not this emblem have great significance to a Seneca chief's wife?

Yes, it would mean that she herself was of the Hawk clan. She would proudly wear the emblem for everyone to see.

But she could not wear it today, not because she

wasn't yet Shadow Hawk's wife, but because she had to wear her usual disguise when she returned home to talk to her mother.

Even though Shadow Hawk would be with her, and even though she planned to marry him soon, there was always the chance that things would go awry and she would be thrust into that same ugly world she had known before being introduced into Shadow Hawk's.

Having made her decision, she slid the breeches up her thin, yet shapely legs. She winced as she took the time to bind her breasts to make her disguise foolproof.

After getting the clothes on, and tying her hair back with the usual thong, she sat down to yank on her boots, but stopped when she became aware of something happening outside the longhouse.

The village was no longer silent. There were voices, laughter, and girlish squeals. The sounds made her too curious not to investigate.

She went barefoot to the front door of the longhouse and opened it. She gazed around and saw men entering the village, bending low under heavy loads of game. Several other men had strings of fish.

But what held her attention was a group of girls in a clearing not far from Shadow Hawk's lodge. They were participating in some sort of ball game.

Something tugged at Shawndee's heart. It was a

mixture of sadness and envy. She was keenly aware of the fun, the joy, and the laughter that the game was bringing the girls.

She looked from girl to girl. Some were much younger than Shawndee, and some appeared to be the same age as she.

Having been kept away from other girls all of her life, Shawndee longed to join the fun today.

If she approached the girls, would they allow her to play the game with them? She could play until Shadow Hawk came for her.

Her heart thudded in her chest as she edged slowly away from the door of the longhouse. Her knees were weak with fear of being rejected by the girls. She knew that she was an oddity in their eyes.

She wondered how they would react if they discovered that she had slept with their chief. Would they see her in a different, approving light? Or would they resent and hate her even more than they might already because she was white?

Sighing deeply, and deciding it was worth it to chance rejection if it meant that she could share just a few moments of the girls' fun, Shawndee went onward. When she reached the place where the ball game was being played, she stopped. She grew even more nervous when the girls suddenly realized she was there and turned to stare at her.

The sudden silence and the many sets of eyes

now on Shawndee made her take a shaky step away from them.

Shawndee swallowed hard and started to turn and run away, but she stopped when one of the girls stepped away from the others and came hurriedly to Shawndee.

"Your name is Shawndee," the pretty girl said as she stopped only a few inches away. She lifted a hand toward Shawndee. "I am called Dancing Snow. Would you like to join us in the game called football?"

Realizing that this pretty, olive-skinned girl, with dark, piercing eyes that seemed to smile as she talked, was offering a hand of friendship, Shawndee was momentarily stunned.

Surely they all knew that she had been brought to their village as a captive. And she was dressed as a boy, whereas they wore lovely fringed skirts and blouses.

Yet they were willing to look past all of that to include her in their game. She realized then that not only was Shadow Hawk special and kind, so were the Seneca girls.

Shawndee was even more anxious now to return to the Seneca village after her mother was safe.

Yet she wondered if they would be as kind, as generous, if they knew she had slept with their chief last night, and that she would soon be his wife.

Casting all of those thoughts aside, wanting to

accept this moment of friendship and join them at play, Shawndee reached her hand out and accepted Dancing Snow's handshake.

"Dancing Snow, thank you. Yes, I would love to play the game with you," Shawndee said, breathless and elated over being included in the lives of the Seneca girls.

"Come, then," Dancing Snow said, easing her hand from Shawndee's. "I shall explain how it is done."

"Football?" Shawndee said as she ran beside Dancing Snow toward the waiting, quiet girls. "I watched you playing. It is done mostly with the feet."

"That is why it is called football," Dancing Snow said, laughing softly. She stepped amid the other girls and reached a hand out for Shawndee.

Shawndee felt bashful to be the center of attention. She sorely wished she had the dress and moccasins on, which would have made it easier for her to fit in with the other girls.

"Shawndee is going to join us," Dancing Snow said, smiling from girl to girl. She turned to Shawndee. "You have watched us. Do you know from that how the game is played?"

"Yes, somewhat," Shawndee said, smiling awkwardly as one of the girls brought the small ball and handed it to her.

"The football is stuffed with deer hair," Dancing

Snow explained. "As we play the game, no hands are allowed to touch it." She glanced down at Shawndee's bare feet, frowning. "You should wear moccasins or your toes might get injured."

"I shall go for mine," Shawndee said excitedly, blushing when she realized that she'd referred to the moccasins that Shadow Hawk had given to her as hers.

She gave Dancing Snow a nervous smile, handed her the ball so the game could continue, and rushed back to Shadow Hawk's longhouse to retrieve the moccasins.

When Dancing Snow saw Shawndee returning, she shouted at everyone to stop playing.

Soon Shawndee was a part of the group, laughing, squealing, shouting, kicking at the ball, often missing and striking each other's shins with their moccasined feet.

Shawndee did not even feel the pain that came with those kicks. She was too elated over being a part of the group.

Despite her enjoyment of the game, she kept close watch on Shadow Hawk's longhouse.

When she saw him, she must stop this lighthearted fun and attend to more serious concerns.

Her mother.

She must get to her mother today. Shadow Hawk had promised her. She couldn't understand why he wasn't with her now.

Where was he?

What had drawn him from his longhouse?

She cast a quick glance toward the council house and saw warriors coming and going from it. Shadow Hawk must have been called there for a meeting about something. When he left there, he would surely come for her.

When the football suddenly crashed into her belly, momentarily robbing Shawndee of her breath, she felt gentle hands on her arm and found Dancing Snow beside her, her eyes filled with concern.

"Are you alright?" Dancing Snow asked as the girls continued their game without them.

Shawndee's breath finally returned. She laughed and nodded. "I'm fine," she said, then ran with Dancing Snow, hand in hand, into the melee again.

There were great peals of laughter as one and then another girl fell onto the ball, which other eager players strove to extricate with their feet.

Again forgetting everything but being a part of other girls' activities for the first time in her life, Shawndee squealed and laughed as the game increased in its ferocity. It was rough and tumble, yet no one was injured, for the kicking feet that flew about were clad in soft moccasins.

Then the game came to an end. The girls' chests heaved from their hard play. Some still laughed.

Others hugged their friends.

Shawndee was delighted when Dancing Snow came and hugged her. Shawndee marveled over this first hug from a friend. She felt a joy she had never known before, and returned the hug.

Then as Dancing Snow stepped away and ran off with the girls, Shawndee stood alone. She turned and stared at the forest and realized that she could leave now if she wanted. There was no one to stop her. She could go to her mother and warn her about things to come.

Yet she truly did not want to leave the village alone. She wanted Shadow Hawk at her side. She wanted to feel his comforting presence when she told her mother about the women.

"Shawndee?"

When Shawndee heard her name spoken behind her, her heart soared with memories of that voice speaking love words in the darkness.

She turned smiling eyes to Shadow Hawk as she spun around and saw him approaching.

She ran to him and stopped just short of flinging herself into his arms. There were too many people outside their lodges who might witness such fondness shown their chief by a white woman.

Shadow Hawk saw her hesitate, and he understood. He refrained from holding her, for he, too, felt many eyes on them.

"I watched you with the girls," he said. "You are good at ball playing. And I saw how quickly you have made friends. That is good. They will be your friends for life once you join our people."

"I did enjoy the game so much," Shawndee said, turning and walking with him toward his lodge. She gave him a questioning look. "But can we leave now? I wish to go to my mother. I want to see if she is alright. I want to warn her—"

"We cannot leave just yet," Shadow Hawk said, gently interrupting her.

She stopped abruptly.

"But you said . . ." She paused, her voice breaking.

"My father's health has worsened," Shadow Hawk said, his own voice husky. "My sister and I have sat with him since before sunrise. I left long enough to find you, to explain things to you."

"I am so sorry about your father," Shawndee said. She was sorry, yet she was also concerned about her mother. "And I understand why you don't want to leave." She squared her shoulders. "I shall go on ahead, without you," she said.

"No, that is not possible," Shadow Hawk said firmly.

Taken aback by Shadow Hawk's refusal to let her go on without him, especially after what they had shared the night before, Shawndee moved away from him. Her eyes narrowed. Her breathing was coming in quick, angry pants.

"Was all that we shared and said to one another

a lie?" she demanded, making certain that her voice was steady this time. "Do you not trust me enough to allow me to leave? Do you think I slept with you only to get something from you . . . to ensure my freedom? Do you not know the difference between truth and lies? If you do, and if you made love with me for all the right reasons, for love's sake alone, then you would not hesitate to allow me to go ahead of you to my mother's home. You . . . would . . . let me go!"

Seeing that Shawndee's angry voice was drawing quizzical looks their way, Shadow Hawk took her by the elbow and quickly ushered her into the privacy of his longhouse. Then he closed the door between them and the rest of the world and placed gentle hands on her shoulders.

He winced when she yanked herself back, her eyes filled with mistrust.

"You did not allow me to tell you everything," he said, his voice drawn. "I was about to explain that our departure will be delayed for only a little while longer. I want to wait until Father is sleeping comfortably. That should not be much longer, Shawndee, and then we can travel together."

"But you still do not trust me to go alone," Shawndee snapped, only half believing his explanation.

"I do not trust those who might see you alone," Shadow Hawk said.

253

He reached for her hands and was glad when she allowed him to take them. "Yes, you will be dressed as a boy," he said. "And you believe this disguise will protect you from being attacked by women-hungry men. But there are also men who might still want you, for there are vile men in this world who desire boys over women."

"I know," Shawndee gulped out, reminded of those awful moments with Chester, and of what he had in mind for her.

She *was* afraid of running into Chester again, for she knew that he hungered for the boy, Andrew.

She understood, now, that it was in her best interest to wait for Shadow Hawk.

"And, Shawndee, if the women of Silver Creek are planning harm to your mother, then does that not include you, her child?" Shadow Hawk said. "I hope to protect you from anything they might have planned for you."

"Yes, I'm certain those women have nothing good in mind for me," Shawndee said. She swallowed hard as she recalled their hateful voices at the town hall, and how they had voiced their hatred of Shawndee's mother, and even of Tootiba.

"Then be patient while I go now and see how my father is faring," Shadow Hawk said.

He reached a hand up and gently touched her cheek. "You see, my father will soon leave this place and go to the heaven world. He will be with his wife, my mother, and so many more who are dear to him."

Glad that he did still have her welfare in mind, Shawndee leaned her face into his palm, then sighed with pure joy when he lowered his hand and twined both his arms around her waist.

"My beautiful Shawndee," Shadow Hawk said. He smiled mischievously. "My pretty ball player."

She giggled, but when he hurried away from her down the dark corridor, Shawndee felt at a loss as to what to do while waiting for him. She kept remembering the fun she had had with the girls.

Hoping to see Dancing Snow again, Shawndee went outside into the morning sunshine. She was disappointed when she didn't see Dancing Snow anywhere.

But she was aware of something else—the smell of roses wafting toward her from the forest. An idea sprang to mind that made her smile.

Roses.

She could take her mother a bouquet that might help lighten her mother's mood once she was confronted with the bad news she and Shadow Hawk must bring her.

Smiling, she ran back inside the longhouse and yanked on her boots. Then without hesitating, she went back outside and hurried toward the beckoning aroma of roses. Although her mother was tough and cold in many ways, she did love roses. They were her mother's favorite flower.

Shawndee hoped to find many roses for her bouquet.

Chapter Twenty-two

Chester Hawkins had seen all of the morning activity at the Seneca village, how Andrew joined the girls playing some sort of ball game, and how the girls seemed taken by him, especially a pretty one who befriended Andrew.

Chester had also seen Shadow Hawk come from his longhouse to watch the game, and then go to Andrew and say something to the boy that angered him.

Chester had then watched Shadow Hawk take Andrew back inside his longhouse.

Now he couldn't believe his luck as he watched Andrew leave the longhouse again, alone, and venture into the forest. He was this very minute kneeling on the ground, picking wild roses.

Chester decided that Andrew had become smitten with the pretty Indian girl. Surely the roses were for her.

But what puzzled him was that Shadow Hawk trusted the boy enough to let him run free. Did they have some sort of understanding? Was the Seneca chief himself smitten with Andrew?

Did Andrew see life among the Seneca as better than with his crazy witch of a mother?

Chester chuckled as he grabbed a scarf from his pocket as well as a bit of rope. He was going to spoil the boy's plans today, whatever they were, as well as Chief Shadow Hawk's.

"Sweet, pretty Andy, come to Chester," he whispered to himself, his eyes gleaming insanely as he crept closer and closer to where Shawndee so innocently plucked roses for her mother.

Chapter Twenty-three

Roses tumbled from Shawndee's hands and her eyes widened with fright when an arm circled around her and held her in a tight grip, while a hand quickly covered her mouth, stifling her scream.

Memories of another time, another arm, came to her. But Shawndee knew that this time it wasn't Shadow Hawk's. No, he would have no reason to treat her in such a way.

There could be only one other person who would do this.

Chester Hawkins!

She had stepped right into his trap by foolishly leaving the safety of Shadow Hawk's lodge to pick roses.

Before Shawndee had a chance to wrestle herself free of Chester, he slammed her down onto the ground on her back. The hard impact of her head hitting the ground stunned her long enough for Chester to straddle her and roughly tie the scarf around her mouth.

After her mind had cleared and she was fully conscious again, Shawndee glared at Chester over the gag.

She reached up to remove it, but he was too quick. He forced her wrists up over her head and leered at her.

"Pretty as a picture," Chester said thickly, his eyes filled with lust. "They just don't make boys as pretty as you very often, now do they?"

Disgusted by what he was saying, Shawndee tried to raise her hips from the ground to shove him from atop her, but it was wasted effort. He jumped off her and flipped her over on her belly.

Shawndee's breath caught in her throat as fear and revulsion swept through her at being in this position with this vile man leaning over her.

She clenched her eyes as she waited for him to yank her breeches down, but was relieved when she discovered that he had turned her over only to make it easier for him to tie her wrists together behind her.

Once that was done, he grabbed her by an arm and yanked her to her feet, then gave her a shove toward the river, which was visible through the towering trees.

Shawndee believed she was possibly living the last moments of her life. Once Chester had her where he could do anything with her that he pleased without being caught, he would perform his vile acts and then kill her. Tears fell from her eyes. She couldn't believe that she had placed herself in this sort of danger. Only moments ago she had been in Shadow Hawk's arms, safe, loved, and looking forward to a future with him.

Now? She doubted that she had a future, and she had ruined Shadow Hawk's, as well.

And what about her mother? What would happen to her?

She tried to squirm free when Chester began shoving her into a small boat, but all efforts failed as she fell awkwardly to the bottom, her elbows throbbing from the impact.

She glared at him above her gag, praying that when this vile man unclothed her and saw the mistake he had made, the shock of it would make him leave her alone.

"Yep, Andy, I've almost got you where I want you," Chester said, chuckling.

He shoved the boat out into deeper water, then leapt inside. He sat down behind Shawndee, picked up a paddle, and began making his way from shore.

"But I promised your ma I'd bring you home

first," he said. "Yep, I feel it's safer to take you home and have my way with you *there*. That's what your ma promised me if I found you and brought you home to her. Yep, I'll be much safer in your home than out here in the open, for I don't want to chance the Seneca chief catching me with you."

What he said about her mother puzzled Shawndee, for she knew that her mother would never allow this vile man to have his way with her.

What her mother had promised Chester must be a ploy to get Shawndee home. Surely then her mother would turn the sick man in to the law.

Sheriff Dawson would probably hang Chester by the neck until he was dead for the vile things he had planned to do to Shawndee. What puzzled Shawndee was why her mother hadn't sent the sheriff and a posse to find her instead of this man.

"No sirree, your ma won't back down on her promise to ol' Chester," he said, drawing Shawndee's attention back to him.

She looked over her shoulder at him.

"Your ma promised me some time with you in exchange for my silence about the sheriff lying dead just outside her home, in the forest," Chester said. "Your ma knows that if she doesn't keep her word, I'll run to the law and tell the deputy sheriff that his boss, Sheriff Tom Dawson, is dead, and that your ma is the one who killed him and left him for the wolves to feast upon."

Shawndee could feel the color drain from her face as his words sank in.

Her mother had killed the sheriff? Why? Oh, why would she do that?

Her mother might be lots of things that made ordinary women frown, but she most certainly was not a cold-blooded killer.

Shawndee lowered her eyes as she turned from Chester. She blinked tears away as she thought more about what Chester had just said.

How well did Shawndee know her mother?

Hadn't she hidden the book about witches from Shawndee?

Not knowing what to think about her mother, and dreading what this terrible man had planned for her, Shawndee thought for a moment that she would be better off dead.

When she had realized that there could be something wonderful at last in her life, with Shadow Hawk and his people, she had thought that God was finally making up for the drudgery of the life that had been forced upon her by her parents.

When she had met and fallen in love with Shadow Hawk, she had finally had hopes of a wonderful, pure future.

Now, one moment of carelessness, when she had ventured into the forest for roses, had changed her life back to the sordidness that she had lived with so many years. Shawndee felt sick to her stomach as she thought of the worst that could happen to her by the end of the day.

Her only chance was that when Shadow Hawk found her gone, he would come immediately to look for her. He would know to come to her mother's home. She prayed he would get there in time.

When she realized just how close she was to her home, and that Chester was steering his boat toward shore, panic grabbed Shawndee.

She looked over her shoulder in the direction of Shadow Hawk's village. Her heart sank when she saw no trace of Shadow Hawk on land, or in his canoe. When the boat began scraping the rocky bottom of the river, and she heard Chester scramble over the side and into the water, she didn't want to see him drag the boat to dry land. She didn't want to feel his filthy hands on her waist as he pulled her out of the boat and placed her on the riverbank.

She tried to run away, but he was there too quickly, grabbing her by her ponytail.

"Behave now, Andy, for no amount of struggling will get you anything except perhaps a knock over your head to make you unconscious so that I won't have to constantly be on guard with you," Chester said.

He dropped his hand away from her hair, then leaned into her face. "If you don't behave, I'll rape you right here on the spot and lie to your ma and tell her I didn't. Then I'll do it again in the privacy of one of your ma's rooms," he growled. "What do you think of that, pretty boy?"

Shawndee tried to speak with the gag in her mouth, but all that came out were dry, mumbling sounds.

She knew she had no choice but to cooperate, at least until she got home.

And then, surely then, her mother would make things right for her. Surely her mother would stop this man's plan.

Chester grabbed her roughly by an arm and forced her to walk beside him.

When she saw her mother's house in the clearing up ahead, she was torn with conflicting feelings— elation to know that she was this close to her home, and dread at not knowing what to expect.

If Chester did manage to rape her, then Shawndee would lose all hopes of ever having a normal life with Shadow Hawk. Once wrongly touched by this vile, filthy man, she would not even want to go to Shadow Hawk. She felt her body would be too unfit ever to be touched by someone like Shadow Hawk, who stood for everything pure and good on this earth.

"Come over here with me and let me show you somethin'," Chester said, giving a hard yank on Shawndee's arm.

She stumbled along beside him, then felt she might retch when she saw the lifeless body of Sheriff Dawson, which was half hidden beneath a layer of last year's dried-up autumn leaves.

Feeling bitterness rising into her throat, Shawndee closed her eyes and looked quickly away from the dead body. Up until now she had hoped that Chester was lying about the sheriff being dead.

Now that she knew he hadn't lied about that, she feared he was telling the truth when he had said that her mother had killed this man.

"And so you see just how wicked your mother can be?" Chester taunted, yanking on Shawndee's arm again until she cried out with pain.

"Come on, Andy, let's go on to your house so I can get my reward for bringin' you home, and for keepin' my silence about your ma havin' killed the sheriff," Chester said, releasing his hold on Shawndee's arm and giving her a hard shove toward her house. "Yep, everyone heard the sheriff take your ma down a notch or two and will know that she was out for blood—*his*. Yep, she'll sure as hell hang for the deed, but first ol' Chester has got to have his way with *you*, pretty little thing."

Sobbing, truly wishing she were dead now, Shawndee went with Chester to the back door of her house.

Feeling faint, she teetered, then fell into the

house when Chester opened the door and gave her a shove.

She heard the familiar hard and heavy footsteps of her mother coming down the hallway, and then heard her mother gasp with horror when she saw Shawndee stretched out on the floor, her eyes pleading up at her. Jane bent hurriedly to her knees and gathered Shawndee into her arms.

"Shawndee, oh, Shawndee, you're safe," Jane murmured, caressing her daughter's back as she glared at Chester.

"Remember your promise," Chester warned darkly. "I get to take Andy on upstairs. You said I'd earn a night's stay with Andrew if I found him and brought him home to you. You'd best keep that promise. The sheriff's body is still out there. I'd waste no time turnin' you in to the law for the crime."

Jane eased an arm around Shawndee's waist. She gently helped her up from the floor, then stepped away from her.

"Take him," Jane said as she nodded toward Shawndee. Her jaw was tight. Her eyes were narrowed and filled with angry fire. She nodded toward the back stairs. "Go on. I said you'd have time with Andrew. I'm a woman of my word."

She turned to Shawndee. "Go on, Andrew. I don't have any choice but to let this man do what he wants with you, and then tomorrow we'll head out for a new life," Jane said tightly. "We'll leave all of this behind us, do you hear? All of it."

With the gag still covering her mouth, Shawndee couldn't plead with her mother.

And her heart tore in shreds as Chester grabbed her by an arm and forced her up the stairs, then pushed her toward the room next to Shawndee's.

While he fumbled at the door, Shawndee was suddenly aware that her mother had followed them up the stairs with silent footsteps. She stood at the far end of the second-floor corridor, where candles in wall sconces revealed her mother motioning to Shawndee with hand gestures and nods of assurance. Shawndee realized now that surely her mother had a plan . . . a plan to save her from an act that would be worse than death at the hands of this vile man.

Shawndee hoped she had interpreted her mother's gestures correctly, and that she wouldn't wait too much longer to save her, for Chester was taking her into the room now.

Chester kicked the door shut almost immediately.

Shawndee turned and stared at him and knew that it would not take long for him to force his way on her!

Her heart throbbing, fear mounting inside her, Shawndee knew that she was helpless until he untied her wrists. With them locked together behind her, there would be no way she could open the door to escape.

Mama! she cried inside her heart. *Please ... please, hurry, Mama!*

Chester yanked the gag from Shawndee's mouth, then gave her a rough turn and soon had her hands untied.

"Don't get any ideas just because your hands are free," Chester said, grabbing her painfully by an arm. He nodded toward the bed against the far wall. "Go over there. Stand beside the bed. I'll watch you undress. I've been wanting to see the litheness of your body. I've dreamed of touching you all over."

Sickened by the very idea of what was on this man's mind, but knowing that surely her mother had some plan to stop him, Shawndee smiled wickedly. She was glad to finally show this man that she was a woman, not a boy. Slowly, she unbuttoned her shirt, and then revealed the bindings that held her breasts.

Shawndee could see his eyes widen as she tossed the shirt aside and then slowly unwound the bindings, her breasts soon falling free—smooth, round, and plump.

Suddenly all of this humiliation, this fear, this degradation was worth it, when she saw Chester's astonishment. He gasped as he stared at her breasts and finally knew that she was anything but a shapeless boy.

"What . . . is . . . this?" Chester stammered, his face suddenly flushed a crimson red. He gestured toward her with a shaky hand as he took slow steps toward her. "You ain't a boy. Why would you be dressed like a boy when you ain't?"

Shawndee didn't get the chance to respond. She screamed when the door quickly opened and her mother rushed into the room and hit Chester over the head with a whiskey bottle, rendering him unconscious.

Shawndee was relieved that the ordeal was finally over.

But all was not yet right. She looked at her mother and now saw her in a strange and different light. She recalled Chester's claim that her mother had killed the sheriff.

As her mother stood over Chester now, laughing in her cackling way, Shawndee was again reminded that her mother might be a witch, and it looked as though her mother was about to kill another man.

Shawndee realized now that she truly didn't know this woman who was her mother.

Something else came to Shawndee that made her heart sink. When Shadow Hawk found her gone, he would not know that she had been taken by force. He might think that she had gone back on her word and left on her own—that she could not be trusted, that she perhaps had been playing him along until she had an opportunity to leave.

No! She couldn't let him believe that she was so deceitful!

Needing time away from her mother now, to sort through her thoughts and feelings, Shawndee felt that she had no choice but to leave. First and foremost, she must go to Shadow Hawk and explain everything to him. He was her life. She couldn't allow herself to lose him over such a misunderstanding as this.

And she was eager to leave this house and everything in it.

Even Tootiba, she thought as Tootiba raced into the room, her dark eyes wide with horror as she gazed down at Chester, and then up at Jane, who had murder in her eyes.

Confused by everything, Shawndee pulled her shirt on, brushed past her mother and Tootiba, and ignoring her mother's shouts to stop, left the house in a panic.

When she reached the forest, she stopped only long enough to get her breath. Then she ran, blinded with tears, in the direction of Shadow Hawk's village.

Abruptly she ran into someone. She looked up and saw that it was Shadow Hawk.

The stress of what she had just been through was

suddenly too much for her. She collapsed in a dead faint in Shadow Hawk's arms.

Stunned, Shadow Hawk lifted her into his arms and held her tenderly.

He turned and stared in the direction of her home. Surely she had been there. He wondered what she had seen or learned that had caused her such distress.

He gazed down at Shawndee. He brushed a soft kiss across her brow, then ran with her to his canoe and laid her on soft pelts at the bottom.

For now she was all that mattered.

The question of why Shawndee had left without him would be answered later. And his meeting with her mother would have to wait.

He had to make things right for Shawndee first. He would be there for her when she awakened, so she would know that she never had anyone, or anything, to fear ever again.

He covered Shawndee with a soft pelt, then hurried into the canoe and sat down close to her.

His jaw tight, his heart filled with love for Shawndee, he lifted his paddle and turned his canoe toward home.

Chapter Twenty-four

Stunned by Shawndee's sudden flight, and by the horror-struck way she had stared at her just before running from the house, Jane stood at the window beside Tootiba, staring blankly into the shadows of the forest. Both were shaken by Shawndee's mysterious behavior. And worst of all, after being home for such a short while, Shawndee was gone again.

"Miss Jane, ol' Tootiba will go afta' sweet baby Shawndee," Tootiba said breathlessly, already turning toward the door.

Jane grabbed Tootiba by an arm, stopping her. "No," she said, her voice drawn. "She's already too far for you to catch up with her, and we both are too unfamiliar with the forest to go there. I don't want you getting lost."

Jane shuddered as she stepped away from Tootiba and gazed at the dark shadows of the forest. "Shawndee has explored enough to know where she's going," she said, swallowing hard.

She turned and stared at Chester. "And with Chester here with us, he's no longer a threat to Shawndee," she said.

Then Jane's eyes widened and she clutched her throat. "Oh, Lord, I hope she doesn't find the sheriff," she gasped out. "Do you think Chester told her I killed him?"

"I 'spect so," Tootiba said, a sob catching in her throat. "Somethin' sure spooked my baby doll."

Tootiba turned slowly and stared at Chester, who still lay on the floor, unconscious. The glass from the whiskey bottle lay in sharp splinters around his head in small pools of blood that had seeped from his many tiny wounds.

"Sweet baby Shawndee might even believe you were gonna kill *dis* man," Tootiba said.

Jane turned sharply and gazed down at Chester. She doubled her hands into tight fists at her sides as she glared at him. "The sonofabitch deserves no less from me," she said venomously. "You just don't know the pleasure it would give me to wrap my hands around his neck and choke his last breath from him."

Tootiba shivered as she gazed at Jane. "Lordy me, Miss Jane, don't talk like that," she gasped out.

"You are already in enough trouble to last a life-time."

"And the worst of it is that my very own daughter looked at me like I was a stranger," Jane said, her voice catching. "If she thinks I killed the sheriff, I might never see her again."

"Where does you t'ink she's been?" Tootiba asked. "Where do you t'ink Chester found her?"

"I was so glad to see her I didn't ask," Jane sighed.

"He had mentioned something about the Seneca chief," Tootiba said, inching away from Chester when he let out a moan.

"I doubt that was where he found her," Jane said, hurrying over to fall to her knees beside Chester. "The Seneca hate me, I'm certain, because I sell liquor to their warriors. But they surely wouldn't chance gettin' the white community after them by abducting my daughter."

"But, Miss Jane, the townspeople believe Shawn-dee is a boy. Dey might even applaud the Indian for riddin' the town of one of us," Tootiba said, shuddering when Chester let out a long list of vile words as he awakened and saw Jane kneeling beside him.

"Tootiba, quit your worrying and go git me a rope," Jane said. She quickly grabbed Chester's wrists and plastered them to the floor when he attempted to get up.

"Hurry, Tootiba," Jane said as she cast her a glance over her shoulder. "We'll get this sonofabitch tied up and then decide what to do with him."

"You whorish witch," Chester hissed out, then winced and gagged when Jane spit on his face.

"I'd watch what you call someone who holds your life in her hands," Jane snapped back at him, her grip tightening and causing him to yowl with pain.

"You're gonna pay for this," Chester dared to say. "I'll get a mob after you when I tell them you killed the sheriff."

"You make me laugh," Jane said, cackling. "When I get through with you, you won't be tellin' anyone anything except the truth. Oh, I'd like nothin' better than to kill you, but you are worth more to me alive than dead, for you've got much to confess to the people of Silver Creek. But for now I'm just going to tie and gag you and leave you in my attic until I have the chance to clear things up with the townsfolk."

"Do you think they'll listen one minute to some-one they think is a witch?" Chester said, laughing sarcastically. "The next time they come to your house, they'll do more than threaten you with those torches. I imagine they'll be burnin' down your house, hoping you and that black woman is in it. That'd save burnin' you at the stake."

Breathing hard from climbing the stairs much too quickly, Tootiba came into the room with a coil of rope.

Jane nodded toward her. "Come and tie his wrists

together behind him after I flip him over," she said.

Jane grabbed Chester around the waist and in one movement turned him on his stomach, her knee pressed into his back to hold him in place.

When Tootiba hesitated, her eyes wide and wild as she stared down at Chester, who was now yelling obscenities at her, Jane looked quickly up at her.

"Come on, Tootiba," she said in a softer and more coaxing tone. "Let's get him tied and then I'll see what I can do to clear my name. Once Shawndee hears that I'm not wanted for murder, she'll come home."

"Shawndee?" Chester hissed. "So that's what her name is, huh? Not Alexander or Andy. It's Shawndee? A girl you made pose as a boy?"

"Yes. Shawndee, my daughter, who I had to force to dress like a boy to keep her protected from . . ." Jane said.

She stopped and cackled.

She leaned down into Chester's face. "I started to say I made her dress like that to keep her protected from the likes of you," she said, her eyes dancing. "But when it comes to you, that didn't work, did it? *You* thought you were ogling a pretty little *boy*."

She shivered and gagged. "How disgusting you are," she said. "The townsfolk are going to learn what sort of man you are. They'll give me a reward for riddin' their lives of the likes of you. No young boy is safe while you are loose and roamin' the streets with your eyes searching for your next victim."

"You've got your likes, I've got mine," Chester said, chuckling.

"Like I said, you're a disgusting, vile man."

Jane gave Tootiba a quick glance. "Tootiba, give me your apron," she said.

"Why on earth does you need my apron?" Tootiba said, arching an eyebrow.

"What better way to gag this man, wouldn't you say?" Jane replied. "A woman's apron gagging a man who hates women. Why, he probably even hated his mother."

Tootiba untied her white apron and handed it to Jane.

"Yep, that'll do just fine," Jane said, shaping the apron into a gag and then tying it around Chester's mouth.

She cackled when he gagged and choked as she shoved a portion of the apron inside his mouth.

"There, now don't he look ready to hide in the attic with all of my witch's equipment?" Jane said, watching his eyes go wild with fright. "Yep, my broom, my black dress and hat, and my black cat."

She leaned down into his face. "You ain't seen my black cat, have you?" she said, enjoying teasing him about things that were far from the truth.

"Yep, my cat," she said, again cackling. "It's got the greenest eyes imaginable. Ah, how they shine in the night when he is stalkin' his victim. But the one thing my cat is surely proud of is his claws. They are long and sharp enough to scratch out the eyes of a man."

She ran her hand across Chester's brow. "My, oh, my, look at your eyes," she said, cackling. "Soon they might be my cat's next meal."

She got up from the floor and stood over Chester, her fists on her hips. "Enough of fooling with this man," she said, glancing at Tootiba. "We'll get him in the attic and then proceed with trying to clear my name, and Shawndee's. She doesn't deserve what she's had to deal with."

"But, Miss Jane, will dey listen?" Tootiba asked, her voice breaking. "I so badly want to move to another town and have another start and leave the whiskey business outa it."

"Yes, Tootiba, I believe it's time to wipe the slate clean, especially for Shawndee, for of late *she's* had to pay for my mistakes," Jane said soberly. "After she discovers the truth about everything, that I didn't kill the sheriff, and I've had a chance to explain why my grandmother's name is listed with those who died at Salem, then we can all have a fresh start. It'll be hard, though, for I don't have much money put away."

"But we'll make do, won't we?" Tootiba said, her eyes eagerly wide.

"Yes, Tootiba, we'll make do," Jane said, nodding. "But first I've got to go into town and request a town meeting with the ladies and gents of Silver Creek. I'll explain everything and tell them I plan to leave town real soon with my daughter, to begin life anew."

"They don' know Shawndee is Shawndee," Tootiba said, sighing.

"Yes, I know," Jane said, also sighing. "But they will, and then they'll realize just how far this mother went to protect her daughter, by hiding her identity from men who might harm her. Surely they will sympathize with me."

"And you'll also tell them about Chester, what he tried to do with Shawndee, and about him killin' the sheriff?" Tootiba said, wincing when Chester shot her a sour glance from above the gag.

"Yes, that too," Jane said. She frowned down at Chester. "I'll leave him in the attic until I know everyone believes my story. And then I'll direct the deputy sheriff to the attic so he can take Chester away and do whatever they do to criminals like him."

"And Shawndee?" Tootiba asked, tears filling her eyes. "My precious Shawndee. Where do you think she's gone? She's in danger all the while she's out there all alone."

Jane went to the window and gazed again into the forest. "I'm not sure where she thought she was goin', but she did seem to have a place in mind, for she didn't hesitate one iota to choose a direction," she said, nodding. "Yep, I believe she's found a friend out there somehow and she's goin' to that friend even now. I've got to believe that, and that she'll be safe until I discover a means to find her, or I'd not be able to face what lies ahead for me. The townsfolk? Oh, Lord, how they do despise me and everything I stand for."

Tootiba went and stood beside Jane, taking one of her hands. "We'll all get through this, you'll see," she said reassuringly. "And Shawndee is smart. She's read many a book. Book learnin' makes for smartness."

She squeezed Jane's hand affectionately. "And, Miss Jane, don't you fret none about our Shawndee t'inkin' dose bad t'ings about you for long," she said. "Surely after she t'inks things over she'll know you ain't capable of murder, or anyt'ing else dat's dark and sinister. Shawndee knows you only sold whiskey 'cause you had to, to survive, to make a livin' to support a daughter."

"I know she will think things through and know the truth, but I pray that Shawndee comes to her senses and returns home soon," Jane said, her voice drawn. "I'd love nothin' more than puttin' a pretty dress on my daughter and showin' up at the town hall with Shawndee, so that the people could see with their own eyes the truth about her bein' a girl. With Shawndee at my side, I could have more courage to say what must be said to clear my name. And then we can leave this dreadful town and start life anew."

"But, Miss Jane, what if dey *don't* listen?" Tootiba said anxiously. "What if dey believe you murdered the sheriff? If dey see you as a liar, none of us will be free to do anyt'ing."

Tootiba swallowed hard as she stepped away from Jane. She lifted her hands to her throat. "What if dey hang us all?" she gulped out. Color drained from her face. "Or what . . . if . . . dey burn us on stakes?"

Jane turned and smiled crookedly down at Chester. She folded her arms across her chest. "Well, now, Tootiba, I don't think you have any of that to worry about," she said, her eyes meeting and holding Chester's. "That's where Chester comes into the picture. By the time we need him to tell the truth, I will have him convinced, one way or the other, to do it. He'll tell how he killed the sheriff, and why, and about how he has a sickness that makes him like boys."

She bent down over Chester, grabbed a handful of his hair, and gave it a yank, bringing a moan of pain from the depths of his throat.

"Yep, I'll make Chester admit to all of those truths . . . or else," she hissed out.

She saw fear enter Chester's eyes.

She cackled and yanked her hand away from

him, his head dropping to the floor with a hollow thud.

"Let's get this sonofabitch to the attic," Jane said, grabbing hold of one of his arms. "Take his other arm, Tootiba. Let's get this vile creature into hiding."

They dragged him from the room, then down to the far end of the corridor and up the steep steps into the darkness above.

When they left him alone, they took the gag off. No one could hear him up here. His eyes were wide as he heard a strange noise above him. He died a slow death inside when a bat lunged down from its hiding place and began slowly circling his head.

Then he flinched and his heart grew cold when he looked into the darker shadows of the attic and thought he saw the green eyes of Jane's black cat peering out at him.

What Jane had said about her cat eating eyes for dinner made Chester so terrified he fell back into a dead faint.

Chapter Twenty-five

Even before opening her eyes, Shawndee was aware of strong arms holding her, and whose lap she lay upon, and whose longhouse she had been taken to.

She recalled having seen Shadow Hawk before she collapsed. The recollection of everything that had caused her to faint brought tears anew into Shawndee's eyes.

"It's almost too much for me to bear," Shawndee sobbed out, and proceeded to tell Shadow Hawk everything.

"You are here with me now," Shadow Hawk said, holding her, slowly rocking her back and forth on his lap. "You do not have to think any more about those things. You are safe. You are with a man who loves you. No one will ever get a chance to harm you again. You know you can put your full trust in Shadow Hawk, the man who will soon be your husband."

"I want that so badly," Shawndee murmured, another sob catching in her throat. "I do feel safe. I do feel wanted. And . . . I . . . have never felt so loved in my life until you gave your love to me."

Then another hideous thought came to her mind. She tried to force it away, but she could not help rembering: those scalps that she had seen in Shadow Hawk's chest.

She shivered when she thought of how she had made love with Shadow Hawk in the very room where the scalps were stored. She had slept in his arms the entire night and had not once thought about the scalps that lay so close to her and Shadow Hawk beneath his bed!

But now she *was* thinking of them. She could not get them off her mind.

She was glad when a soft voice spoke up, stilling her thoughts at least for a while.

She leaned away from Shadow Hawk and beheld a lovely woman in a long doeskin robe, her hair hanging long and loose around her shoulders, her eyes and face revealing a serenity she surely felt inside her heart.

"Shadow Hawk, *no-tha* is asking for you," Song of the Moon said as she came and knelt beside

Shadow Hawk before the lodge fire, her eyes filled with sympathy for Shawndee. "I will stay with Shawndee as you go to him."

"Will you be alright?" Shadow Hawk asked Shawndee as he framed her face between his gentle hands. His eyes searched hers. "I will be gone for only a short while. Do you mind my sister, Song of the Moon, sitting with you?"

"Please do sit with me," Shawndee murmured, smiling weakly at Song of the Moon. She cast Shadow Hawk a quick look as he gently placed her on mats beside his sister. "I will be all right. I . . . I . . . have just had so much happen so quickly to me, it's hard to adjust to." She gulped hard. "And my mother. I love her so. I just don't know what to do with that love now."

"No matter what your mother is guilty of, you cannot abandon her in her time of trouble," Shadow Hawk said. "I will find a way for you to help her, and I will try to offer her my own help. If all that you say about her is true, she is a lost woman who needs to find her way back. Shawndee, you and I will find a way to lead her."

"You are too kind," Shawndee said, stifling a sob behind a hand. "How can you be . . . this . . . kind?"

"Because my love for you is true, and when I see you hurt, I hurt," Shadow Hawk answered. "I will go and see Father now. Soon you and I will plan ways to help your mother."

He brushed a soft, comforting kiss across her brow, gave Song of the Moon a nod, then left the room.

"My brother is a good man, a man who strives to spread goodness to others," Song of the Moon said. She took one of Shawndee's hands. "I know you are confused by what you have recently discovered about your mother. But in time you will find ways to forgive her even the worst of her transgressions."

"How . . . do . . . you know . . . about my mother?" Shawndee gasped out.

"I hope you do not mind, but I stood and listened before I came in to send my brother to our father," Song of the Moon said. "Have faith in my brother. Trust what he says and does. In time you will find a way to look past those things your mother is guilty of. And pray, Shawndee, to your God that He, too, will guide her to a life that is rewarding."

Feeling completely at ease with Song of the Moon, and knowing that she was a person who was good and pure of heart, Shawndee decided to ask her about Shadow Hawk.

"Song of the Moon, I am so troubled by something else," Shawndee blurted out. She eased her hand away from Song of the Moon's, then moved to her knees before the Seneca priestess. Her pulse raced as she found herself under the close scrutiny of bewitching, beautiful eyes.

"Tell me what else is troubling you," Song of the

Moon said, resting her long, lean fingers on her lap as she crossed her legs beneath her robe.

"It's about Shadow Hawk," Shawndee gulped out.

"What about Shadow Hawk?" Song of the Moon asked.

Shawndee lowered her eyes. "I did something that your Seneca people would say is wicked," she said, her voice breaking.

Slowly she lifted her eyes and gazed into Song of the Moon's once again. She was surprised to see that the priestess's expression had not changed. There was still gentleness, understanding, even holiness there.

"I snooped in Shadow Hawk's room," Shawndee said softly. "I . . . I . . . opened the trunk that he stores beneath his bed. And what I saw there frightened me. I . . . need . . . to know why the scalps were there. Was Shadow Hawk a party to such a crime as that?"

When Song of the Moon said nothing, Shawndee again began feeling uneasy.

"Please forgive me for what I did," Shawndee said, placing her hands together before her as though in prayer. "Please tell Shadow Hawk to forgive me."

"What you did was very wrong," Song of the Moon finally said. "You should never have gone behind Shadow Hawk's back by looking through his private belongings. To the Seneca, you have committed a sin not only against Shadow Hawk, but against his people, for he is his people's chief, a man revered by them."

"I know that what I did was wrong, but I don't feel I should be totally condemned for having done it," Shawndee said.

"Why do you say you should not be condemned for what you have done?" Song of the Moon asked, her voice still as steady and sweet as before. Even when she had openly criticized Shawndee, her voice had not become ugly and scolding.

"I feel I shouldn't be condemned, because all of this is new to me," Shawndee murmured. "And I wouldn't have even been in the village, or in Shadow Hawk's house, if he had not abducted me and brought me here against my will."

"Are you here now against your will?" Song of the Moon asked softly. "Were you forced to return to my brother's lodge tonight?"

Shawndee lowered her eyes. "No. I am here out of the goodness of Shadow Hawk's heart, not otherwise," Shawndee said.

"He brought me to his lodge because he loves me, and because . . . he . . . knows that I love him," she murmured.

She stopped, paused, and then said, "But I am somewhat hesitant to allowing myself to love him if he has a dark side. Only moments ago I ran away from someone I have loved all of my life, but who may be evil and sinister. I can't chance learning later that the man I married is also evil."

She leaned closer to Song of the Moon. "Did he take those scalps?" she asked, her voice drawn. "If so, will he take others?"

Song of the Moon reached a gentle hand to Shawndee's face. "Sweet one, listen well to what I say," she murmured. "The scalps that you found are Shadow Hawk's and Song of the Moon's great-grandfather's treasures—trophies from a time long ago, when there were wars with whites and it was an honor, a *savage* honor, to take scalps as trophies of war."

Relieved, Shawndee sighed and joy soared inside her heart as Song of the Moon said the words to confirm that Shadow Hawk had never taken any-one's scalp.

"Shawndee, my brother is a gentle man, a kind leader, a man who does not see taking scalps as something honorable," Song of the Moon said. "He is a man of peace . . . a man of love."

"Thank you, oh, thank you, for sharing this with me," Shawndee said, reaching for Song of the Moon's hands, affectionately taking them in hers. "Please believe me when I say I am so very, very sorry for what I did. My doubts about Shadow Hawk are proof of why it is best not to snoop among things that are not yours, for wrong impressions can come of it."

She smiled softly at Song of the Moon. "Do you accept my apology?" she asked.

"Yes," Song of the Moon said, then slid her hands free and gave Shawndee a gentle hug.

Song of the Moon leaned closer to the fire and slid a log into the dying flames. "I understand that you did not know the true extent of your crime, how it is our people's custom to keep personal belongings sacred to those who own them," she murmured. "Just as Song of the Moon would not know your customs."

Song of the Moon settled down on the mats again and with slow strokes of her hands smoothed out the wrinkles in her gown. "Yes, I forgive you and so will my brother, for his love for you is much stronger than any resentment he might feel because you did something you did not know was so terribly wrong."

Shawndee blushed and looked away from Song of the Moon into the flames of the fire. Song of the Moon didn't know that Shadow Hawk *had* warned her about going through people's things.

She wondered now if she should confess this to her?

She decided not to.

It was up to Shadow Hawk to forgive her.

When she felt a presence behind her, Shawndee

looked over her shoulder and found Shadow Hawk standing in the doorway.

She went cold inside, for surely he had heard her confession about the crime she had committed against him. She truly hoped he was as forgiving as his sister. Even more so, for he had more to forgive, did he not?

Chapter Twenty-six

Shawndee was relieved when she realized that Shadow Hawk apparently had not heard the conversation between herself and Song of the Moon, for he did not say anything about it. Instead, he went to her, taking her hands and urging her to her feet.

"My *no-tha* has asked to have council with you," Shadow Hawk said, his eyes revealing his silent, personal pain at his father's worsening health. "He knows he does not have much time left for such introductions and he feels it is only right that he should know the woman who will soon be his son's wife, who will be princess of our Hawk clan, and who will give birth to his grandchildren."

Shawndee was nervous to hear that his father understood how things were between herself and Shadow Hawk, and that there would be a marriage ceremony soon.

There was a chance that he would openly reveal his dislike of his son's choice, and that would cut through her heart like a knife. She had gone through so much these past few days. How could she stand rejection from this ailing, powerful man who was the father of the man she loved and adored?

"I see fear and uneasiness in your eyes," Shadow Hawk said, affectionately squeezing her hands. "And that is understandable. It is only normal for a woman, even a man, to feel apprehension in this circumstance. If things were different in your family, and there were a father and mother I was required to meet, I would feel the same way you are feeling now. But know this, Shawndee, I will be at your side. I will be there to support you."

"If your father openly disapproves of me, will you be free to marry me? Do you not need your father's approval since you are your people's leader?"

"I am my own man and, no, I do not absolutely need anyone's approval for the choices I make," Shadow Hawk answered. "Of course, it would make things more joyous if he approved. But if he still has reservations about who you are, a white woman whose parents have brought sadness into our people's lives, know this, Shawndee—I will still take you as my wife."

"But—" she stammered out, her eyes wavering.

"There are no buts about this decision," Shadow Hawk said, his jaw tightening. "I love you with all my heart. I want to protect you. I want to share children with you. I want to grow old with you."

Tears filled Shawndee's eyes. She eased her hands from his, then flung herself into his arms and clung to him. "I do not deserve such love, such loyalty," she sobbed. "But I shall, Shadow Hawk. I will do everything possible to make you proud of me."

She glanced sideways at Song of the Moon, then leaned away from Shadow Hawk and gazed into his eyes. "And I shall never doubt anything about you again," she blurted out.

His eyebrows lifted, and she realized that what she had just said had aroused his curiosity. When Song of the Moon also saw his bewilderment, she went to her brother and drew him around.

"Go with Shawndee to Father," she encouraged. "He is waiting."

Nodding, Shadow Hawk swept a comforting, encouraging arm around Shawndee's waist and led her from the room.

"My knees are shaking," Shawndee said. She swallowed hard.

Shadow Hawk stopped, turned her to face him, and placed gentle hands on her shoulders. "Be not intimidated by my father's standing," he said. "Be yourself. Who could not help loving you?"

He glanced down at her clothes and sighed, then smiled at her. "It would have been better if you were dressed in doeskin when you met my father," he said softly. "But time does not allow the change. My father will look past the clothes and see the gentle, beautiful lady that you are."

"I truly do not think he will pay attention to my clothes," Shawndee said solemnly. "It is my parentage . . . my skin color . . . that will prejudice him against me."

"We shall see this through together however my father leans," Shadow Hawk said. He drew her into his embrace. "Take a deep breath now. Think of butterflies. Do you not see their beautiful wings in your mind's eye instead of the face of an old, ailing man? Or do you prefer to see the rainbow in the sky after a summer rain? Would that bring you more peace than butterflies?"

Shawndee laughed softly. "Do you truly want to know what I am telling myself to see when I close my eyes and seek something for solace?" she said, stepping away from him so that their eyes could meet.

"What is it that you see?" Shadow Hawk asked, a slow smile quivering on his lips.

"You, my love," Shawndee said, her eyes dancing.

"It is your face that brings such peace, such joy, such love into my very soul."

Touched to the core by her words, Shadow Hawk pulled her into his arms and gave her a deep kiss.

He held her for a moment longer, then took her hand and led her toward his father, who waited with what Shadow Hawk already knew was stubbornness and resentment of Shawndee in his heart.

But Shadow Hawk knew that this meeting must be held, for it was only right that his future wife and his father come face to face before his father's last breath was taken.

Yes, it was necessary, no matter the outcome.

Whatever occurred in his father's room today, Shadow Hawk would still be spending the rest of his life with Shawndee and the children that would be born of their special love. He would arrange a wedding ceremony as soon as possible. He hoped it could come before the burial rites of his father. . . .

Shawndee gave Shadow Hawk a quick, pleading look when he stopped with her before a partially closed door.

"Remember to put things in your mind that make you happy, and soon this meeting with my father will be behind you," Shadow Hawk said only loud enough for Shawndee to hear.

Shawndee smiled weakly, then took a deep

breath and went into the semidark room with Shadow Hawk.

A lone candle flickered on a table beside the platform bed upon which the elderly man lay. A beautiful pelt was drawn up over him to rest beneath his armpits.

Shawndee noticed that Purple Cloud's chest was bare, revealing his leanness. The skin was drawn tautly over his chest and the bones of his ribs could be counted.

But it was his face, with its deep lines and sunken eyes, that made Shawndee's heart ache suddenly for this man whom she doubted would live long enough to see her as his daughter-in-law. His health had deteriorated dramatically since she had watched him telling his beloved stories beside the fire.

She could tell, by the way his breath caught almost every time he inhaled, that his pain was great. Shadow Hawk had told her that his father's ailment had something to do with his lungs.

But it was not the purplish hue of his lips, nor the pallor of his skin, nor the pain he was so obviously suffering, that caused Shawndee to be uneasy. It was the way his old, sunken eyes had remained fixed on her since she had entered his room. She could see great resentment in their depths.

It was hard to stand there and be so closely scrutinized by the father of the man she would soon marry, and to realize he would never approve of her in any respect.

"*No-tha*, as you requested, I have brought Shawndee to you," Shadow Hawk said, regretting his father's behavior, which revealed his intense dislike of Shadow Hawk's choice of wives.

But Shadow Hawk stood his ground, knowing this meeting was necessary. He sorely wished for approval, yet had prepared himself for the opposite. His father had witnessed many wrongs committed by the whites against the Seneca.

Shadow Hawk had never imagined himself falling in love with someone of a different skin color and culture, either.

But this woman standing at his side was far removed from the habits and customs of most whites. She had been forced to live a life of degradation and had been treated as badly by her own kind as they treated the Seneca.

He wished he could make his father understand this about Shawndee—that she needed to be loved, protected, that no one had really appreciated her.

Not until now. But he would never let her feel anything less than loved and proud!

"Shadow Hawk, I have now seen this woman up close, and I have studied her from afar, and I have questioned those of our warriors who sometimes trade among whites at Silver Creek. I know of this

woman and her family, and I have come to the con-
clusion that she is of undistinguished birth, a com-
moner, someone who is far beneath our Hawk clan,
especially you, who are *hasennowane*, chief," Purple Cloud said in a rush of words that soon left him
breathless.

Shadow Hawk, on the other hand, was at a loss
for words. He was absolutely stunned by what his
father had said. He feared his father's attitude
would hurt Shawndee deeply, whereas Shadow
Hawk was doing everything within his power to restore her pride, her feeling of worthiness.

Shawndee was so stunned, so hurt, she couldn't
even find the strength in her wobbly knees to turn
and flee.

Surely Shadow Hawk had not expected such ver-
bal abuse; otherwise he would not have brought her
here for this tongue-lashing.

As it was, she did not now believe that she would
ever be able to marry Shadow Hawk.

She gasped and paled when Purple Cloud began
to speak again.

"My son, if you marry this woman, you, who are
a sachem, will be marrying a woman out of your
class," Purple Cloud said, his eyes slowly moving
over Shawndee. The attire she was wearing made
him visibly shudder.

Shadow Hawk was shocked by his father's rude

behavior, by his frankness, which was not necessary in the presence of Shawndee.

It was hard for Shadow Hawk to find the right words to answer his father. He had never seen his father like this—prejudiced, cold, and absolutely unkind.

Shadow Hawk had to believe that because his father was on his deathbed, he was acting in ways that were abnormal for a man who was usually kind, sometimes even to a fault.

But still, his father had said those unkind things to Shawndee, and she had stood there and taken it, surely because she was as much at a loss of what to say or do as Shadow Hawk.

Shadow Hawk was relieved about one thing. His father had not out-and-out told him that he could not marry Shawndee. He had not asked Shadow Hawk to promise not to marry her. Only such a deathbed request as that could make Shadow Hawk feel obligated to turn his back on the woman he loved.

His father had suffered so much due to the ailment that would soon rob him of his life. He was like a tree whose branches had been broken by storms and whose trunk had become weather-beaten and decayed. Surely that was why he was so bitter.

Shadow Hawk's thoughts were stilled as Shawndee stepped away from him and moved closer to his father's bed.

"Sir, I am so very, very sorry that you feel as you do about me," Shawndee said, glad to have found the courage to speak her mind.

"And, sir, I am so very sorry that you are ill. I will pray to my God for you."

A sob stopped her words momentarily, and then she spoke again. "I forgive what you have said to me today, and how you said it, for I know how concerned you must be about the woman your son has chosen for a wife," she said, her voice quavering as she fought the urge to cry.

Oh, Lord, she needed one more moment, she despaired to herself. And then she could leave this room . . . and cry her heart out.

But never would she cry in the presence of this man who obviously hated and resented her with all his being.

She was too proud, for she did not see herself as beneath Shadow Hawk. She believed that in his eyes she was his equal, for their hearts were joined now, as one. Their very souls had come together.

Their hearts were going to sing and rejoice when their first child lay at her breast, suckling nourishment into its tiny body. Their lives were going to be filled with love and respect.

She only wished that his father could understand

what they shared. But she knew now that that was something that would never be.

"But I promise you, I would be the most faithful, the most loving wife to your son that you could ever want," she went on. "I . . . if you would give me your blessing, I would be the best mother for your grandchildren."

She turned to leave, then paused, looking back at Purple Cloud as tears she had not wanted to shed swept down across her burning cheeks. "And, sir, I do so truly love . . . and . . . respect your son," she blurted out.

She covered her mouth with a hand as the tears blinded her.

"Please, oh, please give us your blessing, for I shall die without Shadow Hawk's love," she begged between deep, gulping sobs.

Her head lowered, she ran past Shadow Hawk, ignoring his arms as he reached out for her. She feared that she had said too much.

Suddenly she was afraid that Shadow Hawk would feel he had no choice but to choose his father over her.

If he did, she would die a slow death inside, knowing that she had come so close to paradise only to lose it. If she lost Shadow Hawk, she would never allow herself to trust, or to love, again!

Chapter Twenty-seven

Shadow Hawk started to go after Shawndee but first looked down at his father with a hurt glance. When he saw his father's gaze waver, Shadow Hawk knew he already regretted what he had said.

Shadow Hawk fell to his knees beside his father's bed and wrapped his arms around the old man, whose body was now racked with sobs.

"I was wrong," Purple Cloud said. He clung to Shadow Hawk, his arms and hands trembling. "I do not even know where those words came from. I never purposely hurt people. But . . . it . . . was so easy to hurt her. Do you forgive me, my son? She . . . she . . . said that *she* forgave me."

"*No-tha*, you are not the same as you once were. Minute by minute, the illness robs you of your former self," Shadow Hawk said thickly. His father's bony fingers bit into the flesh of Shadow Hawk's shoulders.

"Please do not fret any longer over what you said," Shadow Hawk continued, hoping to lift his father's shame. "You did hear Shawndee tell you that she forgave you . . . that she would even pray for you. Does that not prove the goodness of my woman? Does that not prove that she would make your son a caring, thoughtful, loving wife? Do you not see that she will be a good mother to your grandchildren?"

"I want to see good in this woman, and I shall try harder to do so. I do not want you to turn your back on this love you have finally found," Purple Cloud said, his voice steady now, his sobs having subsided. "Go to her. Tell her that I regret my words. Carry to her my apology. Tell her . . . that . . . she even has my blessing, and . . ."

His father removed his hands from Shadow Hawk's shoulders and gazed into his son's eyes. "Also tell her to burn those clothes that rob her of her true, lovely self," he said, smiling. "Tell her that someone as lovely as she should wear beautiful doeskin dresses."

Relieved, even stunned, at his father's changed mood, Shadow Hawk smiled back at his father.

"Yes, I shall tell her, and she will be happy to wear the dress of our people," Shadow Hawk said.

"When you see her next, she will look as beautiful as the stars twinkling in the heavens on a clear summer night."

"I do wish to see her like that," Purple Cloud said, nodding. His eyes slowly closed. His head bobbed as he sought the comfort of his cattail-floss-filled pillows. He curled up onto his right side in a fetal position and slowly closed his eyes.

"Sleep well, my *no-tha*," Shadow Hawk said softly as he covered his father warmly with rabbit-skin pelts that were white as a winter snow.

"I shall," Purple Cloud said, his voice hardly more than a whisper. "Go now, my son. Make things right with your Shawndee. I shall sleep, sleep, sleep . . ."

His father drifted off. The gentle snoring made Shadow Hawk smile, for his father had snored since Shadow Hawk had been old enough to ask his mother what that strange rumbling sound was.

Then Shadow Hawk's smile waned, for now he heard another sort of rumbling coming from his father's lungs. He did not want to think about what was causing it. It could not be the death rattles that came some hours before a man's death.

No! He would not accept that he might lose his father this very night. He would put it from his mind. He would fill his thoughts and heart with other things.

"With Shawndee," he whispered.

He looked quickly toward the door that she had

left ajar when she had fled from the room.

Shadow Hawk must convince Shawndee that his father had not been aware of how hurtful he was being. He also had to deliver his father's message of apology.

He hoped she would accept it.

He gave his father one last glance. He was relieved to hear only snoring instead of the rumbling that he had heard for a brief moment. He left the room and closed the door behind him.

He searched until he found Shawndee in her room, sobbing on her bed. She wasn't aware of him entering the room, not until he sat on the bed beside her, placed gentle hands on her waist, and turned her to face him.

Gently his hands went to her cheeks and wiped away the wetness of her tears with his palms.

He brushed a soft kiss across her brow, then drew her onto his lap and slowly rocked her as he explained about his father's mood changes, and about how deeply his father regretted what he had said.

He continued to talk comfortingly to her, telling her things that he knew would erase the hurt his father had inflicted. He could tell her pain was easing by the way she smiled, sighed, and pressed more closely against him, snuggling nearer as his hands caressed her back.

"And now is the hurt lifted from your heart?"

Shadow Hawk softly asked, smiling into her eyes as she smiled up at him.

"Yes, it is lifted, and I do not feel any resentment toward your father over what happened in his room," Shawndee murmured. "Thank you for explaining his condition to me, though."

Then her smile wavered. "But what he said did give me reason to think more about our situation," she said warily. "How can you want me, a white woman, when white people have betrayed your people so badly in the past? How can you want me, someone whose mother has done things that have displeased you?"

"Shawndee, your skin might be white, but you are not like whites, especially your mother," Shadow Hawk said. "Are you not shunned by whites because of who your mother is? Marry me, Shawndee, and in turn, shun those who have shunned you. When you marry me you will become Seneca. All Seneca women hold high positions of honor, especially a chief's woman. You will be a princess!"

"A princess?" she gasped, her eyes widening. "Truly, I . . . will . . . be a princess, like those I have read about in books? A true living, breathing princess?"

"I am not certain about those princesses you read of in books," Shadow Hawk said, "but as for my people's princess, yes, you will be honored . . . revered."

He placed a gentle hand on her cheek. "As you sit beside me during our celebrations and councils, you will be envied by all other women," he said, smiling proudly at her.

"I do not wish to be envied," Shawndee replied. "That would make me disliked by the women of your village. I want to be as one with the women, with your Seneca people as a whole."

"Do not fear," Shadow Hawk said. "My people will adore you because you are who you are, not because you are married to their chief."

"Adored?" Shawndee said. She reached a hand up to her hair and shuddered when she felt the ponytail.

She was glad when Shadow Hawk quickly untied the thong, tossed it aside, then ran his fingers through her thick, golden tresses as he arranged them to lie across her shoulders.

He placed his hands at her waist and lifted her to stand on the earthen floor.

He smiled at her as he slowly undressed her. A happiness she had only discovered with him bubbled over anew inside her.

After her clothes were tossed aside, Shadow Hawk stood back and drank in her nakedness with his passion-filled eyes. Then he went to her and placed her hands at the waistband of his breech-clout.

"Make me nude, as well," he said, his voice thick.

A blush rushed into Shawndee's cheeks. As he nodded at her, urging her on, her breath quickened. Slowly she began easing his breechclout down across his hips.

His thick, ready manhood sprang out as it was freed from the garment. She shoved the breech-clout down his muscled legs until it finally fell to the floor and was kicked aside by Shadow Hawk.

Endlessly spiraling passion overwhelmed Shawn-dee as Shadow Hawk bent lower so that his mouth, lips, and tongue could claim first one breast and then another until her nipples were hard and her pulse was racing.

Shadow Hawk's hands ran up and down Shawn-dee's fiery flesh, teasing and stroking the supple lines of her body. When he knelt on the floor before her and stroked the satiny flesh of her inner thighs, Shawndee threw her head back in a sigh of ecstasy.

She almost melted on the spot when she suddenly felt his tongue on her sex, flicking, caressing. Her mind spun gloriously with the building of rapture.

His eyes glazed, the red-hot embers of passion leaping at his loins, Shadow Hawk reached his hands up to Shawndee's waist and positioned her on the bed on her back.

He mounted her and did not hesitate to thrust himself deep into her waiting folds.

Shawndee's senses reeled in drunken pleasure as her body moved with his, and his mouth came down hard on hers with a series of feverishly hot kisses.

Shadow Hawk trembled with readiness.

He drove in swiftly and surely, his quivering awareness of the approaching climax causing his mouth and hands to become more urgent.

Shawndee felt the savagery in his kiss. He now took her mouth by storm, his hands molding her breasts, kneading.

She went wild as his lovemaking again filled that hollow ache inside her. He gathered her into his arms and held her fiercely close while their bodies danced together, ecstasy claiming them with bone-weakening intensity.

Knowing that the ultimate pleasure was so very near, Shawndee caught her breath, ready; then they both went over the edge into blissful abandon.

Afterwards they still clung together, joyous, fulfilled, and breathtakingly happy.

But now that Shawndee was back on earth, she could not help being troubled by something she had yet to share with Shadow Hawk. It suddenly troubled her so much she did not see how she could keep such a secret from him any longer, especially since they were now promised to one another.

She bolted to a sitting position, causing Shadow Hawk to look up at her with surprise.

"What is it?" he asked. He reached a hand out and stroked one of her breasts. "What causes you to look at me in such a way . . . as though you have something difficult to say?"

"I'm not at all comfortable with what I have to tell you, but nevertheless it must be said," she blurted out.

She closed her eyes as he leaned up and swept his tongue over one of her nipples, then reached for her and brought her down beside him again, holding her sweetly close.

"Say it, for you know that nothing you say will change how things are between us," Shadow Hawk said.

"Shadow Hawk, I am so ashamed of something I did," Shawndee confessed, pushing herself up into a sitting position.

She watched his expression as she poured her heart out to him, telling him about having gone through his things, and how for a while she had thought the scalps were his, taken by him.

She was surprised when he didn't get angry.

"I would have soon showed you the scalps, and everything else that is in my chests, because I would never want to keep any secret from you," he said. "What is mine is now yours."

He reached for her hands and held them. "The

scalps?" he said. "They belonged to my ancestors. I only keep them as a reminder of how things can go wrong . . . how things can be bad between the Seneca and whites. The scalps are a reminder to me to work harder to keep that from coming to pass . . . to keep such a bad time in history from being repeated."

Shawndee snuggled closer to him. She was relieved that he wasn't angry with her, yet sad because she knew the violence between their peoples was not yet over.

"Perhaps you should display those scalps on a scalp pole outside your lodge," Shawndee found herself saying without thinking first.

He eased her slightly away from him so their eyes could meet.

"Why would you say that?" he asked.

"I believe whites should see the scalps, to know what the end result of a war with the Seneca could be," she said, with a seriousness in her voice that surprised Shadow Hawk. "Scalps could be a reminder to whites about the horrors of war, do you not think so?"

Hearing her explanation of what she said, and knowing she was sincere in wanting to discourage whites from interfering in the lives of the Seneca ever again, Shadow Hawk smiled.

"I will think about what you have suggested," he said, nodding. "But for now, my woman, I would rather not talk any more about scalps, or anything but my love for you," Shadow Hawk said, gently shoving her beneath him as he knelt over her.

He gave her an all-consuming kiss.

She twined her arms around his neck, and once again they soared amid the clouds as their bodies joined, their hearts pounding, their lovemaking utterly wondrous.

Chapter Twenty-eight

The crowd around the coroner's office was thick. Everyone was strained and silent as they watched the coroner step out onto his porch in his black attire. His face was solemn and his long, lean fingers were clasped together behind him as he looked from one citizen to another.

"Sheriff Dawson's body was found today. He was stabbed," Coroner Smith growled out. "Citizens of Silver Creek, we have as nasty a murder on our hands as we did when Caleb Sibley was found knifed in the back, but I do not believe the same knife was used on Sheriff Dawson as killed Caleb Sibley. The person who killed the sheriff did it because the sheriff stepped on her toes a mite too hard by siding with the community over her bein' a witch. The killing of Sheriff Dawson was an out-and-out act of vengeance. And I don't have to spell out the name of the culprit who stabbed the knife over and over again into Sheriff Dawson's back. It was the very same woman who we now know is practicing witchcraft in our fair town of Silver Creek."

He raised a hand in the air and doubled it into a tight fist. "I say, let's not treat this murderer in the traditional way," he shouted, his eyes narrowing angrily as he talked. "Let's treat her like the witch she is. And I don't mean burn her at the stake! I say let's go and set fire to her whole damn house while she's got her doors closed to business. Let's make sure neither she nor anybody who's kin to her comes out of that burning house alive!"

The attention of the crowd shifted to the deputy sheriff as he stepped up onto the porch with his slouchy manner, his tight pants and shirt making him look even thinner than he truly was. His coal-black hair was long and uneven as it hung down his back.

He spat over his shoulder and then glared at everyone. "It's always been my practice, as it was Sheriff Dawson's, to enforce the law," he shouted. "But my friend now lies on a cold slab of granite, the victim of a vicious murder, and I say to hell with what's proper and lawful. I agree with the coroner. Let's all take torches and rid this town of Jane Sibley once and for all. That goes for her son, as well as her black voodoo companion. I say let's set fire to that damnable place and finally restore peace, and wholesomeness to our town."

With both the coroner and the deputy sheriff inciting the crowd, there were loud shouts of "Burn 'em, burn 'em."

Then all hell broke loose as the people scrambled over themselves in their rush to the general store to make the necessary torches.

The people of Silver Creek had made themselves judge and jury.

And this time it wasn't only the women. Almost every man who resided in Silver Creek joined the melee.

The one person who didn't condone what was about to happen stood in his black robe on the porch of his church, holding a Bible, praying for the souls of those who were blinded by hate and fear.

Chapter Twenty-nine

Shadow Hawk could not get enough of looking at Shawndee. He was dressed now. Having crept from the bed where he had left Shawndee sleeping, he now stood at the door, watching her as she lay, smiling sweetly in her sleep.

He was so in awe of this woman, of her loveliness, of her sweetness, he could not believe that he had been blessed with knowing and loving her.

"*Wee-nighh*, I shall always love you," he whispered.

He turned with a start when there was a knock on the front door. He heard the voice of Blue Night, one of his warriors who for a while had taken the wrong path. His friend had vowed never to go that way again, and was again Shadow Hawk's favored warrior.

Wondering what might bring Blue Night to his lodge, Shadow Hawk noiselessly closed the door between Shawndee and the rest of the world so that she could get her rest.

When she awakened, their trek to her mother's home must be made at last.

Then he would bring Shawndee home with him again, this time forever.

He would make certain that her life was one of pure happiness and joy, and that his people accepted her completely.

He went to the front door and opened it, only now aware of the length of time he and Shawndee had spent making love. The sky was showing the first signs of dusk. Streamers of orange were all that remained of the sun, which had dipped down out of sight behind the horizon.

He gazed questioningly at Blue Night, who seemed uneasy, shifting his moccasined feet so nervously.

"Blue Night, what have you come to tell me?" Shadow Hawk asked. He stepped outside and closed the door behind him. "Tell me, Blue Night, why you are here, and what is it that you are trying so hard to say?"

Blue Night clasped his hands together behind him, his breechclout stirring in the wind as the evening breeze picked up. "Earlier this evening, as I approached Silver Creek in my canoe, planning to trade at the general store before it closed for the night, I saw something I have never seen before," he said worriedly.

"What did you see?" Shadow Hawk asked, arching an eyebrow.

"Is Shawndee still here?" Blue Night asked guardedly.

"Yes. She is asleep," Shadow Hawk said.

He took Blue Night gently by an elbow and ushered him farther from the longhouse toward the light of the outdoor fire.

"Tell me, Blue Night," he said thickly. "Tell me why you ask about Shawndee in the same breath you speak about something you saw in Silver Creek."

"While in Silver Creek, I beached my canoe and very stealthily went to stand where whites would not see me. I listened to what was being said," Blue Night explained. "You see, Shadow Hawk, a large crowd of whites, more than I have ever before seen gathered in one place, was standing outside the coroner's office."

"There was a large council of white eyes?" Shadow Hawk asked, his heart skipping a beat.

"It looked like the whole town had congregated there," Blue Night said, nodding. "The coroner, who I know well, since he so often sits in the general store sharing talk and smokes with other white menfolk, seemed to be the first man in charge tonight. When he finished what he had to say, Deputy Boyd took over the meeting."

"Get on with telling me why they were there," Shadow Hawk said, his patience running thin.

"The sheriff's body was found," Blue Night said, his voice drawn. "It was found close to Jane Sibley's house. She is being accused of the murder. The people of Silver Creek have decided to make her pay for the crime by burning her house down while she and those she lives with are in it. It is fortunate that Shawndee is here, safe in our village."

Shadow Hawk was stunned speechless. Should he awaken Shawndee and tell her what was going to happen so that she could go and warn her mother of the danger?

But, no. If he did that, he would be sending Shawndee into the face of danger. The white people who were taking the law into their own hands tonight would only make sure that Shawndee died with her mother.

"Shadow Hawk, what are you going to do?" Blue Night asked. "What can I do to help you?"

Shadow Hawk placed a hand on Blue Night's shoulder. "I must have time to think this through," he said, his voice tight. "If I make the wrong decision, I might lose my Shawndee."

Should he go and warn Shawndee's mother without alerting Shawndee to the danger? Or should he pretend he knew nothing of it and allow the townsfolk to rid the area of an evil influence?

Yet this woman was Shawndee's mother, her flesh and blood. He knew the sorrow one felt when one's mother passed on to the other side. He had felt it when his own mother died.

He stopped pacing and inhaled deeply. Although torn, he knew what must be done.

"Blue Night, no matter how this turns out, because Jane Sibley is Shawndee's mother, I have no choice but to go and do what I can to save her," Shadow Hawk said, bringing a look of shock into Blue Night's eyes.

"By doing this, you chance bringing our people into the middle of the whites' quarrel," Blue Night dared to say to a chief whose decisions he had never questioned before.

"I understand your worry," Shadow Hawk said, placing his hands on Blue Night's muscled shoulders. "But can you truthfully say that you can stand by and watch a whole community go against a lone woman in such a way? Do you not see that they would be killing Jane Sibley without giving her a chance to defend herself? The whites do not have proof of this woman's guilt."

"They did not say they had proof of her guilt," Blue Night said, nodding. "It was obvious to me they were looking for an excuse to rid their lives of the whiskey woman."

"As well as her family, which includes my Shawn-dee," Shadow Hawk said, his voice filled with fire. He dropped his hands to his sides. "I cannot let such injustice happen, even if I am protecting a woman I despise. I went so far as to abduct some-one to try to right the wrong this woman has caused in our people's lives, even though I have always taught that taking captives is wrong."

He spun around and went to the door, then turned to Blue Night. "I must do this thing alone," he said thickly. "What I ask of you is to let nothing happen to Shawndee while I am gone. If she awak-ens and asks for me, send my sister to her to sit with her until I return, but do not tell her where I am, or why."

"Whatever you ask I will do," Blue Night said. "But are you certain you should go alone?"

"Under these circumstances, yes," Shadow Hawk answered. "Too much attention would be drawn to the rescue if more than one of us do it."

Blue Night nodded and positioned himself beside the outdoor fire as Shadow Hawk went inside his lodge and strapped on his sheathed knife.

Hurrying from the lodge and boarding his canoe, he headed for Silver Creek, the moon high and bright and making a path of white for him to follow in the river.

"Please let what I am doing be right," Shadow Hawk prayed as he gazed heavenward.

When a star fell suddenly from the sky in a streak of silver, he smiled and felt relieved, for he saw it as a sign of good things to come.

Chapter Thirty

Thinking about Shawndee out there somewhere all alone, and not knowing what to do to find her, Jane Sibley stood at her front parlor window wringing her hands. Night had fallen with its dark, sinister shadows. She had grown to hate the dark, especially now, when Shawndee was lost in it.

She did not feel comfortable opening her doors to the menfolk of Silver Creek, knowing that Sheriff Dawson lay dead in the forest nearby, and with a man tied up in her attic. As a result, she had decided not to allow drinkers in her establishment tonight.

She had sent one man away with the news that she was closed, but she had not thought that he would spread the word so quickly. She had expected to be sending men away all evening.

But no one else had shown up, and she was puzzled as to why no other men had come. It was as though the world had stopped dead in its tracks, as though something terrible were about to happen. She felt doom pressing in on her and she could not help being afraid.

Filled with dread at meeting the townsfolk of Silver Creek to plead her case, Jane had decided to wait one more day to do it. She had hoped that by then Shawndee would have returned home.

"Please come away from de window," Tootiba begged, her hand trembling as she held a candle closer to Jane. "Baby doll, you ain't safe standin' there. Anyone could get a good shot at you."

"I can't get Shawndee off my mind," Jane said, holding the sheer curtain farther back to gaze up at the sky. "Thank the Lord, at least there is a full moon to give my daughter some light, wherever she might be."

She shuddered. "But, Tootiba, there's such a strange orange haze circling the moon tonight," she said, her voice breaking. "There is such a strange calm everywhere."

Tootiba set the candle on a table and hurried to Jane. She grabbed her by the hand and gave a frenzied yank. "Come away from de window," she again said, this time her voice almost a shriek. "Don' you know dat de strangeness of the moon is a sign of what is to come? It's a bad wickedness that's coming our way tonight. Let's go to the cellar. Let's hide."

Jane let the curtain flutter back down to cover the window. She eased her hand from Tootiba's, yet in the candle's glow she could see the intense fear in her friend's eyes. She had never seen them so wide. The pupils were so large, their blackness almost washed out all of the white.

"You're scarin' me, Tootiba," Jane said, again shuddering as Tootiba's fear crept through her and entered her heart.

"I'm glad you're afraid, if dat's what it'll take to get you to go into hidin' with Tootiba," Tootiba said, her thick jaw squared with determination.

Then Jane became aware of something else.

Her spine stiffened when she recalled seeing the same thing—how the reflection of a fire danced on the walls and ceilings of her house when the women of Silver Creek had brought torches, and with them, threats.

Her heart pounding, Jane spun around and saw, through the sheer curtain, torches once more moving toward her home.

"No, not again," Jane moaned as she swept the curtain aside to get a better look.

Her knees grew weak and her heart seemed to drop down to her toes when she saw that this time there weren't only women brandishing the torches, but also men. Now she understood why no men had come tonight to drink at her establishment. They had been busy making torches, surely coerced to do so by their wives.

It looked like the whole population of the town had decided to come tonight to rid themselves of a woman they despised. Perhaps they were also afraid of her, if they truly believed the claim that she was a witch.

"We've waited too long," Tootiba sobbed as she clung to the skirt of Jane's dress. "No matter now if we do get into hidin', they're going to make sure we never see the light of another day. They're gonna burn us, Jane, the house and all. Even hidin' in the cellar won't be protection enough. As the house burns, we'll suffocate from the smoke the fire gives off, and then the rubble and ashes will spill down on us and bury us."

Tootiba yanked on the dress. "Come with me," she cried. "We might have time to escape out the back way. Dey are still just in front of de house."

When they heard chants of "Burn the witch, burn the witch," as the crowd came closer, tears sprang to Jane's eyes. She turned and hurried to the hallway.

"Tootiba, come with me to my study," she said with determination. "Hurry! We don't have much time."

"We should leave through de back," Tootiba argued as she followed Jane down the hallway. "Please, Jane. There ain't much time."

"Hush up," Jane said in a scolding voice that Tootiba knew not to ignore.

Panting and sobbing, Tootiba followed Jane into the study at the front of the house.

Stopping at her large oak desk, where a mirror reflected the glow from the torches, Jane quickly opened a top drawer, then removed a book that Tootiba recognized.

"De book about de Salem witches," Tootiba gasped out.

"Take it," Jane said, forcing the book into Tootiba's trembling hands.

"Why are you givin' dis to me now?" Tootiba asked, a lone candle on the desk revealing the title of the book. The word "Witch" stood out as though it were alive and ready to grab her.

"I brought the book from the attic this morning," Jane said, trying to ignore the shouts and the reflections of fire, and with them the threat that she might not live much longer.

"Why did you bring de book down here?" Tootiba asked.

"I had planned to explain everything about the book to Shawndee," Jane said, her voice drawn. "I felt that I no longer had a choice. Now it must be you who tells her, Tootiba. I won't be here to do it.

But *you* will, Tootiba. Take the book and run out the back door. Leave, Tootiba. Now!"

"No, I can't do dat," Tootiba said, her eyes begging Jane. "I won't leave without you."

"Tootiba, you've always done anything I have asked of you," Jane said, taking Tootiba by an elbow and leading her from the room and down the hall toward the back door. "Now is no different. Run, Tootiba. Escape. Find Shawndee. Give her the book. Teach Shawndee what she should know about her ancestors, and how only one was connected with the Salem tragedy . . . how her great-grandmother died because of it."

"Please, Jane, please don't make me leave without you," Tootiba sobbed as they reached the back door and Jane opened it for Tootiba's exit. "I beg you, Jane. Come with me! The people are still just at the front. No one will see you leave with Tootiba!"

"Don't you see, Tootiba?" Jane said, a sob lodging in her throat. "There is no escape for me now. When I die in the burning inferno of my home, perhaps the townsfolk will think that Shawndee died with me. Shawndee will then be free to go and seek a new life for herself elsewhere. The people of this town will think a boy has died—a *son*, not a young woman, a *daughter*. Don't you see, Tootiba, how that frees Shawndee of all the scandal that has been connected with her because of her parents and the sort of lives they chose to live?"

"It don't have to be dis way," Tootiba cried, still unable to leave.

"Yes, it does," Jane said solemnly. "I am so tired. I . . . am . . . ready to die."

She held her chin high and placed her hands on Tootiba's thick shoulders. "Now, Tootiba, do as I tell you," she said forcefully. "Go and make things right for our Shawndee!"

Seeing that she had no other choice, Tootiba looked through her tears one last time at Jane, then clutched the book to her bosom and fled the house, crying. She soon found shelter and protection against the mob in the dense, dark shadows of the forest.

Sobbing fitfully, and still clutching the book, Tootiba began running as fast as her short, heavy legs would carry her, away from the lapping flames of the torches and the continued shouts of "Burn the witch, burn the witch."

It was hard for Tootiba to believe that she had said a final good-bye to Jane. The only thing that made her go on was Shawndee; it was now up to Tootiba to find Shawndee and see that her life was set right.

Tootiba would see that Shawndee wore beautiful dresses and met the most handsome men! But then she realized that she had no money or means to make those dreams come true. She didn't even have Shawndee.

She continued stumbling through the darkness. She tried not to hear the shouts, or to think of how Jane would soon die.

Back at the house, Jane had watched until Tootiba was safely in the forest, then slowly closed the door, ready to accept her own fate. She was tired of fighting for her mere existence. Even when her husband was alive, she had begun dreading getting up each morning, knowing that a life of drudgery was all that faced her and her daughter.

Now that she was a widow, it was even worse for her.

"Yes, I'm tired of it all," she whispered as she walked numbly back toward her study, where she planned to spend the last moments of her life and die with at least a measure of dignity.

Then her eyes widened as she started to pass by the back stairs; the stairs reminded her of another set of stairs . . . the ones that led up to the attic.

"Chester!" she gasped out, paling, only now remembering that he was in the attic.

And he was helplessly tied to a chair. There would be no way for him to escape the flames once the torches were thrown through the windows. No, she couldn't allow the man to die this way, no matter what he'd done.

And she didn't want to be accountable for his death. She was already being accused of one death—the sheriff's. She did not want to go to the grave with people blaming her for two.

Her heart pounding, Jane rushed up the first flight of stairs. Just as she reached the second floor, with the attic steps far down at the other end of the corridor, torches crashed through the windows of the bedrooms on each side of the hallway, and landed with thuds on the roof. The smoke quickly spread along with the flames, filling the long, narrow corridor.

Half blinded by the smoke, Jane realized that she could not even see the attic stairs. She covered her mouth and nose with her hands, but nothing would keep the smoke from reaching her.

Overcome by the smoke before she was halfway to the attic steps, Jane collapsed. But just before she slipped into the dark void of unconsciousness, she was aware of a figure rushing through the smoke-filled corridor toward her.

"Shawndee?" Jane managed in a whisper, thinking that she was seeing her daughter. Then she blacked out.

Shadow Hawk had seen the first torch thrown into a window as he had come to the back of the house, unseen by those who did their dirty deed at the front.

Realizing that time was short, and that he might

perish in the flames that would spread like wildfire through the house, he had hurried in the back door and quickly checked each room on the lower floor, finding no one there.

Knowing that it was risky to stay much longer in the smoky, burning house, yet wanting to do what he could to save Shawndee's mother, Shadow Hawk had grabbed up a towel, soaked it with water, and tied it around his nose and mouth, then raced up the back steps to the second floor just in time to see great bursts of smoke rushing from the opened doors. Through that smoke he had seen Jane Sibley collapse in the hallway.

His pulse racing, knowing that he did not have much more time since even the damp cloth was not keeping the smoke out of his lungs, he groaned as he lifted Jane's heavy body into his arms, then carried her down the back steps.

He was grateful when he finally reached the fresh night air, hurrying from the house to the back yard.

After carrying Jane to the forest without being seen by anyone in the crowd, Shadow Hawk laid her beneath the towering trees.

He yanked the damp cloth from his face and used it to wipe Jane's brow. He hoped that this might awaken her so she could tell him where to find Tootiba.

He hoped to save her, as well, for when Shawndee talked about Tootiba, it was with fondness. He knew how much the black woman meant to her.

"Please wake up," Shadow Hawk urged, yet Jane's eyes were still closed and there weren't any signs of her waking up.

Sighing, and knowing he could wait no longer to ask Jane where Tootiba was, he leapt to his feet to return to the house.

Just as he tied the damp cloth around his nose and mouth again, Shadow Hawk's eyes widened in horror when he saw that the house had been totally consumed by flames. The crackling sounds of the wood burning sent goosebumps up and down Shadow Hawk's spine.

Then something else caused even more goosebumps. The air was suddenly filled with a loud scream coming from the burning house.

Horrified, Shadow Hawk continued staring at the house as it fell in on itself in monstrous flames.

The scream. Surely it was Tootiba! Shadow Hawk's heart ached that he had not been able to save her.

Shadow Hawk could see through a break in the trees that the people who had done this terrible deed were gazing in stunned silence at the burning debris. They, too, must have heard the scream, forcing upon them a realization of the monstrous thing they had done tonight.

A shudder ran through Shadow Hawk to see just how cold-heartedly those people had killed tonight.

He was appalled to think that his village was so close to such people. It made him rethink the future of his own people. He must move them away from the area. He must find a new place for the Seneca children to grow up in. He could not take a chance that these same heartless people might decide to go against the Seneca someday.

He sighed heavily and turned to gaze down at Shawndee's mother. She was still unconscious. He had to get her where she was safe, and then he would go to Shawndee and tell her what had happened.

He would then take Shawndee to her mother, for he had decided to take Jane Sibley to his hunting lodge for protection. No white man knew about Shadow Hawk's private, special place where he went when he needed to pray and hunt.

Lifting Jane into his arms, he broke into a run toward his waiting canoe.

When he had Jane safely in the canoe, laid out on pelts and covered with a warm blanket, Shadow Hawk guided the craft out into the middle of the water. A short while later he had Jane comfortably settled on a bed of pelts beside a warm fire in his hunting lodge.

Shadow Hawk had taken a quick dip in the river to cleanse his body of the smoke. He now knelt over Jane, who was still unconscious, gently washing the black from her face and arms.

As he studied her, he noted how different she was from Shawndee. This woman was hefty and hard-looking, whereas her daughter was tiny and delicate.

He blamed the hardness of Shawndee's mother on the way she had made her living, which could not be good for any woman.

Shadow Hawk was glad to have saved Shawndee from such a fate as that, for when she became his wife, his people's princess, she would never have to worry about anything but enjoying her womanhood and motherhood.

She would not have to lift a hand. All would be done for her.

He lifted the damp cloth away from Jane's arm and stiffened when her eyelashes began to flutter. He watched her guardedly as she awakened, for he knew she would be alarmed when she discovered she was with a red man, someone hated by most whites.

Shadow Hawk saw the instant alarm that leapt into her eyes when she saw him. Even though it was white people who had tried to kill her tonight, he could tell that she feared him just as much as she had feared the mob that had thrown burning torches into her home.

"Who . . . are . . . you?" Jane gulped out, her heart racing. She looked quickly around her, yanking the blanket up to her chin. "Where . . . am . . . I?"

343

"You are safe and you are with a friend," Shadow Hawk quickly reassured her. "You are in the presence of a friend of your daughter, Shawndee."

Hearing him speak Shawndee's name, Jane turned questioning eyes on him again. "How could you know my daughter?" she said warily.

Then she went pale and recoiled away from him. "Oh, no, don't tell me you're the Seneca chief Chester Hawkins told me about, the one he blamed for Shawndee's disappearance, the one who—" she said, but he interrupted her.

"I am Chief Shadow Hawk, yes. And yes, I did abduct Shawndee, but while she was with me in my lodge we became more than captive and captor," Shadow Hawk explained, trying to say it as easily as he could so he would not alarm her too much.

"More than . . . ?" Jane gasped.

"For now, let me just say that your daughter and I have become close. Know that she is safe. She is no longer at my village as a captive. She is there because it is her choice to be."

He started to place a gentle hand on Jane's arm but saw her flinch and drew it quickly away. "Tonight? Do you remember what happened tonight at your house?" he asked.

Terror appeared on Jane's face.

She closed her eyes and gritted her teeth, for she knew that someone had died in that house tonight, and although she despised the very ground Chester had walked on, she did not enjoy thinking about the unmerciful way he must have died in the fire.

"Yes, I remember it very well," she said, a sob catching in her throat.

"I am sorry about your friend Tootiba," Shadow Hawk said solemnly.

Jane opened her eyes and looked wildly up at him. She grabbed his arm. "What do you mean?" she gasped out. "What about Tootiba?"

"After I rescued you, I did not have time to go back into the house to save Tootiba," Shadow Hawk said, lowering his eyes. "When I heard her scream . . ."

Jane sighed deeply. "The scream? If it came from the house, it was not Tootiba," she said, swallowing hard.

"The person you heard screaming was Chester Hawkins," she said softly. "I . . . I . . . had him locked in the attic. I could not get to him in time. I . . . am responsible for his death. I sent Tootiba away in time. She is safe, I hope."

Then she gazed incredulously at Shadow Hawk. "You saved me," she said, her voice drawn. "You must hate me, yet you risked your life and went into that house to save me."

"You are Shawndee's mother. How could I not save you?" Shadow Hawk said.

"You care that much for Shawndee that you would save the woman who . . ." she began, then sat up and looked at the door. "Shawndee? Where is she?"

"She is back at my village," Shadow Hawk explained. "I have brought you to my hunting lodge, a safe haven from whites. I believe you should stay here for a while, at least until things in Silver Creek have simmered down. I even think it is best that you never allow them to know you lived through the fire, for would they not seek ways to destroy you again?"

"You would allow me to stay here?" Jane asked in wonder. "You would be so kind to someone who traded firewater freely with your warriors?"

"Again, you are Shawndee's mother, and I know that Shawndee will be grateful that I saved you and brought you to a safe shelter," Shadow Hawk said. He rose to his feet. "I shall go for Shawndee now. She will want to know that you are alive and well. Then, if you wish, I will send warriors out to search for Tootiba. I will also have her brought here."

He bent down beside her again. He gazed intently into her eyes. "I will be leaving now, but I advise you to stay here, where I know you will be safe," he said. "I will bring your daughter to you. Soon."

Amazed by his kindness, by his gentleness, and by his forgiveness, Jane broke into deep sobs.

"Thank you," she cried. "Thank you for everything. I am so sorry for having wronged your people. I . . . won't . . . do it again. I have no interest in getting involved in selling whiskey again. All I wish for now is to see my daughter happy. I will find a way to see that happen."

"You have to look no farther than this man," Shadow Hawk said thickly. "Shadow Hawk is the answer to your daughter's happiness. We are going to be married."

"Marry?" she demanded, her eyes searching his. "You are marrying my Shawndee?"

"In the short time we have known one another, we have discovered that we love one another, and, yes, we discussed marriage. As soon as we can, we will become man and wife," Shadow Hawk said, watching for her reaction.

Jane was too stunned to say anything else for the next moment or two.

An Indian chief, she thought to herself, suddenly aware of being in the presence of a man whom everyone spoke of highly. He was a man of honor . . . of savage honor!

Recalling her dream of her daughter finding and marrying a man who would treat her well, a man of *honor*, she saw this man as the fulfillment of that dream.

The fact that he was an Indian was even better in her view, for she had not seen one white man she would ever want to see her daughter marry.

None were worthy of her. But this man, this proud chief, *was*.

"I, too, see you as the answer to my daughter's happiness," Jane said, tears spilling from her eyes.

"Shawndee will explain to you in more detail, if you wish, how it happened that we fell in love," Shadow Hawk said. He reached a hand out for hers.

He smiled when she twined her coarse, thick fingers through his, knowing this was proof of the genuiness of her feelings about becoming his mother-in-law.

"Rest while I go for Shawndee," he said, slowly slipping his hand free of hers.

"Yes, I do believe I can rest now," Jane said, easing down onto the pelts and pulling a warm blanket up to her chin. "Perhaps I am finally free of my demons." Her eyes slowly closed. "Thank you, Shadow Hawk. Thank you."

He nodded, then fed more wood into the flames of the lodge fire, took one last look at Jane Sibley, and hurried from the lodge. He could not get to Shawndee quickly enough to tell her that life was going to be beautiful for her, that she was free to love and to marry him, and that she had nothing to dread, or fear, as far as her mother was concerned.

"I am coming, my pretty little innocent one," he whispered as he climbed into his canoe and headed toward his home, and her.

Chapter Thirty-one

As Shadow Hawk stood over Shawndee and saw how peacefully she slept, he was glad he was going to awaken her with good news instead of bad. He hoped never to see her life filled with sadness again. She had had enough trouble to last a lifetime.

He wished now that all he had to do was climb into bed with her and hold her and tell her just how much he loved her, as he had earlier in the evening when they made love.

But that would come later. Her mother was waiting for her, along with news that she had a new life.

The townsfolk of Silver Creek thought that Shawndee had died with her mother in the fire tonight. They would never know that Andrew was in truth a lovely, soft-spoken woman who was very much alive, and who would soon be Shadow Hawk's wife—a Seneca princess!

Her mother was free of the past as well.

Shadow Hawk hoped that Shawndee's mother would use that freedom well and walk the good road now, not the bad.

He would encourage Shawndee and her mother to talk over the terrible thing that had been done to them, then let it lie . . . let it remain in the past and never discuss it, or the ones who'd wronged them, again.

"Shadow Hawk?"

He was shaken from his reverie by Shawndee's voice. He had not even been aware of Shawndee waking up, for he had gone to the door and was staring into his lodge fire as he thought everything through.

He spun on a heel and hurried to Shawndee. He knelt down beside the bed, reaching for her and holding her close as he explained what had happened at her home, and how he had saved her mother.

He gave her the news that Tootiba hadn't been injured in the fire either, because her mother had sent her away in time.

He told her about Chester dying in the fire, and why, and how her mother had tried to save him.

"I will take you to your mother now," Shadow Hawk said as she eased from his arms and looked

350

with wide eyes into his. It was obvious to him that she was still absorbing all that he had told her.

"Where is my mother?" Shawndee asked finally.

"At my hunting lodge," Shadow Hawk said. He took her by the hand as she stepped from the bed, her body soft and pink in its nudity. "She will be safe there until she decides what she will do with the rest of her life . . . where she will go."

Shawndee was stunned by all he had revealed. "You are the kindest, biggest-hearted man I have ever known," she murmured. "You have your own concerns—your father's ailing health, and your warriors whose lives have been torn asunder by firewater—yet you have put all of this aside and saved the very woman you wanted to get rid of."

"No matter what, I could not let your mother die, for she *is* your mother," Shadow Hawk said. "When word came to me about what the people of Silver Creek had planned for your mother, I had no choice but to save her. I didn't awaken you to take you with me because I didn't want to chance your getting involved in something that might harm you."

"You are amazing," Shawndee said, more in awe of him now than ever before.

"When people heard someone screaming in the inferno, they must have believed it was your mother, or perhaps even you," Shadow Hawk said. "Now the townsfolk believe they are rid of your mother once and for all."

"The scream was Chester's," Shawndee said, shuddering. "He finally got his comeuppance. But what a horrible way to die."

"He was a man who wrote his own death sentence by choosing the wrong road of life long ago," Shadow Hawk said. "He was a man whose life was wasted, and who will not be missed by anyone."

Shawndee stepped hurriedly away from him. She did not have to think twice before choosing the lovely beaded doeskin dress over her dreaded boy's attire. Her mother would see right away that Shawndee would never take on a false identity again.

She was Shawndee!

Not Andrew!

And she would soon be a Seneca princess!

"You said the crowd was shouting, 'Burn the witch'?" Shawndee said, shuddering.

"Yes."

Shawndee gasped, trembling again, then hurried into the dress, reveling in the softness and warmth of the doeskin as it clung to her shapely figure.

She turned to Shadow Hawk. The glow from the firepit lit his face, giving Shawndee the opportunity to watch his expression as she asked, "How do you feel about what the people were saying to my mother . . . about how they labeled her a witch? You heard them calling her that. You even know there is a possibility that she is a witch. And you know she is guilty of having caused your warriors to take the wrong road of life, yet . . . you . . . saved her life?"

Shadow Hawk stepped up to her and gently placed his hands on her shoulders. "My woman, in life there are many things that one finds alarming, distasteful, and hard to accept, yet one must learn to forgive, perhaps even accept, in order to move forward. Tonight I saved the mother of the woman I love. That is how I see it. Nothing more or less. The rest is left up to you, for she *is* your mother. Whether or not you forgive her will come from deep inside you. It is your choice. As for my warriors? Tonight the paths of their lives became straight again. They will be alright."

"But what if my mother decides to trade in alcohol again and settles close enough to your village to lure your warriors to her establishment?" Shawndee asked.

"I do not anticipate your mother doing that, for tonight she faced her own mortality," Shadow Hawk said solemnly. "She still lives, does she not? She will not want to test her mortality again anytime soon."

"Take me to her?" Shawndee asked, tears filling her eyes at the knowledge of just how close she had come to losing her mother. She felt ashamed now for having abandoned her in her time of trouble.

And even though Shawndee still did not know

whether her mother was a witch, somehow it no longer mattered. Her mother had come through all of this alive. Surely God would not have allowed it if she were the monster so many believed her to be.

Shawndee had always put her trust in the Lord. She would do so now.

"Yes, I will take you to her," Shadow Hawk said. He bent over, picked up Shawndee's moccasins, and handed them to her. "Will you also wear these, not the boots?"

Shawndee laughed softly. "Yes, these too," she said, momentarily hugging them to her bosom.

"Look what I'm going to do with those awful boy's clothes and stiff, uncomfortable boots," Shawndee said, hurrying into her moccasins. Her jaw tight with determination and her eyes dancing, she grabbed up the shirt and breeches and draped them over an arm, then yanked the boots from the floor.

With Shadow Hawk beside her, she left the longhouse and walked directly to the communal fire that burned bright and high into the dark heavens.

Several elders sat on blankets around the fire, smoking their long-stemmed pipes, while mothers gathered their children to take them inside for their stories before putting them into their beds. Shawndee stepped up to the huge fire and piece by piece fed her clothes and boots into the flames.

When they had been consumed, Shawndee

turned to Shadow Hawk, beaming. "Now my past is truly that," she said.

She flung herself into his arms and hugged him, not caring that everyone could see their display of affection.

"Thank you, darling," she said just loudly enough for him to hear. "Thank you for making all of this possible."

"How could I not?" he replied equally softly. "Not after falling in love with you the moment I realized you were not a boy, but a woman who was surely sent to me from the One above."

"I hope I never disappoint you," Shawndee said. She leaned away from him and gazed into his eyes. "Will you tell me if I do?"

"I promise to, only because I know it will never be necessary," Shadow Hawk said, chuckling. He took her hand. "Now come with Shadow Hawk. Your mother awaits your arrival."

Smiling, and anxious to make amends with her mother, Shawndee walked with him toward the river, then proudly sat with him in his canoe as he paddled down the river.

After the canoe was beached and hidden behind tall shrubs, Shadow Hawk held Shawndee's hand as he led her to his lodge.

Beneath the moon's glow, the magnificent landscape was clearly visible. It was a region of many wonders. To the south were splashing waterfalls, loamy bluffs, and beautiful, wonderful-smelling cedars and pines stretching high toward the bright and shining moon.

And then she saw it. The hunting lodge sat near one of the waterfalls, where water roared and spilled over cavernous rocks into a body of water that stretched out, finger-like, in many directions, dissecting the land with springs and creeks.

The lodge was situated beside one of those springs. In the moonlight she could see that the spring was wide, and surely deep. Water was gushing forth from the middle, with tiny bubbles bursting to the surface as if there were some living force beneath that drove the water upward.

In the light of the moon, each bubble seemed to change color. Purple became red. Blues became green. The rainbow colors seemed to spread out until they reached the banks on all sides, and only then dissolved into nothingness.

"I have never seen anything so beautiful or so fascinating," Shawndee said.

Entranced by the spring, Shawndee broke away from Shadow Hawk and ran to kneel beside it. Again she watched the gushing burst of water, and then the bubbles that followed it.

Shadow Hawk knelt down beside her. "It is magic water," he said. He reached a hand into the soft coolness, running his fingers through it.

"Why do you call it magic?" Shawndee asked,

gazing at him. "Because of what it does?"

"It is water with magical qualities because the Great Spirit has spoken to it," Shadow Hawk said. "Many legends have been told about this pool of water, and all Seneca believe in its magical qualities."

He leaned closer and cupped his hands together, dipping them into the water and bringing some out to offer to Shawndee. "Taste, drink," he said. "The taste is stimulating."

He brought his hands to her mouth, and Shawndee drank. She felt a strange warmth spiral downward into her stomach.

"Do you feel it?" Shadow Hawk said, wiping his hands dry on his breechclout. "Do you feel the warmth—the stimulation of it?"

"Yes, I do," Shawndee said, her eyes widening.

"Then you have known the magic that until now only my people have known," Shadow Hawk said. He took her hand and urged her back to her feet.

"But I thought your hunting lodge was private," Shawndee said, walking toward it and seeing that it was as large and impressive as his personal lodge back at the village.

"Private to the Hawk clan of Seneca, but no one else," Shadow Hawk said, nodding. "When my people need private time for prayers, they come and kneel around this water. When they leave, they are filled with hope again."

Shawndee only half heard what he had said, for suddenly the door opened before her and her mother was standing there, her arms outstretched for Shawndee.

"Your voices awakened me," Jane said, rushing to Shawndee and enveloping her in a hug. "Shawndee, oh, Shawndee, you are alright. I wasn't sure if I should believe Shadow Hawk. I'm glad that I did."

"He saved your life, Mother, so how could you have doubted him?" Shawndee said, enjoying this rare moment in her mother's arms. She could almost count on her ten fingers the number of times her mother had hugged her, for such shows of affection were rare for Jane.

"I doubted because he had just cause to hate me," Jane said, her voice breaking.

She stepped away from Shawndee, yet still held her hands as she took in the way Shawndee was dressed. "And look at you," she said, smiling crookedly. "A dress?"

"Not only a dress, Mother," Shawndee said, hoping that what she was going to reveal to her mother would not arouse her disapproval. "It is the sort of dress I intend to wear from now on." She paused, inhaled a nervous breath, then continued. "Mother, this man who saved you tonight will soon be my husband."

Shawndee was shocked when her mother did not

react in any way except to exchange smiles with Shadow Hawk.

"Mother?" Shawndee said, then turned to Shadow Hawk. "Shadow Hawk?"

"He told me, and I do not disapprove," Jane said, cackling when she saw the look of amazement in her daughter's eyes.

That cackle, that strange laugh of her mother's, banished the joy of the moment for Shawndee.

She slid her hands free of her mother's, took a slow step away from her, then went and clung to Shadow Hawk.

"What's wrong?" Jane asked, placing a hand to her throat. "What did I say to make you behave so strangely?"

"Mother, of late I have felt that I've never known the real you," Shawndee said, her voice drawn. "Your laugh, Mother. It . . . it . . . reminds me . . ."

"Of what?" Jane asked, bewildered.

Shawndee stepped away from Shadow Hawk. "I need to talk with my mother about something," she said, her voice filled with apology.

"I understand," Shadow Hawk said. He brushed a kiss across her lips, then turned and gave Jane a stern look. Then he walked toward the door. "I will go and add wood to the fire," he said. "Come inside when you are finished."

Shawndee sat down beside the water, where she felt a strange sort of peace.

"Mother, there is so much I need to know," she began. "First, I need to know about the sheriff. Chester and you were discussing his death as though you had killed him. Mother, I have not wanted to believe that you could, but—"

"Is that why you ran away after I hit Chester over the head to stop him from raping you?" Jane asked, her voice somber.

"Yes, that, and . . ."

"The talk of me being a witch was something else that bothered you?" Jane said, searching her daughter's eyes.

"Yes," Shawndee said, swallowing hard. "Mother, do you have things you wish to share with me?"

Jane sighed. "I didn't kill Sheriff Dawson," she said, her voice drawn. "Chester killed him and placed his body close to our house to make me look guilty of the crime. He had even plotted as far as to say he would tell the people of Silver Creek that I did it, unless I let him have his way with you."

Jane shivered, then continued. "The sonofabitch had me cornered for a while, because I knew that if he told the townspeople that I'd killed the sheriff, they'd believe him, only because they'd want to so they'd have more ammunition against me," Jane said in a rush of words. "I swear on a stack of Bibles, Shawndee, I didn't harm the sheriff, and I truly regret that Chester died in the attic in the fire.

I tried to save him. The smoke claimed me too quickly."

"And Shadow Hawk saved you," Shawndee said softly.

"Yes, and brought me to this enchanting place," Jane agreed, slowly looking around her, where the moon shone its silver light on the loveliness of the surroundings.

"Mother, tell me about the book about witches," Shawndee said.

"I sent Tootiba away from the house with the book, so that she could give it to you when she found you, and explain everything," Jane said. "I shouldn't have kept these things from you."

"No, you shouldn't have kept so much from me," Shawndee murmured. "We are alone, Mother. Please tell me now."

"Shawndee, your great-grandmother died because of rumors that she was a witch, as did so many others in Salem who were accused of practicing witchcraft," Jane said.

Jane looked quickly away from Shawndee, making Shawndee wonder why she was avoiding eye contact.

"Your grandmother's name was listed in the book along with the others who died that day," Jane said.

"But she wasn't a witch?" Shawndee asked, still wondering why her mother would not look her in the eye. Was her mother lying? She didn't want to think so. This was the time for honesty . . . for sharing between a mother and daughter who had not had time through the years to discuss many important things. It had always been Tootiba who had taken time with Shawndee, not Shawndee's mother.

"No, your grandmother wasn't a witch," Jane said, only briefly glancing at Shawndee. This discussion made Jane terribly uneasy. There had been so much about her past that she had been forced to accept. She had wished to protect Shawndee from all of this.

"It wasn't true about my grandmother being a witch," Jane murmured. "It was just a rumor that got out of hand, as it did for many other innocent people who died in Salem that day. So many were wrongly persecuted. There were false tales. When one story began, it was expanded upon, just as you saw in Silver Creek. One mention of me being a witch, and see what happened?"

"But the book, Mother," Shawndee persisted. "Why would you keep the book if you didn't want anyone to connect you with witchcraft? My great-grandmother's name was listed with those who died at Salem."

"I kept the book through the years to show you if the need arose, as it did recently," Jane said. "After you read the book and see how wrong the people of Salem were, you will understand better than if I tried to elaborate on it myself. The important thing is that we are both alive. The people of Silver Creek will never know the truth. We are both free to begin life anew."

"I feel so ashamed for ever having doubted you," Shawndee cried. She turned to her mother and leaned into her embrace, loving the feel of her mother's arms around her again.

"It's not surprising that you jumped to conclusions after you found the book, and then heard me tell Chester that I'd witch him," Jane said, choking on a sob.

Shawndee had never seen her mother cry before. She was deeply touched when she felt her mother's tears on her face as they clung together, cheek to cheek.

"Things are going to be alright now," Shawndee sobbed. "And please don't go somewhere where I will never see you again."

"Your mother can stay at our village," Shadow Hawk said as he stepped up behind them. He had seen their embraces and tears, and guessed that everything was cleared up between them.

Shawndee and Jane moved out of each other's arms with a start, then smiled as Shadow Hawk bent and offered them each a comforting arm around their waists.

"Jane, you can become a part of not only your

daughter's life at our new village, but also her husband's and your grandchildren's."

"You truly wish to include me in that way?" Jane gulped out. "You want me to live among your people?"

"It is something that would please your daughter, so, yes, it would also please Shadow Hawk, who will soon be your son-in-law," he said, smiling from Jane to Shawndee.

"Mother, please?" Shawndee pleaded.

"And Tootiba?" Jane asked warily.

"Tootiba, as well," Shadow Hawk said, nodding. "We will find her soon and bring her to this lodge, where the two of you will be safe until my people leave for their new home, away from Silver Creek."

"I didn't know you were leaving the area," Shawndee gasped out.

"I did not know this myself until tonight, when I saw the viciousness of Silver Creek's people," Shadow Hawk said tightly. "I cannot chance them turning on my people in the same way. But I cannot travel yet. My father's life lies in the balance. Now that your life has been put right, I must focus entirely on my father."

"Thank you, Shadow Hawk. I will love staying here at your lodge," Jane said. "There is such serenity here. It will be good for me to know such goodness after . . . after . . ."

"Say no more about anything that pains you,"

Shadow Hawk said, interrupting her. He gestured with a wide sweep of his hand around him. "You can feel at peace here, especially near the magic water."

He lowered his hand and trailed it through the warm water. "The Great Spirit created this water," he said, looking from Shawndee to her mother. "He made it with a tear because two brothers would not be peaceful. Then he urged all of the Seneca clans to drink from his water. When they did, peace came among our people's clans forever after."

He smiled and looked at Shawndee. "The old people used to say that any Seneca who drank of the water would live happily in the world hereafter," he said. "I have carried this water to my father many times during his illness. I know now that when he is gone from me, he will be happy."

He cupped his hands in the water, brought some out, and offered it to Jane. "Your daughter drank from this water tonight; so should you," he said, the water dripping between his fingers.

Jane's eyes met Shadow Hawk's for a moment, and then she glanced at Shawndee questioningly.

When tears came to Shawndee's eyes and she nodded to her mother to encourage her to drink the offered water, her mother returned the nod, then moved closer to Shadow Hawk and drank.

"I must return home now," Shadow Hawk said, lowering his empty hands to his sides. "Shawndee,

I wish you would come with me. I want you with me as my father slips away."

Shawndee nodded, then gave her mother a soft hug.

Jane returned the hug, then stepped away and watched them walk off in the direction of the river. She was stunned by what she had just experienced, and touched to know the sort of man her daughter was going to marry. She couldn't believe that any man could be as wonderful as Shadow Hawk—as caring, as thoughtful, as good. Her daughter was blessed to have him!

She felt blessed herself, because her life was finally going to be filled with peace and love!

Chapter Thirty-two

Many years later.

The Seneca had established a new village far enough from the people of Silver Creek to feel safe from their wicked ways, yet near enough to the magical stream near Shadow Hawk's hunting lodge to travel there by canoe whenever one needed renewal of strength and hope.

The village of the Hawk clan lay just inside the Canadian border, safe from depredations by the United States government.

It was the time of *Nisha*, the January moon, and the Hawk clan was celebrating the Mid-Winter Ceremony which marked the beginning of the Seneca new year.

Cassie Edwards

Shawndee and Shadow Hawk had left the celebration at the large council house long enough to return to their longhouse to place Moon Shadow, their very tired six-year-old daughter, in her bed.

Shawndee and Shadow Hawk planned to rest awhile themselves before returning to the excitement of the celebration.

Shawndee had celebrated the Mid-Winter Ceremony many times with the Seneca. She smiled as she recalled the first time she had seen the members of the False Face Society, and how frightened she had been of the grotesquely carved masks they wore during the celebration.

"Up you go," Shadow Hawk said, helping his daughter climb the notched ladder to her overhead loft.

"Will I dream of Grandfather again tonight?" Moon Shadow asked as she climbed up into the loft while her father waited just far enough up the ladder so that she could see his head.

Moon Shadow leaped onto her thick bed of pelts and blankets. She stretched out on her tummy and rested her chin in her hands, the light from a candle beside the bed illuminating her long golden hair and large dark eyes.

"Your grandfather would be pleased to join your dreams again tonight," Shadow Hawk said, smiling. He was sorry that his daughter had never met his father, for Purple Cloud had died shortly after his marriage to Shawndee.

But Shadow Hawk had drawn a portrait of his father in his daughter's mind to keep him alive in her heart.

"Also Grandmother?" Moon Shadow asked.

"Also Grandmother," Shadow Hawk said, for he had told Moon Shadow many stories about his mother. She knew her other grandmother very well, since Jane Sibley lived in the Seneca village.

"Then I shall sleep well tonight," Moon Shadow said, sighing as she rolled over onto her back and curled up while Shadow Hawk climbed farther up the ladder and covered her with a pelt of rabbit fur.

"Tomorrow I will spend the day with Grandmother Jane, and Aunt Tootiba," Moon Shadow said as she slowly drifted to sleep. "I have fun with them. I love their stories."

Shadow Hawk sighed, then backed down the ladder. Jane and Tootiba had promised that they would never tell Moon Shadow anything that had to do with witchcraft or voodoo, yet he sometimes wondered if they might slip in a tale or two, since those were stories that intrigued little ones.

"What's wrong?" Shawndee asked as Shadow Hawk came into their bedroom.

"Are you certain your mother and Tootiba are not teaching Moon Shadow things she should not

know?" he asked as he drew Shawndee into his
arms.

"They have promised never to speak of witches
or voodoo to our daughter," Shawndee said. "I trust
them. But Tootiba and Mother are good at elabo-
rating on things that interest Moon Shadow. They
love to hear her squeal with delight, or see her eyes
widen in wonder."

"As long as you trust them, then I shall continue
to, as well," Shadow Hawk said.

He gently pulled Shawndee's doeskin dress over
her head, revealing a figure that was not so petite
anymore. Her belly was again swollen with child.
Shadow Hawk wished for a son, but if he had another daughter, that would satisfy him, as well.

Shawndee reached for Shadow Hawk's breechclout and lowered it past his waist, then watched
him step out of it as it fell around his ankles.

She giggled when he reached for her and swept
her into his arms. "We will be missed at the celebration," she murmured, already breathless from
anticipation of making love again with the man she
adored.

"We will be with them again in time for the Great
Feather Dance," Shadow Hawk said huskily as he
placed Shawndee on their bed, then moved over
her.

"But for now, my *neio*, we are the only two people
in the universe," Shadow Hawk said, pressing gen-

tly into her slowly yielding folds. He began his rhythmic strokes within her.

As her gasps of pleasure became long, soft whimpers, he kissed her breasts, sucking, then flicked her nipples with his tongue.

And then he kissed her long and deep, his hands beneath her buttocks, cupping them and lifting her so that she would be closer to his heat. Their naked flesh fused, their bodies moving, flesh against flesh in gentle rhythm.

She arched toward him as she felt the bliss rising inside her, her entire body becoming warm, all senses yearning for that great burst of energy when ecstasy would surge through her.

"I love you so," Shawndee whispered against Shadow Hawk's lips, then caught her breath when she went over the edge with him.

Shadow Hawk held her close for a moment longer, then rolled away from her and lay on his back, breathing hard.

Shawndee turned and molded her body next to his. "I believe I am hearing the thump-thump of turtle-shell rattles coming from the council house," she said, though she hated to leave this bed of wondrous pleasure. "The Great Feather Dance is about to start."

"Yes, I know," Shadow Hawk said, sighing.

He crawled from the bed. "And we must go and participate," he said, offering her a hand.

She took it and moved from the bed with him.

Her hands went to her hair. "My braid is a mess," she murmured. She wore her hair in a single braid now, as was required of married women.

"I shall rebraid it for you," Shadow Hawk said, turning her back to him. His fingers soon had the braid undone, and then redone.

She was soon dressed again in her doeskin attire, and he in his buckskins.

They left the bedroom and stopped to look up the ladder.

They heard no sounds.

"Yes, she dreams," Shadow Hawk said. "The dream god is guiding her soul on its journey."

Smiling, Shadow Hawk slipped a fur cape around Shawndee's shoulders and then one around his own. They went outside and hurried through the snow that had blanketed the ground early that day. They soon entered the council house, where women sat on one side of the building and men on the other. They arrived just in time, for Shadow Hawk's name had just been announced.

Shawndee sat down between her mother and Tootiba, who had been invited to sit with the Seneca women.

Shawndee smiled as she watched her husband join the dance after his name had been proclaimed to the four winds and he had slipped on a costume of feathers.

Shawndee was caught up in the wonders of the dance as the men in all their feathered finery circled the benches in the center of the lodge. The ritual conveyed thankfulness and hope—thankfulness to the spirit beings for past benefits to the community, and hope that the spirit beings would continue to care for the Seneca.

Singers sang and thumped their painted turtle-shell rattles, cheering at the end of each part of the ceremony.

"*Who-eey!*" they shouted in a high voice, dragging out the word.

The shout was followed by chanters thanking the Creator for everything that he had made—for water under the earth, grass and shrubs, trees, and everything that was of value to the Seneca.

"*Nyahweh*," they sang as they continued to dance, and the rattles rattled, and the feet stamped in rhythm, and feathers bounced and swayed. Shadow Hawk's sister, the Hawk clan's head priestess, presided over the ceremony.

As snow began to fall again outside the council house, covering the earth with an even deeper blanket of white, Shawndee became lost in thought, musing over how good life was under her husband's guidance.

She gazed at the warriors who were dancing with her husband and recognized the faces of those who had found their way back to the good road of life.

Because of Shadow Hawk, his warriors had regained their *savage honor*. Because of her husband, all was well for everyone!

And she felt proud for what she had brought to the Seneca children. She had managed to get some discarded books from a library in a nearby Canadian town and had brought them to the village.

Each day now she sat with those children who wished to be read to. In one room of her longhouse she was building a vast library of books that she would acquire little by little.

She beamed to know that although she was not a true librarian, she owned many books and performed all the services of one.

Those children who could read came and checked out the books they desired. For Shawndee, there could be no greater reward than watching the children's eyes light up as they chose books for themselves.

She was brought back to the moment, and the celebration at hand, when Shadow Hawk gave her a smile as he continued to swing and sway and move his feet in the dance steps of his ancestors.

As always, his smile, and the wonders of his love that it conveyed, made Shawndee melt, for her husband still affected her in such a way.

She returned his smile and formed the words *I*

love you forever on her lips, shivering when he whispered them back to her, then resumed dancing, on his face a look of radiant joy, a joy that matched Shawndee's.

Dear Reader:

I hope you enjoyed reading *Savage Honor.* The next book in my *Savage* Indian series will be *Savage Moon,* which is about the Shoshone and the Bannock tribes. You will find much romance and adventure in this novel. I hope you will enjoy reading it as much as I enjoyed writing about the interesting customs and lives of both tribes.

For those of you who collect my Indian romances and want to hear more about them, you can send for my latest newsletter, autographed black-and-white photograph, and bookmark, at: Cassie Edwards, 6709 North Country Club Road, Mattoon, IL 61938.

For a prompt reply, please send a self-addressed, stamped legal-size envelope. Thanks for your support!

Always,
Cassie Edwards